CW01391630

Rachel married at nineteen and went to university in her thirties where she gained a first-class degree in English Literature. She penned her debut novel *Sex in the Shires* as she juggled her time as a single mum with a career in media and celebrity recruitment in the charity sector.

In loving memory of my mum, Doreen Gamble, and artist, Geoff Beasley.

Rachel Attewell

SEX IN THE SHIRES

AUSTIN MACAULEY PUBLISHERS™

LONDON * CAMBRIDGE * NEW YORK * SHARJAH

Copyright © Rachel Attewell 2023

The right of Rachel Attewell to be identified as author of this work has been asserted by the author in accordance with sections 77 and 78 of the Copyright, Designs and Patents Act 1988.

All rights reserved. No part of this publication may be reproduced, stored in a retrieval system, or transmitted in any form or by any means, electronic, mechanical, photocopying, recording, or otherwise, without the prior permission of the publishers.

Any person who commits any unauthorised act in relation to this publication may be liable to criminal prosecution and civil claims for damages.

This is a work of fiction. Names, characters, businesses, places, events, locales, and incidents are either the products of the author's imagination or used in a fictitious manner. Any resemblance to actual persons, living or dead, or actual events is purely coincidental.

A CIP catalogue record for this title is available from the British Library.

ISBN 9781035844005 (Paperback)
ISBN 9781035844012 (ePub e-book)

www.austinmacauley.com

First Published 2023
Austin Macauley Publishers Ltd®
1 Canada Square
Canary Wharf
London
E14 5AA

Chapter 1

I woke up this morning feeling like a defrosted mammoth, looked in the mirror, saw the head of Medusa and recoiled in horror. Last night was a not-to-be-repeated event where a favour for a friend resulted in me soaking up enough duty free to compete with a trifle sponge.

It's no consolation that my malady is the result of an altruistic gesture and maybe, I have to concede, a teensy-weensy little bit because I was lured out, against my better judgement, to meet a man. It's not as if I indulged that much, but when you get to a certain age, you have to grapple with the realisation that carnal sin is cumulative. Once, in the first flush of youth, you could stuff your face with chips, go from one year to the next without so much as a sliver of fruit or vegetable passing between your teeth, stay up till dawn and still operate like a human being. But eventually, it all catches up with you.

Hit forty and lick a biscuit, and your face breaks out in pustulating sores whilst a layer of fat in the shape of a rubber ring suddenly appears beneath your ribs. Sniff a whisky and you can be mistaken for your great granny. That reminds me, I must remember to avoid going near a naked flame because one spark from a lighted match in a public place and I'd be turned into an incendiary device and a suspected suicide bomber. Am I crazy or what?

I have within my sights one of the most eligible men in Wethershire who isn't old, impotent or gay and I go and reduce my chances of success by helping a friend get their leg over; how ironic is that? I am offered a rare window of opportunity and I slam it shut on my own little paws. So ungrateful.

Last night, I should have been sorting out my slap and waxing my bikini line for a potentially steamy session with Charles Smythe Bothum-Wethem (pronounced Bottom Wettum)—he's got 2,000 Wethershire acres and a pied-à-terre in Hampstead and he's coming here for dinner tonight—with moi!

Delia says he's an awful snob and makes King Charles sound like an old lag off a sink estate. But she's just jealous. He's got everything a girl could want except hair and a chin; but let's face it, at my age, I can't afford to be picky.

Or blasé for that matter. Goodness only knows what he'd think if he caught sight of me now, a sozzled slattern sitting at my kitchen table obscured by packets of supermarket own brand and the floor littered with tat. I must remember to push all the pot noodles to the back of the pantry, buy some sun-dried tomatoes, avocados for the fruit bowl, put a few strategically placed country magazines around the place and sling some jodhpurs over the back of the sofa.

If only I didn't feel quite so depressed that I feel the urge to eat an industrial supply of Smarties to raise my serotonin levels. It's all the fault of Delia and her toy boy. Gorgeous Delia—fit, fifty and rich, asked me out on a blind date to amuse Toy Boy's cousin Mervin a local loss adjuster. She drools over Toy Boy. Says he's the must-have accessory for every woman. He's got low mileage, runs on one brain cell and comes complete with a 40-year guarantee. So how come I got Mervin? We decided to meet in a pub in the nearby town of Broadmarket. I set off fired up with a sense of optimism, driving dreamily all the way there with romantic visions of Mervin in my head. I imagined our first encounter, eyes meeting across a crowded room, a frisson of sexual chemistry as our hands touched and the delightful discovery that we share common ground about music, politics, religion, child-rearing and the best way to save the world.

I parked the car in one of Broadmarket's beautiful, ancient, tree-lined streets and headed for the Cock and Bull, a once venerable chapel recently converted into a trendy bar where hopeful people congregate, eager to meet potential partners for nocturnal fornication fests. I could hear the thump, thump, thump of house music one hundred yards before I reached the door, which, on opening revealed a tightly packed throng bathed in a kaleidoscope of coloured lights which swirled swiftly around the room before leaping up and arching across the chapel's lofty vaulted ceiling.

My eyes expertly searched the crowds with more precision than a barcode scanner at a supermarket checkout, for any noticeably decent men. I immediately eliminated the usual native male crew of spotty teenagers, red necked invaders from the moors and the gorgeous groups of fit, twenty-something guys eyeing up equally gorgeous gaggles of strikingly pretty girls.

My eyes skimmed fleetingly over a solitary figure standing at the bar with one hand nursing a pint of beer while his other was vainly trying to block out the din by poking a fat finger very firmly inside one of his not inconsiderably sized ears. I immediately thought of an elephant. My attention was riveted by a pair of gruesome 'easy rider' specs circa 1970 which shrieked 'loser' and his polyester clothes in various shades of drab, from beige shirt to dog-shit brown slacks confirmed that he was a stylistic dodo. Bless. My gaze drifted down his body until they reached his feet clad in those weird faux walking boots with eyelet holes that you see advertised in Sunday supplements. Sheer heresy in such a trendy joint. I almost instinctively genuflected at his complete crucifixion of decency and taste.

Then, I spotted Delia who was waving in the general direction of this person and I realised with mounting horror that it could only be Mervin. My dreams of romantic harmony were dispelled in an instant. Here was a classic case of Spam Man. Just like junk mail, guys like this are ubiquitous, popping up all the time in singles clubs, on the Internet, newspaper lonely heart columns and on blind dates. Your hopes get raised in anticipation only to have them dashed to the ground when you see what's on offer.

Beer in one hand, he raised his arms above his head and moved like a circular saw through the tightly packed crowds which melted apart like the Red Sea for the children of Israel, as his sweaty armpits passed them uncomfortably close by at sniffing range.

"Pleased to meet you Rebecca," he said, as he executed a final turn to stop directly in front of me, extending his free hand and enveloping mine in a flabby, sweaty grip.

Definitely no sexual frisson there, it was like shaking hands with a dead haddock.

"You too," I lied as I bleakly assessed the merchandise at close quarters with 'bargain basement big time' registering instantly in my mind.

Every atom in his body had gone south including his stomach and moustache. His hair, apart from the bald patch, was so frizzy it looked as if it had been wired up to the National Grid. Delia whispered in my ear: "He's got nice eyes."

I replied through stiff lips: "Yes—for a walrus."

Laughing, she sauntered off and attached herself around Toy Boy like a boa constrictor and left me to it. We managed to find two spare seats in a dingy corner. Realising my chances of coming into snogging range of anyone half decent was virtually nil, I tucked into a massive 'Big Bag' of cheese and onion crisps and resigned myself to my fate over half of Guinness.

"And how do you know Delia?" asked Mervin politely.

"We met as mature students at a local university," I explained. I took a sip of Guinness, hoping to go on and tell him how it had transformed our lives from bored, depressed housewives, to liberated, well educated women. But I never got the chance. As far as Mervin was concerned, I'd had my say and now it was his turn. I spent the whole evening hearing how loss adjusters use psychology to convince distraught housewives that their charred burnt-out kitchens will brush up as good as new with a squirt of Mr Sheen and a bit of elbow grease.

I said witheringly, "I never get taken in by cheap sales routines," only to realise later that I ended up buying all his drinks.

He then proceeded to deliver a character assassination on his ex-wife, who it transpired had a shoe shopping habit that made Imelda Marcos seem frugal by comparison, and she was heavily into tantric sex—with her personal trainer.

Finishing my bag of crisps, I managed to stifle a yawn only to sniff vestiges of Mervin's earwax on my fingers. I thought the crisps had tasted extra spicy. I sat there practically fluorescently green with envy as Delia disentangled herself from Toy Boy and sauntered over to skewer my foot with her Jimmy Choo stiletto to say they'd love to meet back at my place for coffee. I poked her viciously in the ribs as we left and hissed: "Don't you dare abandon me with Merv."

Smiling she arched one perfectly plucked eyebrow and said half reprovingly: "Now would I?"

"Yes," I replied through gritted teeth.

I got home first with Mervin. And, as I had suspected, minutes turned to hours. No Delia and no Toy Boy. Mervin decided to elaborate further on his ex-wife's foibles and when he'd put her thoroughly through the metaphorical mincer moved on to her mother, then a daughter by her first marriage and a menagerie of pet dogs and cats who were all part of a conspiracy to part him from his wallet. Fat chance, I thought, as I reached for the duty-free in despair to stop my brain from turning into a cabbage as he droned on and on and on ad nauseam.

I never, for one nanosecond, thought Delia and Toy Boy had got lost or been mangled in some gruesome pile-up as Spam Man kept fretting on and on about at various intervals in his narrative about Mervin versus the rest of the bloody world.

No. They'd probably found a convenient lay-by and Delia was being deliciously and vigorously rogered by Toy Boy. And here I sat in a sex-free zone with a lump of worried lard—with bristles.

I couldn't tell him that Delia was married, could I? Metaphysics and ethics was never my strongest point, especially at 2 am in the morning entertaining an emotional dumbo. I'll rephrase that—a completely sexless, physically amorphous, emotional dumbo, not even shaggable when utterly and irredeemably rat-arsed.

When Delia did eventually turn up with Toy Boy, her face was so red it looked as if she'd had a close encounter with an industrial sander. Their excuse was as farfetched as it was ingenious. Delia, waving one hand airily while squeezing Toy Boy's buttocks affectionately with the other, said blithely: "Oh, we took a two-hour detour to settle a dispute over whether a house in Hartborne was roofed in Collyweston or Welsh slate."

She relinquished her grip on Toy Boy's arse for a split second, to slap him across the head for grinning and saying it actually turned out to be 'thatched.'

I eventually managed to get rid of them all after a heated and fantastical debate on genetic engineering. Delia and I thought it had potential, zapping out unsavoury male characteristics such as an inability to differentiate between the threat of World War III and England being knocked out of the Rugby World Cup. Toy Boy thought it could revolutionise the mental health of the male population by eliminating unsightly chest and back hair and the trauma of de-fuzzing, while Mervin thought it could wipe-out an inbuilt default mechanism to mistrust men who built model railways. He's got one as big as Clapham Junction in his shed apparently. Yawn.

Warning bells began to ring as they left, and Mervin casually said: "I'll call you." Throwing my arms theatrically wide above my head I slurred: "Well, why not when you're such a nice spam?" Then I started to titter convulsively. Delia flashed me a warning look before Mervin bent to kiss me. I engaged the infallible trick of leaning forward to wipe a non-existent speck of dirt off the light switch. Even so, the whiskers of his moustache brushed past my ear—sufficient contact to shrivel my libido like a man's bits suddenly being immersed in liquid nitrogen. Not nice.

I meandered my wobbly way back to the kitchen which looked like squatters had moved in and out while my back was turned. I put my hands over my eyes to blot out the devastation before making my way, with great difficulty, upstairs to bed. I only remembered to remove my hands from my eyes after I tripped over a hole in the stair carpet and my body made painful contact with the bedroom door.

The sheets were cold like my heart and my cheeks were hot like my fanny which suddenly revved into gear due to a combination of intoxicating liquor and neglect. One of these days, raced the thoughts in my fuddled mind, it will go into overdrive like the car and stall, never to start again without help from a nice AA man with a big spanner. And with that pleasant thought I fell soundly asleep like a baby.

Five hours later and I look like a raddled old hag, I've got a splitting headache and worse of all—stale onion breath. This is the price I'm paying for my altruistic gesture to a friend in need and my inability to deal decisively with a member of the opposite sex who can bore for England, Europe and the universe. Let's face it, last night, a man in my place faced with a female equivalent of Mervin would have yawned—said: "Sorry luv, I'm bushed," and beetled off to bed leaving them alone with the TV remote control. But women haven't yet mastered the fine art of bludgeoning other people's feelings into a mash until the pips squeak while congratulating themselves on their magnanimity in condescending to speak to them in the first place.

Well, all this musing and ruminating like a toothless camel isn't going to get any housework done or the meal organised for my tête-à-tête with Charles. If I want to get more than the table laid tonight, I've got to get motivated, sparkle, and sweep away the cobwebs of obfuscation and procrastination from my mind and then get my fat arse in gear. Yes. Just one more cuppa and then it's action stations.

Chapter 2

I can't quite remember the exact moment when it all started to go horribly wrong, when the cruel finger of fate, maliciously and mischievously pressed the 'crush' button, so that all my dreams, glistening like some phantom silver cypher in the sun, crumpled into a dull metallic clod to disappear unceremoniously down life's metaphorical shute to dumpsville. Not that I'm feeling sorry for myself or anything. Could I, if I had handled things differently, be now looking forward to date number two with Charles instead of analysing the inflection of every little word, the body language of every gesture, for the moment when our burgeoning relationship was nipped in the bud, trodden under foot and flushed down the proverbial toilet?

It called for a serious dose of therapy from my closest friend—the telephone.

I rang Delia.

"Hi darling," she said. "Did he get his rocks off then?"

I took a deep breath and started the circuitous route from the mundane account of the earlier part of the day to the juicy bits in the evening.

"I had a premonition that it was all doomed when I burnt the dinner after gossiping with Cesspool," I explained.

"Sorry darling, but where does that smelly old man fit in the grand scheme of things—lost me I'm afraid," Delia replied.

Farm worker Cess Poole, affectionately known as Cesspool on account of the manure trapped in his turn-ups, is a living legend. He really ought to get an agent and go on reality TV. His rivetingly entertaining encyclopaedic knowledge of the sexual antics and peccadilloes of almost every toff in the county is unsurpassable.

He tells his tales with such relish and it's all backed up with anecdotal evidence that goes back donkeys' years. To before the war. The Boer War that is. But then, why should Delia know that? Although she's lived in the small and picturesque county of Wethershire since marrying 30 years ago, she isn't a local.

13

For that distinction, you need to be able to trace your family's name, carved for generation after generation, on the stone and slate gravestones in the hillocky churchyards, or carved on the village war memorials, names carried away on the wind as the rector calls them out on Remembrance Sunday while old soldiers stand like black crows amongst the gnarled ancient yews.

"Cecil Poole is our village one-stop-gossip-shop," I told her. You can't stop him talking mid-flow in case you miss some vital salacious anecdote.

"I see," Delia drawled.

I ploughed on explaining how Cess had stopped by for a chat as I was en-route to put all my old red-topped newspapers in the car for recycling in case Charles saw them and realised I had tabloid tendencies. I smugly explained to Cess that I was expecting Charles for dinner.

"Scratching his head under his cap," he said—"What that drip?" and went on to tell me some really, really, juicy gossip involving the Wethershire upper crust that would make a gossip columnist's mouth water.

"Really—do tell," said Delia intrigued. "Did it involve Squire Percy and that new stable hand of his with the bleached highlights?"

Exasperated at her inability to grasp the vital crux of the conversation I ploughed on with my tale of woe upon woe.

"No, no, nothing as interesting as that, but the point is, I forgot that I'd left some raspberries in kirsch warming over a low heat on the stove. I stood there with my ears flapping, quivering with moral indignation—I promise, I imagined I could smell the smoke of hell fire."

"That's what a Calvinist background does for you," said Delia sympathetically. "That and vaginismus."

I told her mournfully how I had suddenly sniffed the air, screamed and rushed back inside to the kitchen where acrid black smoke was billowing from my best saucepan which was buckling from the heat. As I vainly poked the charred remains of the raspberries, I became aware of Cess standing behind me rubbing his stubbly beard.

"Dead loss, old girl, if you ask me," he said. "If you can resurrect that, my name's Jamie Oliver."

"It was awful D," I wailed. "I could almost see the auto cue rolling in his eyes as he stored the titbits of my misfortune to entertain his cronies over the dominoes and a pint in the Doom and Gloom, you know, the pub in Hartborne, the Horse and Groom."

Yet, despite Cess' apparent perkiness over my predicament he came up trumps by suggesting he asked his wife Gladys to defrost some of her legendary melting moments, biscuits that always take first prize at the village show, much to the consternation and bitterness of the rest of the village WI ladies who mutter dark accounts of culinary gerrymandering and sexual intrigue of past yore. All fascinating stuff but peripheral to the urgent nature of my tale.

"I felt so grateful, but the stress of it all had made everything go pear-shaped, including my waistline which had expanded with stress. I looked like Victoria Beckham expecting twins," I groaned.

Delia laughed: "Shame they weren't conceived by David Beckham—God, I wouldn't kick him out of bed in a hurry!"

I went on to explain that pressed for time, I scurried round doing all the essential jobs such as changing the sheets, painting my toenails and waxing my bikini line. But due to my deformed waistline I abandoned plans to wear my slinky black sexy dress and instead defied the laws of physics by squeezing myself into black velvet jeans by pulling up the zip with a coat hanger. The pressure nearly perforated my ear drums. I felt positively lightheaded as I opened the door to Charles as he stood there smiling with a bottle of Bolly in one hand, the violin strings of his hair wafting over his bald pate in the breeze.

"It was then that I felt the first twinge of misgivings, but I dismissed it as wind on account of my tight waistband," I elaborated to Delia.

I said 'hi' as we self-consciously 'air kissed.' He sauntered in and plonked himself down on the sofa.

"Nice place," he remarked looking round the room, liberally sprinkled with new county touches including a copy of Country Life, a battered old wicker basket with a tartan scarf in it and a pair of old riding boots casually tucked under a table. I poured out glasses of Bolly, giving myself a generous slug before inviting him into the kitchen while I fiddled around with the meal. The conversation started benignly, circling round safe topics like what he'd been doing that day. He'd had a 'jolly' day at a Point-to-Point then he'd waited around for the vet to arrive to geld one of his favourite nags.

"Doesn't it bring tears to your eyes in sympathy?" I queried. He threw back his head and laughed so heartily I could see his tonsils quiver.

"Never thought about it really—nature's way you see. Anyway, my tackle's in fine fettle—good enough for a hard day in the saddle without it putting me off my stride," he winked saucily. Things were looking up.

"Delia, I almost had him in the bag."

"Oh," she squeaked.

I swapped the phone from one ear to the other, a subconscious move that signalled a sudden change in the direction of events.

"Err, not quite," I said slowly.

"You don't mean you blew him out—just as he was within shagging distance," Delia exclaimed in horror.

"Well," I wheedled. "Things sort of escalated and before I knew where I was, he was on one side of the front door and I was on the other. Things just suddenly started to wobble when we got on to politics."

The saying that goes 'the path to hell is paved with good intentions' is one that aptly described the moment when I realised that, although he was eligible, we were about as compatible as Margaret Thatcher and Lenin and the evening was hurtling towards a scene straight out of Dante's Inferno, rather than Hironimus Bosch's 'Garden of Delights'.

"Shame," Delia murmured.

"The candles on the table were lit and I felt we were cruising, two forty somethings having an intelligent, rational debate about the political issues of the day until he dropped a bombshell."

I paused for dramatic effect to impress upon Delia the yawning chasm that had opened between Charles and myself.

He sat up as stiff as a poker in his chair and snapped, "Margaret Thatcher, bless her, if only she were still here to sort out that rabid lot in the Commons, load of swivel-eyed socialists, impostors, all rampant sex mad hypocrites,' and then reverently raised his glass to the woman he called his favourite leader of all time!"

"So?" queried Delia in a puzzled tone.

"Whadya mean, so?" I shrieked.

I drew in a sharp breath and tried patiently to explain that ideological differences could pose a barrier to a more intimate relationship and I was so irritated with him it made me chew extra hard on my pasta balls.

I really tried hard to sound like a meek, demure Tory wife but I ended up squawking in his face like a parrot on speed.

"I called him a capitalist rent lord, among other things," I said, remembering that I followed my remark by spiking a succulent piece of garlic sausage and popping it into my mouth—a classic case of Freudian penis castration if ever there was one.

"He's so up himself you know; he could polish the backs of his eyeballs." Delia tittered.

Charles' hand froze, his fork poised midway to his mouth, he looked like some android whose batteries had gone flat on Star Trek. "You don't mean you're a feminist—a woman with balls," he whispered hoarsely.

"If you mean, am I a woman who values her independence, am I a woman who doesn't defer to a man simply because he has a penis, then the answer is 'yes'," I said brazenly. I heard Delia groan.

Obviously fazed to find himself in such close proximity to a feminist, he started to look wary, eying the backdoor in case he needed to make a sharp exit. Suddenly realising the enormity of the damage done, I decided to embark on a limitation exercise.

Giving out a big sigh, I told Delia how I had looked deeply into his eyes, smiled my most winning smile and said as innocently as I could: "Who cares about politics anyway, let's just forget it shall we?" Then, desperate to fill the awkward silence, I lisped provocatively: "Do you fancy a melting moment?"

His mouth dropped to reveal partially masticated pasta and his head turned purple, it was enough to dampen the ardour of a Turkish courtesan. Funnily enough it seemed to break the ice and from then on, we managed to scramble back from outright war to a truce. Differences forgotten we retired to the sofa.

Charles, obviously thinking feminism is akin to whoredom pounced and started to breathe heavily like a cart horse with asthma. But the tingling sensation I felt in my loins was caused by a lack of circulation to my vital organs from my crutch-strangling jeans which felt as if they were getting tighter by the minute. I feigned virtue and said I never slept with a man on the first date.

Frantic to regain his composure, Charles rearranged his trousers with one hand to hide his hard-on and smoothed the strings of his hair back into place on his sweaty head with the other.

"Worth a try," he muttered as he rose to go. We stood embarrassed and dejected on the doorstep saying our hurried good-byes, where only a few hours earlier we had greeted each other with shy curiosity.

"Why do we put ourselves through such emotional contortions to snare a man when we worked so hard to win our liberation?" I asked Delia plaintively. "I feel as if I've just had a severe dose of the emotional trots."

"Because it's fun darling, celibacy is so debilitating and admit it, you love the fun of the chase, you lead all these poor hapless men such a merry dance, reducing them to tears of frustration. Revenge darling, revenge."

"I must admit Charles is a bit of a DUD, you know, dull, ugly and desperate, but I thought I'd give him a whirl, sale on return, after all he might have hidden talents."

"Well, if I were you, I would have given him a few rounds. Check out his credentials in the trouser department. You and your principles. Who cares he if loves Maggie, he's obviously the sort who likes to be dominated, sounds as if he's got potential to me."

I started to giggle. "You're so naughty D—which reminds me. You know I mentioned some juicy gossip that Cecil was telling me about? Well, apparently, Digger Manners was out lamping for rabbits last night when he saw this navy Freelander in a lay-by between Newton Saucey and Hartborne. It was bumping rhythmically up and down, and he could hear a faint buzzing noise coming from the back window. He daren't go too near, because, well you never know these days. But he said the car was familiar.

Hey, it wasn't you was it with Toy Boy, trying out that new sex toy—the penis ring with the battery-operated remote control?"

"Oh my God," shrieked Delia. And then the line went dead. I think she must have dropped the phone.

Chapter 3

Everything's easy in retrospect. You can spot life's mistakes like black boulders littering a snow-covered hillside or as neon lights phosphorus in the gloom—the hieroglyphics of your existence carved out in sharp relief on your memory. Sometimes in your dreams you feel as if you can run your hand over them and feel the scars.

One such scar—or rather a running sore, is my ex—not my ex-husband but my last ex-but-one boyfriend, Jake, a politics lecturer. Such a face ache. One of his most irritating traits was to smile condescendingly at me saying: "I know exactly what you want, what you think, what you think I think and what you want me to think you think."

And I would reply: "I don't think so."

And so it went on. But one of the most painful lessons I learned from that experience is I rather like men like that, urban intellectuals, who are often not particularly eligible, kind or deeply spiritual.

But on the plus side, much more adventurous in bed than any far-right Tory. They can't handle feisty women; they prefer the sort that do it with their tights on and the lights out. Listen carefully and watch my lips: "That's why I don't fancy Charles. I might as well flog a dead horse. Preferably his."

How things have changed since Jane Austen's day. It's no longer a truth universally acknowledged, that a single man in possession of a good fortune must be in want of a wife. On the contrary. A sensible loaded single bloke won't risk burdening himself with a wife who could push off and hoover up half his cash, and a spinster's no longer a marriage market commodity perched prettily on the shelf branded 'unmarked goods.' Unless you believe what's in the Daily Wail.

In Mrs Bennett's heyday, Charles would have been a monster catch. But now poor Charlie Boy is a mere minnow in the lido of life, a dying breed that will soon be extinct, incapable of adapting to mating with women with highly developed brains, voracious sexual appetites and capable of independent thought. Oh yeah, and very low boredom thresholds. A bit like me.

Which means it could be a wise move to keep old hairless but heir-to-loadsa-dosh 'warm' as a reserve relationship—just to amuse myself with until someone more interesting shows up. Keep him dangling on a string, as my granny used to say. Let's face it, despite my vocal protestations that I've got a full buzzy social life, a brill job, a fantastic kid and great friends I've still got an empty bed.

Thinking about kids, Joey will be home soon from his dad's and I must grit my teeth while I hear about this paragon of virtue who has seemingly endless patience, a bottomless wallet and is so nice that he allows Joey to stay up late to watch Netflix—unlike his evil mother who resembles an ogre—on a good day.

Joey is looking forward to this afternoon when we make our weekly pilgrimage to take tea at my mum's house in the next village, its picture postcard streets resonate with the sounds of baaing sheep and lowing cows grazing in nearby fuzzy-felt fields.

It's the perfect vision of an olde-world country utopia that shatters on close acquaintance when you realise that it's been taken over by a swarm of townies. Their imported urban values now dominate the parish council which goes into a spasm every time a piece of horse poo desecrates the immaculately mown wildflower-free verges, or mud from the farm splatters their BMWs as they drive through the village. 'And do the animals have to be so loud and smelly?' they whimper.

Grrrrrrrrrrr.

My mother fortunately is not one of those kinds of people. But she does have other irredeemably bad habits. The whole afternoon takes on the form of a ritual which I take as a sort of faint disapproval and a chiding reminder of the chaotic state of my own life. She defers to ten-year-old Joey, who admires his smug reflection in the gleaming silver teapot when granny pours the tea, preening over her reference to him as the 'man of the house,' "seeing as Grandpa has passed over to the other side—until the Rapture."

My mother Vera is a curious mixture of execrable snob combined with low church evangelical leanings due to the fact that she married into money but couldn't shake off the childhood shackles that bind her to the Bible and 'The Lord.' One of my earliest memories is the regular visits we paid to my auntie Nora and her mynah bird.

They lived in a prefab in Leeds, since swept away in the name of 'progress' to make way for a retail park. Auntie Nora was a Methodist and a war widow whose husband Cyril was slaughtered on the Somme.

"The Lord will provide," she said as she packed me and my cousin Debbie off to the front room to listen to Burl Ives LPs while the pair of them drank orange coloured tea with two sugars. Mum would then pour out her troubles to wise old auntie Nora, usually over my dad's latest fall from grace—mainly sexually deviant in nature like looking at the girl at the till in the Co-op in 'that way'.

We'd listen at the door and then bored, turn up the volume of 'When the roll is called up Yonder' so we could teach auntie Nora's mynah bird to say 'bugger'. "We amused ourselves when we were children," I say self-righteously to Joey, following his regular mantra of 'I'm bored' to the strains of Snoop Dogg. Poor kid, I sound just like my mum years ago when Debbie and me begged her for the bus fare to go into Leeds to have egg and chips in C&A's Cafe. Scary.

"Well, now," my mum's voice interjected into my musing. "How did it go with Charles Smythe Bothum-Wethem. Any wedding bells yet?"

We'd arrived slightly late for tea to find her anxiously scanning the street for our arrival through lead latticed windows peeping out from underneath the low thatched eaves of a former farm labourer's cottage, tarted up for commuters hungry for a taste of the good life.

"Well, if there are, you'll need ears with sonic stereo to pick them up," I replied as I tucked into my second homemade scone with jam and cream.

"Really darling, you are a ninny you know, it's not as if you are getting any younger and if you don't heed my advice about staying out of the sun you'll get as leathery as, as," she waved her arms about vaguely as she searched for a suitable synonym, "as an old cow," piped in Joey, feigning innocence.

"Yes, well, whatever dear," mum replied a tad sharply, not quite sure if Joey had transgressed the boundaries of good taste.

I gave him a wink.

"Charles is a sweetie mum," I explained. "But he's so conventional and predictable."

And short and bald and probably in possession of a small penis, I thought to myself.

"But his uncle Sir Howgrave is president of the Wethershire Conservative Association and I do Meals on Wheels with his mother on a Friday, they are so our sort of people." I sensed a faint rebuke.

I could feel the conversation drifting into its familiar groove, the declining drop in today's standards, the sheer horror at the way the government has dismantled the country, fond reminiscences of the Queen Mother and the scandal at the indiscriminate axing of condensed milk.

"The country is falling apart, and your father always loved condensed milk on his tinned peaches, people just don't know what's good for them these days." She fell into a quiet reverie as her mind struggled to make sense of the frightening new world that seemed to menace her from all sides.

"I know Mum," I answered gently, loving her in her bewilderment and nostalgia for a lost organicist world. Everything was so easy then; men were right and women invariably wrong.

Women in her day knew when to be thankful, most of the eligible men had been killed during the war, so if any man showed any interest, it offered an escape from a sexless and childless spinsterhood where you became more and more invisible with the passing years.

Mind you, there's always the option today of trading in your independence to marry an ancient sugar daddy. The problem is they are invariably physically repulsive, wear incontinence pads or are chronically unfaithful.

Or like Charles; kind, wet, sexless, worthy and dull. Or maybe not. For all I know, old Charlie boy could be so turbo-charged in bed I'd be his willing and grateful slave. But I doubt it. Mind you, it could be that my scarred and troubled relationship history has made me so wary of commitment I will find fault with every man I meet until I shrivel up like a dried old prune and no one will want me anyway. I will become such a lonely old biddie I will settle for any old codger I meet in the Post Office pension queue.

Mum and I sat there, quietly musing our own private thoughts on opposite sides of the coffee table littered with the detritus that defined her existence, her doilies, china cups and saucers, jam spoons and crocheted tablecloth. Suddenly the leaden silence was shattered by the ring of my mobile phone.

It was Charles.

"Oh hello," I said, mouthing Charles' name and pointing at the phone to Mum. She sat bolt upright and listened so attentively that she mouthed every syllable as I ummed and arrhed, yes and no'd and finally said goodbye.

"Is it back on?" she queried hopefully after I triumphantly put the phone back in my bag with a flourish.

"Well, I don't know about that," I laughed. "But he's invited me to go as his partner to a dinner party at Hartborne Hall. Obviously, my resistance to his right-wing rantings and his amorous advances has only spurred him on."

Mum put a warning finger to her lips and her eyes glanced sideways at Joey at the oblique reference to sexual relations, in case it sullied his innocence.

"Is he rich?" asked Joey.

"He's a nice gentleman and your mother should thank her lucky stars," said my mum.

"Breeding and money, the perfect combination."

I felt well chuffed; this dinner party was going to be a perfect opportunity to put myself about to scan around for other talent.

"Delia and her husband will be there," I offered as a titbit of information.

Mum reveres and worships Delia's husband Henry Fielding who reads the lesson in church with the same dramatic delivery as Lawrence Oliver's rendition of Henry V's 'into the breach.' She sees him as the epitome of all that's great about England, good old gentry farming stock, backbone of almost every village committee and a paragon of self-restraint, susceptible only to the odd glass of whisky a little more often than is good for him. But then, for mum, men are allowed their little foibles.

Little does she know that he's humped more stable girls than hay bales during his marriage to Delia, hurls crockery at the wall if the dinner isn't to his liking, and now, thanks to the drink, can't get his willy up without Viagra.

Delia says she indulges him with the occasional humping session to keep him quiet. Apparently, he pops his pill, waits for the desired effect and then lays down with it sticking up like a poker and then roars at Delia to, "Hop on quick," as if she's a jockey.

Delia's worked out that for a five-minute gallop on top she burns off at least two hundred and fifty calories so it's not that different from an aerobics workout and it's great for toning the thighs.

"And, credit where it's due," Delia conceded with awe. "He's hung like a bloody horse!"

"Of course, Henry's wife's a bit of Tartar," Mum said suddenly.

"How's that then?" I replied, my tolerance level dropping faster than a flasher's trousers.

23

"Well, have you seen her shoes—for a woman that age! Bleached hair, and jeans with her tummy on show, it's positively indecent. And these 'adult' art education classes she teaches sound very suspect to me and she never closes her eyes during confession in church, poor, poor, Henry what a heavy cross to bear."

Joey suddenly looked up from a comic he was idly flicking though and adopted his most innocent stare. "Cesspool says Mr Fielding is as randy as an old goat and he's had his leg over more women than five bar gates. He told me when we took Horace the bull to mate with Squire Percy's heifers."

His announcement had the desired effect. Mum positively swooned from the shock, spilling tea down the front of her twin set.

"I knew it!" she moaned. "It was only a matter of time before this innocent defenceless, fatherless child got drawn into the wrong company."

"Joey is neither fatherless nor defenceless, in fact he's a machinatory little menace," I replied, trying hard not to laugh. "And he doesn't understand a word of it," I lied. Driving home in the car, I read Joey the riot act, warning him in sepulchral tones that a repeat of such a heinous crime would result in unspeakable punishment.

"Yeah, yeah," he replied wearily, casually picking his nose and eyeing a particularly juicy bogie before popping it into his mouth, "There's no need to go into orbit." As I instinctively slapped his wrist, I caught his eye and we shared a furtive smile, and then looked fixedly at the road ahead until we reached home.

Chapter 4

I lay in a state of suspended animation dreaming of a sun kissed balcony overlooking the Mediterranean. A flawless blue sky hung like a banner between two sheer white apartment blocks, framing pink floor tiles surrounding the vivid blue slash of a swimming pool; clean, angular lines broken only by the sharp umbrella fronds of green palms, a vista as flat, surreal and silent as a Hockney.

"Mum! Where are my football socks?" Reality punched its fist through the thin veneer of my consciousness, and I rolled over and groaned. That philosopher guy, Baudrillard who maintained that art is a simulacrum of reality, was talking cobblers. Life is a small child jabbing you in the back at some ungodly hour of the morning as chirpy and bright as a butcher's dog. Paint that and stick it in an art gallery. I crawled out of bed and looked balefully at my tummy cruncher exerciser lying supinely on the carpet with arms outstretched, ready to embrace my flabby body and convert it into a toned, rippling sex machine. I made a vow to start a strict early morning regime—tomorrow.

I dressed in two seconds flat except for my tights, opened the relevant drawer with trepidation in anticipation of the tentacles that erupted in a tangled skein of coloured nylon. I frantically choose from three hundred assorted pairs tangled in knots in various stages of decay, ladders, holes and lacy patterns, that are too expensive to chuck out, but too naff to wear. I also rejected various sizes and shades of stockings which a champion Krypton Factor contestant would struggle to match up.

Fifteen minutes later and wearing a pair of tights with an ozone-sized hole in the crutch, I extricated Joey's football socks from a damp pile of washing in the bath.

Damn, I'd forgotten to put them on the radiator to dry last night.

The hands on the clock whizzed round alarmingly as I vainly tried to iron the damn things dry with one hand while eating a bowl of cereal with the other. Guilt coursed through my veins as I imagined Joey pale and prostrate against the sheets, ravaged with pneumonia, rickets or the onset of premature arthritis caused through my wanton neglect.

Fortunately, it was dispelled instantly after I rushed upstairs expecting to find him pristinely dressed in his school uniform, satchel at the ready, but instead found him in his pyjamas grimy and dishevelled with sleep, on his Play Station ruthlessly slaying hostile mobs.

I'd only been awake for an hour, but it already seemed like a lifetime. What bliss it must be to wake up and only have yourself to get ready. A hassle-free start to the morning, casually sauntering down to breakfast, a leisurely read of the newspaper, before cruising off to work arriving at your desk on time, alert and relaxed, ready for a productive day.

After a bout of hysterical arm waving persuading Joey to co-operate and get ready, I zoomed round like a dervish, packing his bag, my bag, his lunch box, my lunch box, fed Gums the goldfish and shoved some dirty clothes into the washing machine. Smug with satisfaction I opened the front door with a sigh of relief only to feel the dog shoot between my legs as it made a dash for freedom and next door's cat. I've always thought that people who believe they are the reincarnation of some famous long-dead illustrious person like Cleopatra or Napoleon must have a really exalted view of themselves. Why, out of all the zillions of people that have inhabited the earth, should they have been singled out to have been someone memorable in a past life instead of a sheep stealer or a circus freak?

But sometimes, such as an occasion like this, I do have an irrational conviction that the whole world is conspiring against me. God wakes up in a capricious mood, yawns, scratches his arse and on a whim, revolves his clenched hand in a circular motion over the world before singling out with his finger some unfortunate soul to suffer an off day. This morning it was my turn.

Abandoning all decorum, I made an undignified dash around the village as Flossie zig-zagged down the main street yapping excitedly after the cat. After three fruitless circuits, Squire Percy de Albion-Hartborne came into view riding a magnificent hunter with a bull mastiff loping alongside. Fortunately, Flossie made a beeline for the mastiff's bum and was so distracted having a good sniff that I was able to grab her by the collar and retreat crab-like, dragging her away from the horse's hooves. I looked up and managed a forced smile at Percy between tortured gasps for breath, peering up at him through bedraggled matted hair, before gabbling an apology like some mediaeval witch. The shame of it.

He smiled munificently as if at a craven peasant and then suggested it might be a good idea to keep my dog on a lead.

Muttering inanely about being in a frantic rush, I dragged a reluctant Flossie off down the road by her collar, slowed down by the fact that her back legs seemed to be suddenly struck by paralysis. The strain made me go over very inelegantly on the heel of one shoe. Damn. Percy gave me a salute as he went by at a fast trot, his delectable jodhpur-clad backside bouncing up and down in counter rhythm to his horse. It's rumoured he only has eyes for guys, but if he's straight, I'd be in love. I arrived at work really late after depositing Flossie back at home and dropping Joey off at school because he'd missed the school bus in the excitement.

"You look as if you've been dragged through a hedge backwards," said Konnie my friend from accounts, after taking in my dishevelled appearance.

"Funny you should say that," I replied, before regaling her with my morning's adventure and a description of the Perfect Percy.

I then settled down to a hard day's work as a staff reporter on The Broadmarket Herald by working through press releases sent by email that were so boring to read that I lost the will to live after the first paragraph.

I decided instead to spice up the reports on the various village shows that have been happening around the county by writing slightly lewd captions about the size and shape of the prize winners' vegetables. The punters love it.

Not a lot of things happen of national or international importance in the rural backwater of Broadmarket or the neighbouring county town of Newton Saucey, home to our district office run by an inebriate hack called Colin. One week the best headline we could dredge up was when a cow got its hoof stuck in a bog at the local nature reserve. It took three fire engines and an armed response team from the local police force to extract it. It was the most exciting thing they'd had to deal with for years.

We generally resort to torturing the local council by muckraking over their internecine squabbles or stoking the dormant flames of local disputes until they erupt into an inferno of claim and counter claim, over spilling onto the letters' page with juicy accusations so close to the knuckle they give our legal guy palpitations.

I caught up with Konnie in the kitchen at lunchtime and we sat down to share our sandwiches and the more interesting and exciting 'off diary' weekend news bulletins which usually start with a précis of Delia's sexploits.

Konnie and Delia count as my rock-solid friends due to the fact that we all experienced an intellectual hunger that led us to study at a local college, a grey, ugly, concrete dump that nonetheless inspired in us a belief that we weren't after all redundant, hormonal airheads. We were drawn together as we slowly deciphered the contradictions in Haralambos and discovered the lyricism of the Metaphysical Poets, emerging triumphant, liberated in mind and spirit and armed with enough qualifications to get us into decent universities.

We've supported each other ever since through the various trials and tribulations of divorce, bereavement, love affairs and the pecuniary circumstances that have almost driven us back into the slavery of female anonymity, a condition spawned by Jean-Jacques Rousseau, the 17th century writer who launched the blockbuster fantasy fiction genre with the 'Social Contract'.

Konnie was all agog with my tale of Delia and Toy Boy and the potential exposé that could result following her horizontal jogging episode in the back of the Freelander and the unwise deployment of the penis ring.

"A bit of a major cock-up you might say," she laughed.

"Well, if this juicy titbit of tittle tattle ever got out it would create such a scandal that the gossip hounds in the Doom and Gloom would feast off it for weeks," I replied. I suddenly had a horrible thought. "I hope it doesn't come out before next Saturday."

"What, you mean it's still in there?" Konnie quipped.

We fell about laughing and between bouts of bawdy sniggers I told her about my dinner invitation to Hartborne Hall from Charles and the fact that Delia would be there with Henry.

"They could hardly go and make polite conversation at the table if everyone knew that Delia's bits had been buzzed by remote control," I reasoned.

Offering Konnie a Cheesy Wotsit, I went on to explain how it came about that Charles had asked me to go as his date and then described the sequence of events leading up to it including the miserable Mervin miasma.

"I know just how you feel," she sympathised. "I went to a night club in York with some of the girls from accounts and I got chatted up by this bloke whose breath could strip paint at ninety paces. I lied and said I was in a deeply committed relationship with a seismic love life." She sighed sadly.

"He backed off, but unfortunately relayed the information back to his best mate who I'd been eyeing up all evening. He lost interest and disappeared with this woman with cankles."

She suddenly stuck her out own neat ankle and surveyed it keenly. "I hope mine never get like that," she said. It prompted her to tell me about this new holistic diet that she's on that involves drinking lots of herbal tea and sitting in a yoga position meditating on kind karmas and positive images of lithe Naomi Cambellesque limbs. "I didn't lose an ounce actually," she admitted. "But it gave me a great excuse to keep walking past Dick, the dishy new deputy editor, on the way to the ladies."

I must try it I thought.

Suddenly Konnie sat up and clicked her fingers. "I know what I wanted to tell you," She said. But before she could elucidate, Moira, the matronly receptionist, burst into the kitchen.

"There's been a delivery at reception for you Rebecca," she said breathless with excitement.

Curious, I followed her out of the kitchen into the reception area, festooned with pictures of village fetes, school sports days and ruddy faced councillors at civic receptions.

There lying resplendent on the counter was a bouquet of pink carnations, fragile gypsophila and furry ferns all wrapped up in shiny purple paper and tied with a big gaudy ribbon.

"Oh," squeaked Konnie.

My heart leapt. Who could have sent me flowers? I picked them up and buried my face into the petals inhaling their sweet, heady fragrance. "Open the card, open the card," came a chorus of voices.

I extracted a pink card from beneath the ribbon with Rebecca Pearce scrawled on the front. I opened it slowly, my heart beating hard with hope. Who could it be? Maybe, maybe, it was from Jake to say he was sorry for being such a heartless bastard. It wouldn't be a day overdue. The thought flashed across my mind like a comet with a shiny tail of sparkling dust, only to have it evaporate like a bubble when I read out the inscription.

'Thanks for such a lovely evening. I hope this is the start of a beautiful and prosperous friendship. Speak to you soon. All yours, Mervin.'

I dropped the bouquet as if it was contaminated with ricin. "Yuck!" I wailed and walked off leaving the flowers abandoned on the counter. I plonked myself

29

down in front of my computer and started to viciously hit the keys with more force than was necessary.

I heard Moira bustling up solicitously behind me. She thrust the flowers under my nose.

"Now dear," she said soothingly. "It's not often that a woman gets sent such a lovely bouquet of flowers."

Unfortunately for Moira that was true. Not even the most inventive and audacious advertorial writer could call Moira attractive or even 'interesting.' The poor thing had been born with looks to die for—literally. Konnie once jokingly re-christened her, changing her name from Moira Hadman to Moira Never-Had-a-Man and we've called her that behind her back ever since.

"You have them," I said, looking at her kind face. "You love flowers."

She flushed with pleasure. "Are you sure, dear?" she asked.

I answered in the affirmative and she walked off, gently cradling the bouquet to her ample bosom like a child, savouring second hand a romantic gesture from a man to a woman.

I fell into a slough of despond, faced with the familiar problem of how to detach myself from a persistent Spam Man. My reverie was broken as Konnie bounced up behind me like Tigger on acid.

"I take it that was a no?"

I looked up at the high windows where the only view is the sky and pondered dreamily if it would be fairer to Mervin if I were really truthful. I turned to Konnie. "Do you think it would be okay to be brutally honest rather than get his hopes up?"

"Well, it depends on how you phrase it really," said Konnie.

"I thought along the lines of, 'Why don't you get the message and leave me alone as the only way I could have sexual intercourse with you is if I was anaesthetised first."

"I bet you go out with him for a drink next week," Konnie said dryly.

I suddenly remembered that she was just about to impart some spicy piece of information to me in the kitchen before being cruelly interrupted by Moira. I asked her to elaborate.

"Oh yes, I forgot in all the excitement," she said. "Forget about Mervin, we are going to indulge ourselves in some man baiting, I'm taking you speed-dating on Friday and we are going to catch us a man each with maybe a couple to spare."

Well, Konnie's news really cheered me up, here was a ray of light at the end of the tunnel. Surely out of twenty or thirty men I could find at least one-half decent guy?

I returned invigorated to my computer to caption more pictures of proud gardeners fondling their engorged vegetables. Things were certainly looking up at last.

Chapter 5

Mervin's hot beery breath fanned my face as he leant earnestly towards me across the table. I sat and listened impassively wondering how, despite every effort to the contrary, I was having a 'date' with Spam Man. It was so surreal it made me think about Daniel Defoe.

Now Daniel Defoe, according to my old university professor, was the father of the novel and, as a realist writer created an illusion that there is a relationship between 'art' and a hidden reality. The author's job as narrator was to convey, through words, the 'truth,' and, as the author, or 'God' was able to demonstrate the workings of Providence, or fate. It was really quite straightforward. Providence smiled benignly on white, male, rational, adventurous colonialists such as Robinson Crusoe, and they prospered. But a malevolent glare was reserved for enterprising but irrational and morally loose women like Roxana, who invariably came to a sticky end.

But who believes that bullshit anymore I frantically tried to reassure myself as I suddenly became aware that remnants of Mervin's dinner were glued to his moustache? Every enlightened person knows that the novel has been used in the past as a tool by the ruling hegemony to oppress women and the masses in order to maintain a white, middle-class, protestant, capitalist, male dominated society. A fleck of food wafted down onto the table. I idly pushed it around as my thoughts continued to drift. If Providence is merely an illusion I reasoned, why, as the author of my own life, was I sitting here being well and truly spammed?

And, even worse, why could I see Konnie across Mervin's acrylic-clad shoulder, flirting for dear life with a good-looking man whose body language was saying, "Fuck me, I'm yours." A good-looking man who answers to the name of Jake. As in my ex. You really couldn't make it up.

"So you see," said Mervin, his drony voice dispelling my intellectual musings, "Fate has brought us together."

Reality suddenly invaded my thoughts like a wet bum-flannel in the face.

"I think your time's up," I replied as the ear-splitting sound of a bell rent the air—a bell that signalled it was time for Mervin to move on to the woman sitting at the next table, a move that drew Jake inexorably closer to me.

It hadn't taken long for my speed dating hopes to be dashed when I walked expectantly into the retro Neon City bar and bumped straight into Mervin. He was instantly recognisable but looked like a shady sex-tourist as he was wearing these weird clip-on shades attached to his glasses in an attempt to arrive incognito.

As soon as his eyes adjusted to the low lighting and he realised it was me, he lifted up his shades and embraced me in such a tight hug that they dug into my forehead and left scars. Konnie was mystified.

"Do you two know each other or are you taking the term speed dating quite literally?" Mervin's eyes swivelled appreciatively to Konnie.

"We are acquainted," he said. "I'm Mervin Purvis by the way and I was at Rebecca's house until the early hours last Friday where we spent a very enjoyable evening together sharing our life experiences."

"Is that all you shared Rebecca?" she said nudging me in the ribs and giving us both a naughty wink. "Or is there something you're not telling me?"

Konnie and Mervin seemed to find her remark hugely amusing but all I could manage was a thin smile as I made my way to the bar.

"I don't know about you but the level of talent in here seems pretty grim to me," I whispered to Konnie. "If it doesn't improve soon, I'm going to ask for my money back."

"There's always Mervin," she teased. "Have you said a nice thank you for the flowers yet?"

I glared at her as we collected our drinks and then wandered over to queue for our name badges and 'courting' cards. Suddenly, a loud bell rang and a bottle-blonde woman, who introduced herself as Shelly, asked everyone to sit down at one of the small tables scattered around the bar so she could explain the rules of engagement. The women were told to sit tight at a table while the men were instructed to make a three-minute visit for a chat during which time you both had the chance to size each other up and decide whether or not you fancied seeing each other again. If the answer was yes, you put a tick against their name on your card, if you thought they were pants you put a cross.

Matching ticks meant the agency exchanged your e-mail addresses. Pretty ruthless really, but then natural selection never took any passengers. Survival of the fittest has always been the name of the game.

So that's how I came to be having a 'date' with Mervin, the big fat fossil. I breathed out a sigh of relief as our interview finished and he shifted his bulk to the next table and some other poor unsuspecting woman, and then I took a sharp intake of breath as I watched Jake edging closer. It turned my thoughts and stomach into complete turmoil. It didn't help either when a fifty-something man sat down in front of me wearing a wig that looked as if it had been hacked out of an old moth-eaten Afghan coat.

"Hi, the name's Ted," he said extending his hand and smiling widely, revealing a set of ill-fitting dentures.

Ted was number twenty-eight out of thirty men up for interview as a potential lifelong partner or short-term shagger who had paid fifteen quid to meet the woman of his dreams. It was difficult to reconcile the sight of Ted with the blurb in the speed dating literature that hinted obliquely at ranks of testosterone-fuelled men and libidinous women all lined up waiting for a perfect match to ignite their mutual dormant flames of passion.

The only interest passion-wise I'd encountered pre-Ted, could be compared to a paraffin heater that had rusted to extinction in some outside lavatory in a northern slum earmarked for demolition under a government regeneration scheme. I wanted to warm myself by a furnace, a fierce heat that could scorch me from a distance melting my resistance with a sidelong glance that hinted at shared pleasure, tender, raw and desperate, all night long. I thought of Jake and instinctively licked my lips. Ted reached out and squeezed my hand.

"You're a beautiful lassie m' dear," he slathered, as beads of sweat oozed out from underneath the thatch perched on top of his head.

"That's very kind of you to say so," I replied as I swiftly withdrew my hand and sat on it.

"So, are you in the glamour business then?" he enquired hopefully staring at my chest.

"Good god no," I exclaimed indignantly. "I'm a reporter on a well-respected newspaper."

Ted, looking a bit shifty, shuffled uncomfortably in his seat before changing tack and asking me all about my interests. I told him I reserved all my passion and energy for the garden.

His eyes lit up like flash bulbs before launching into an eloquent speech about the beloved half-acre plot behind his cottage that he was going to lose in a divorce settlement. He lovingly described his shallots, his old-fashioned sweet-scented bed of roses and all the flowers and salad stuff he'd reared in his greenhouse.

"I won't miss the wife," he said. "But I won't half-miss my garden, all my own work for the past twenty-five years." I thought he was going to cry.

I reached out and squeezed his hand, offering him my heartfelt sympathy as one gardener to another and then covered up his obvious distress by telling him about my less ambitious but equally loved patch of flower-filled ground.

Before we knew it, our three minutes were up.

"It's been lovely talking to you Rebecca," said Ted.

"You too," I replied truthfully as we warmly shook hands.

Lovely guy I thought as I watched him saunter off to the next table. A kindred spirit talking the universal language of flowers, a mutual, unspoken understanding that only true garden lovers can comprehend, an obsession that crosses every social, cultural and religious divide.

"Obviously smitten."

I turned my head to see a smiling stranger sitting opposite me, his greenish eyes fringed with long brown lashes, twinkling with amusement.

"No, no, no," I spluttered, blushing furiously, emphasising my disinterest by making slow exaggerated scissor movements under my chin. "Absolutely no way." Then leaning forward with my hands splayed on the table I whispered conspiratorially, "He's hideous, hideous, lecherous and bald."

And then backtracking, so as not to sound like a complete cow, I said obscurely, "But he likes gardening," as if that explained everything.

"Well, Rebecca," he replied glancing at my name badge, there's no hope for me then. "What would you say if you knew I'd only got a slab for a backyard?"

"Well," I said, drawing out the vowel sound to give me time to think up a suitable response. "It's not an essential qualification, handy, but I could make allowances if there were other, you know, compensations."

My hot little eyes glanced at the shadow of chest hair exposed between the open collar of his shirt, his clean, sharp cheekbones and lithe body clad in arty clothes.

"You mean, like a nice personality?" he queried.

"Yeah, yeah, something like that," I muttered, wondering if hidden in his remark there was a slight rebuff for my character assassination of Ted. Or was he being ironic because he knew I was a tad interested sex-wise?

I decided to go on the offensive. "So, if you don't spend your time gardening what do you do instead?"

He explained that he liked making things with his hands. I also discovered that he loved sushi, Degas and the Simpsons and he had a ten-year-old daughter called Freya who was the light of his life. And he was named Tor because his father loved walking in mountains. I gave him an edited, slightly sexed-up version of my life and then the bell went and he was gone and Jake sat down in his place.

"Well, well, fancy meeting you here," he said, smiling his familiar heart-stopping smile.

"I could say the same to you," I replied. "Where's the saintly Sabrina, gone off you, has she?"

"I'm here for research purposes actually," he answered pompously. I arched my brows.

"I'm here with Maggie from the department to analyse the political dynamics of social interaction between the sexes in a post-modern syntagmatic scenario."

"You mean you're looking at the new ways people cop off with one another," I answered facetiously.

Jake sighed and his eyes went heavenward. He looked gorgeous as he struggled to rein in his irritation. He took a deep breath.

"So, tell me why you're here then, you obviously haven't managed to snare a knob with a double-barrelled name and Range Rover yet."

Conveniently forgetting about Charles Smythe Bothum-Wethem, I managed to look suitably aggrieved at his assumption that I was only on the lookout for a rich bloke to look after me, a weary bone of contention throughout the whole of our relationship.

Pointing to Konnie I explained that I was actually here with a girlfriend—a relationship Jake used to claim I was incapable of achieving because in his book, women with big tits who told men how to give them an orgasm in bed were incapable of female friendships. Too vain and selfish to share. A ball-shriveller in other words.

No, only 'nice' women can achieve solidarity with other women, the sort who have pasty faces scrubbed clean of makeup and sport a chest as flat as an ironing board. Like Sabrina, who by the way was the biggest bitch in Christendom despite looking as demure as a nun—when it suited her.

"So you're friends with Konnie?" said Jake, his tone changing from one of slight hostility to one of genuine interest.

"Yes, it was Konnie who suggested we came here tonight, actually," I said, casually looking down to examine my fingernails before hiding them when I saw they were black rimmed from the garden.

"Meow," said Jake.

I bristled with indignation, although I had to secretly admit that my remark could be interpreted as a bit un-sisterly and my gesture might be construed as slightly Freudian—an unconscious unsheathing of claws.

Emphasising every word, Jake went, "She is gorgeous." And then, quite casually, "By the way, did I mention that Sabrina was seconded to an Australian university for a year—and she's been there for two?"

"No, you didn't."

"The split's mutual, we'd grown apart emotionally and geographically, literally. Now, tell me all about Konnie."

I spent the last-minute eulogising about her, what a great friend, clever, nice, funny, popular, ten years younger than me, childless and looking for a long-term relationship. Every word felt like a dagger in my heart, almost as bad as that stabbing pain when you lose your mobile phone or when you realise you've left it on a train.

I couldn't work out if I was relieved or sad when he had gone, and the ordeal was over, and Konnie and I sat down with a drink for a post-mortem of the talent on offer.

Konnie was euphoric. "What did you think of the dark-haired chap with the blue eyes who was wearing a floral shirt? Was he gorgeous or what? I wet my pants as soon as he sat down. God, I thought I was going to come he was so sexy. Did he tell you he was a politics lecturer? He's got a PhD you know. Dr Manderson he's called at the university. He said he's never been married, he's got no kids but really wants them, he lived with someone years ago but they split and he's had a string of relationships since but they've all been disastrous."

"I was one of them," I said bleakly.

Konnie's mouth dropped and she smote her forehead with the palm of her hand. "Of course, Jake, politics lecturer, drop-dead gorgeous, I should have

37

known, I can see now why you fell for him and kept him under wraps. Lucky you. Was he good in bed?"

"Fantastic," I said woodenly. We both fell silent.

"Look," Konnie said slowly, "I will understand if you don't want me to put a tick by his name."

I felt her eyes scrutinising me forensically for my reaction and I briefly struggled with my conscience before giving an Oscar winning performance.

"I don't mind a bit," I lied. "It was all over ages ago, and as Jake said, ours was just one disastrous relationship in a string of others. I just hope you have better luck then I did, and anyway, why should I care when I could have that babe magnet Mervin?" Konnie laughed and gave me a hug and I felt a huge sense of warmth and affection towards her and then the conversation thankfully moved on and I asked her advice about the terrible dilemma facing me. Should I be callous and put a big cross by Mervin's name or be kind and give him a tick so as not to hurt his feelings? She advised that the best thing to do was to blow him out or he'd be hanging round like a bad smell for ever and I'd never shake him off.

I didn't mention my other dilemma, whether I should put a cross or a tick by Jake's name. I wanted so much to tick his name, just to see if he ticked mine. If he ticked mine and I didn't tick his I thought, that would really hurt his feelings, and if I didn't tick his, how would I ever know if he ticked mine? Round and round I went until I was in a right tizzy. I managed to avoid filling in my card in front of Konnie as we queued to hand them in. She gave hers in with a flourish, but I lingered, standing there chewing my pen looking as if I was agonising over which man to choose. Turning my back to Konnie I scanned down the list of names. I quickly put a tick by Jake's name and then looked at the other names to put a tick by Tor's. I saw Ted Franks' name followed by Tor Franklin.

"Are you ready?" Konnie asked as she tried to peer over my shoulder.

Panicking, I quickly put a tick by Tor's name and thrust the card into Shelly's hand without checking to see if it was in the right box.

"All done," I smiled.

"So go on then, who tickled your fancy?" Konnie asked.

Luckily, I was able to elaborate in-depth about my interview with Tor. As I recounted our meeting, I realised with surprise that I would in fact really like to see him again.

Yes, I really hoped that I would find his e-mail address in my inbox the next day.

"I just knew you'd fancy him, he's just your sort, creative. He's an artist isn't he, quite successful by the sound of it? Not my type though, not with my analytical brain.

He seemed nice too, coming here for his neighbour's sake, that weirdo in the wig. His wife ran off and left him you know, for a woman, the president of the local WI no less. Apparently, he found them 'at it' in his caravan in Ingoldmells. You'd think they'd be too busy, making all that jam."

I was absolutely speechless. Mute. "Are you all right?" Konnie asked solicitously as she unlocked the car.

"Don't even ask," I said as my thoughts ricocheted from my appalling crucifixion of Ted as to why Tor had pretended he was virtually a labourer. Why, why, why? Did that mean he fancied me or not? It was too, too cruel. Did he want to see if I fancied him for himself, or was he being economical with the truth because he didn't want me to want him.

And then a horrible thought struck me. Was I absolutely sure I ticked Tor's name and not Ted's? I was in such a state. I couldn't remember for sure, but I had a horrible feeling.

I'll soon find out I thought as I lay in bed with the events of the evening playing over and over again in my fevered brain like a sitcom repeat on the BBC. Tossing and turning, my imagination ran riot with images of Konnie and Jake trying out all the sexual positions in the Karma Sutra. I ground my teeth with jealous rage.

I'm going to look like a dog again for Charles tomorrow night, was my last thought as I drifted off to sleep to the sound of the dawn chorus. Konnie phoned me excitedly at lunchtime. "I got Jake's e-mail, that means he wants to see me again. I can't wait. Did you get one from Tor?"

I was still bleary eyed when I told her I didn't realise they would arrive quite so soon so checked my email on my phone as we spoke. I felt apprehensive. What would I find? Would I get an e-mail from Jake, or Tor?

I poked the screen. It seemed to take forever. Then, suddenly there it was. 'Speed Dating.' I clicked. The message read: "Your speed dating evening has been a success. You have one e-mail match." It was from Ted. I relayed the message to Konnie then hung up, rushed upstairs and flung myself down on Joey's bed and howled.

Chapter 6

Joey looked disdainfully at the blue and white plant potholder shaped like a clog that I'd dug out from the back of a cupboard for his school bazaar's tombola stall.

"Ashley's mum does cakes, and cheese straws," he said accusingly.

He stood there, arms akimbo with an accusatory scowl on his face, then, wrinkling up his nose and pursing his lips, he gingerly picked up the offending object from the kitchen table. He examined it closely as if he were an expert from Sotheby's, before discarding it with disgust.

"It's rubbish."

It was difficult to disagree. The clog was crap. Nevertheless, I felt obliged to defend the wretched thing and my magnanimity and generosity in donating it to a good cause.

"It's from Holland," I said defensively, as if this automatically increased its value.

"Aunty Thelma bought it back full of tulip bulbs, from Delft."

Joey considered this piece of information thoughtfully before declaring, "It's still rubbish. You say everything in Aunty Thelma's house is rubbish. You say she's got a heart of gold but taste that's totally excrement."

"Execrable," I corrected hastily, feeling too queasy to explain the difference. I was in a hole but unwisely kept digging.

"I'm sure I wouldn't say that," I continued in an artificially high falsetto voice. "Aunty Thelma's house reflects her personality, it's, it's original." I floundered, waving my arms vaguely in the air as if searching for inspiration, "And it's full of, of…."

"Kitsch," interjected Joey. I glared.

"You've said it lots of times," he reminded me. "And anyway, if all her stuff's so nice and priceless, why are you giving it away?"

I stood there flummoxed. My shoulders sagged and I conceded defeat. "We could fill it with sweets," I implored. "And it wouldn't take five minutes to make some flapjacks."

Sensing victory, Joey decided to push home his advantage to see if he could secure further strategic gains.

"Okay," he sniffed. And then, looking decidedly smug, he overplayed his hand. "Maybe we could make a fancy-dress costume as well. Ashley's mum has made him a hobbit's outfit." He studied my impassive face. "It's got papier-mâché feet and pointy ears."

I rubbed my hands wearily across my eyes, tired and red-rimmed from the copious weeping fit following my speed-dating cock-up.

"Ashley's mum has got a cleaner, a gardener, a husband, she doesn't go out to work and she has all her ironing delivered in a van," I said in a voice laced with envy.

Then a thought suddenly struck me. "Anyway, how long have you known about this fancy-dress costume lark, I can't remember having a note about it from your teacher?"

Joey squirmed.

"It couldn't by any chance be lurking about in the bottom of your school bag, could it?" I asked archly. "The temporal vortex where things just mysteriously disappear?"

"Whatever," he said, shrugging nonchalantly as he wandered over to the pantry.

"I suppose Ashley's mum could rustle you up a fancy dress costume out of thin air," I said, feeling slightly peeved that I would probably be the only mother at the bazaar with a fancy-dress-less child.

"Bet," said Joey.

I felt a grave sense of injustice and it reminded me that despite the fact that Ashley's mum is a thoroughly decent, kind and inoffensive woman, I often wish that she were dead. At least three or four times a week in fact. Whatever feeble efforts I make at motherhood, Ashley's mum always does it better. Heaps. I simply can't compete. She is to me what an Olympic athlete is to a contestant running in a local marathon with the stamina of a truss-wearing octogenarian suffering from a hernia. I followed Joey into the pantry and scanned the shelves for the necessary ingredients; "syrup, flour, sugar, salt, margarine, oats," I muttered as I grabbed stuff from the shelves and the fridge.

I passed Joey the ingredients as I found them, but it soon became obvious that there were no porridge oats.

"Oats, oats, please God let me find some oats," I muttered beseechingly. My search became more and more frenzied as it slowly dawned on me that I hadn't got any.

My pantry is like my life, I thought, smiling bitterly at the cruel analogy, it's an oats-free zone.

"What's so funny?" asked Joey.

"Life," I said.

"Does that mean I can't take any flapjacks to the bazaar?"

His bottom lip began to wobble, and his big blue eyes started to swim with ushered tears.

How odd that a child should sense the correlation between comedy and tragedy I thought as I smoothed back his hair from his broad forehead.

"Of course, not," I said softly, with more hope than conviction.

"But," I added, glancing at the clock. "If you can't make an omelette without breaking eggs, we are not going to make any flapjacks unless I drive like a bat out of hell to the shops in Newton Saucey. The problem is it would waste too much time driving around looking for a non-existent parking space."

Joey's eyes widened in fear.

"Or," I said suddenly inspired. "You could pop round to Aunty Thelma next door to see if she's got any."

Joey was out of the door like a flash.

If anyone's got a spare box of porridge oats floating about, I thought, Thelma's the most likely candidate, because despite the fact that she lives alone, her weekly shop is so huge it could be delivered in a skip. I'm sure she's got a reinforced trolley reserved for her at the local supermarket.

"You never know when you might get caught short," is a favourite Aunty Thelma maxim. Any potential world crisis such as a war in the Middle East, a radioactive leak from a nuclear power station or a pandemic, will spur her into buying industrial quantities of toilet rolls and bottled water. The first flake of snow acts as a trigger to fill her three freezers to bursting point. She's got bottled runner beans going back to the 1980s.

"I lived through the war," she explained to me once. "We used to have to recycle our sanitary towels, scrub them clean with scraps of boiled soap. If the

Germans had reached Wethershire , my dear, we would have been totally unprepared. Mother wasn't a planner."

The only drawback with Thelma's food stash I remembered as I saw Joey running joyfully up the garden path with a packet under his arm, is that everything's usually well past its sell-by-date.

Joey burst into the kitchen bringing with him the scent of autumn and the chill of the dying year.

"I've got some Mum," he panted. "And Aunty Thelma says she will be across soon to help."

I quickly grabbed the clog and shoved it under the sink before getting out the mixing bowl and scales.

"Let's have it then," I said, reaching for the packet as Joey blew a layer of dust off the top. I studied it carefully, only six weeks out of date, insignificant I decided. Surely, any weevils or fungi bits will be incinerated in the oven. Anyway, I reasoned, it's a balance between the negligible health risks and my sanity if I don't get the blasted things made.

Soon the kitchen was a hive of frantic culinary activity with the ingredients being weighed and stirred while Flossie the dog zoomed round hoovering up the crumbs from the floor, wagging her tail with unashamed ecstasy. When aunty Thelma's head popped round the door, it was followed by a pile of folded cereal boxes, coloured paper and a bag of old plastic margarine boxes balanced precariously in her arms.

Within a couple of hours twenty-six delicious flapjacks lay resplendent on the kitchen table and, as if by magic, Joey was transformed into a cardboard pterodactyl complete with a mask and margarine pots slung round his arms like plastic vertebrae sporting magnificent glued-on wings.

"Nigh on fifty years teaching in a primary school comes in handy sometimes," said Thelma as she surveyed her handiwork.

"You're a star," I said as I kissed her, before rushing out the door laden down with two biscuit tins full of flapjacks.

"You're bad," said Joey as he manoeuvred his wings into the car.

"What makes you say that?" I queried as I pulled out of the drive.

"You've got Aunty Thelma's clog hidden in your bag."

I took a deep breath and frantically tried to think up a suitably impressive excuse but failed miserably.

"Do you think we should keep it then?" I asked him.

He shook his head so vigorously in affirmation that his wings rattled.

"Aunty Thelma's kind and it would be rank to chuck it. I want to keep it."

I felt truly chastened by the time we arrived at the school to queue with crowds of bored parents and excited children to get into the main hall. We were confronted with a familiar ragbag assortment of games and stalls selling recycled junk, while teas were being served against a backdrop of the school orchestra screeching like a cacophony of tom cats being castrated simultaneously.

Joey flapped around excitedly in his fancy dress costume. "I want a ticket for the bran tub and a go on the rubber coconut shy," he squawked tugging at my sleeve. I was suddenly overcome with a massive sense of ennui as the noise and an overwhelming smell of wax crayons and stale pee seeped into my brain. I handed over a fiver telling him to spend it wisely and then sank gratefully onto a hard wooden chair to enjoy a cup of tea and a bun.

As I watched him run over to Ashley to show off his fancy dress costume, my mobile phone rang.

"Hi, it's Mervin. We've got to talk."

My heart sank. I don't need this right now I thought as he embarked on an epic emotional saga charting my speed dating betrayal. I could just imagine him, a quivering mass of indignant bristly jelly.

I yawned as I listened to the predictable self-indulgent rant, I'd heard from so many men before, the obvious sexual chemistry between us, thwarted only by my refusal to face up to my repressed sexual urges, how, if I'd only let go, I could climb to untold heights of ecstasy and achieve shuddering multiple orgasms that would make my teeth rattle.

"I'm prepared to give you a second chance," he said, pausing for breath.

"I'll let you know," I said in a bored voice as I turned the phone off and slung it in my bag with irritation. Dream on, I thought.

"Mind if I sit here?" said a voice suddenly.

I turned to see that Ashley's mum, Julia had sat down next to me, her usually placid and perfectly made-up face drawn with school-bazaar-induced stress.

"No," I said smiling politely. "Feel free."

We chatted about this and that before Ashley's mum suddenly dropped a bombshell of nuclear proportions.

"You know I envy you," she said suddenly.

"Me?" I asked with incredulity.

"Yes, Ashley's always going on about you, how you're such a fun mum, so trendy and with-it compared to me. All I hear is 'Joey's mum said this, or Joey's mum said that.' I feel quite dowdy and inferior."

She looked puzzled as I started to laugh and then helpfully thumped me on my back as bits of bun went down the wrong way as I doubled up with mirth.

"I bet you've secretly wished that I would disappear from the face of the planet," I said when I'd recovered my breath and wiped tears of laughter from my eyes. She looked sheepish and blushed. I relieved her of her embarrassment by explaining about my own seething jealousy at her apparent mythical status as 'the perfect mum.' We both realised we'd been 'had' and decided that the best thing to do was to play along with it.

"Mum's the word," I said as we parted the best of friends, agreeing to meet up for a coffee in the future.

I was positively jaunty as Joey and I drove home in the car despite the fact that he'd blown his fiver on the bran tub and accumulated a useless heap of tat worth about 50p.

But then, nothing could have dispelled Joey's joy as he'd won the fancy-dress competition, judged by the mayor of Newton Saucey.

"He'd got a long chain made out of real gold," said a wide-eyed Joey to Aunty Thelma, as he proudly showed off his winner's badge.

"Did you get anything nice dear?" she said turning to me.

"She won a prize on the tombola," interjected Joey.

I held up an orange Gerbera plant for inspection and offered it to her.

"I'd like you to have it actually as a 'thank you' for bailing us out in our hour of need."

"I wouldn't dream of it my dear," she replied. "I don't expect a present every time I give you a hand. I enjoy it."

Turning to Joey she asked if he could find a nice plant pot to put it in. Joey looked at me inscrutably. "We've got just the thing Aunty," he said as he ran from the room. He returned triumphantly with the clog and placed it slap bang in the middle of the coffee table.

"Perfect," said Aunty Thelma as she popped the plant inside. "Just perfect."

Chapter 7

The night air was bitterly cold. Wild vicious easterly winds were whipped into a maelstrom of howling ferocity with driving, horizontal pinpricks of rain that left any skin it came into contact with looking like raw meat on a butcher's slab. I was already feeling slightly dishevelled as we drew up outside Hartborne Hall for Squire Percy's dinner, having unwisely opted to wear a lacy cardigan and pashmina instead of my more suitable, but old and shabby best coat.

"I should wrap up warm dear if I were you," warned Aunty Thelma who had kindly agreed to baby-sit. "You'll catch your death if you go out dressed like that."

I gaily dismissed her wise advice with a wave of my hand as I sashayed round the kitchen, hand on hip, in my satin frock and four-inch stiletto-heeled sling-backs.

"I've got a choice of either cold and glam, or warm and dowdy, and I definitely don't do dowdy," I laughed, before merrily going to open the front door to Charles. My reasoning was that I would only have to walk from my house to the car and then from the car to the Hall. How wrong could I be? I wasn't to know that the remote central locking system on Charles' Range Rover would go haywire the minute I reached for the passenger door handle, was I?

And even though it only took a couple of minutes to right itself, it was long enough to make me feel as cold and stiff as a corpse, while the wind and rain whipped my hair into a veritable bird's nest. It took the three miles to the Hall with the car's heating on full blast to defrost my jaw. We travelled almost half-a-mile down a long drive lined with ancient oaks, before the bleak stone facade of Hartborne Hall loomed out of the inky darkness in the glare of the Range Rover's headlights.

As the wheels scrunched over the gravel, the lights picked out the Hall's architectural idiosyncrasies. Twin medieval circular turrets dominated an eclectic range of styles that had been added on over the centuries to the original timbered great central hall and under croft, built in the 1300s by the founding Albion-Hartborne's. Charles parked a short drive away from the Hall next to a row of cars, including Delia's infamous navy Freelander. I braced myself as I pushed open the car door against the powerful force of the wind, only for a huge gust to swing it open with such violence that I tumbled out in a most unladylike fashion.

Charles rushed round gallantly to pick me up off the ground before opening a huge black umbrella that proved absolutely useless in the teeth of the stormy night as it instantly turned inside out. He grabbed my arm and bent double, we slowly made our way to the cavernous gothic porch with the family motto, 'Rise up and Conquer' inscribed in the stone. I stood huddled against the nail studded door with my pashmina draped unflatteringly around my head framing my pinched and shivering face. I was frozen to the marrow and my teeth chattered so loudly that they sounded like a cacophony of mating grasshoppers.

While Charles pulled the heavy doorbell, I cursed myself for my profound vanity and stupidity in not wearing a coat. The warm interior of the hall looked inviting as it shone out from between the chinks of heavy wooden shutters folded across the inside of the windows to keep out the icy blast. According to the locals it flies unimpeded from the remote and frozen slopes of the Urals in Russia, across the sea and the heather-clad moors of Yorkshire, directly to Wethershire
.

Sometimes, if it's in the right direction, you can stand on a windy ridge overlooking the small, fertile, undulating valleys and taste the salt from the sea pounding along the shore fifty miles to the east.

"Where's that old crone, Mrs Hoare?" I heard Charles mutter through clenched teeth as he pulled on the bell for what seemed like the hundredth time.

"I cannot see the sense in employing a woman to open the door who's as deaf as a post and as slow as a tortoise. We'll have frozen to death before she gets her slippers into gear."

Turning to see me huddled in the corner like a drowned rat, he opened wide his cashmere coat and invited me to cuddle up inside. Sod it, I thought as I wound my frozen arms around his back and pushed my face into the welcoming warmth of his scarf. Just because I've accepted his kind offer of refuge from the storm and the sharing of his body heat, doesn't mean he'll be silly and assume it's an invitation for anything else. Wrong. Soon after our bodies made contact, I became acutely aware that he had a massive hard-on.

How can a man experience a stiffy in sub-zero temperatures? I thought with incredulity. If he knocks it against anything it's likely to snap.

I was saved by any further amorous advances by the sound of the great wooden door opening with a creak of its massive ornate hinges.

The face of Mrs Hoare, lined with more contours than a map of Everest appeared in the gloom, before disappearing behind the door that opened to reveal a magnificent timber roofed hall with black, oak panelled walls and a huge stone fireplace with logs as big as small trees burning in the grate.

Charles, aware of the bulge in his trousers, suddenly looked distinctly discomforted and seemed reluctant to let go of me. As my body temperature had dropped to what seemed like freezing point, my limbs felt locked to Charles like a frozen ice cube to a warm lip.

Unsure of how to proceed, we shuffled sideways into the house like conjoined twins, drawn like magnets to the blazing hearth, under the disapproving glare of Mrs Hoare. It was here that Percy found us as he bounded forward to greet his guests. "Hi Charlie, old boy," he said, slapping his friend heartily on the back. "Is this your latest squeeze then?"

He stared intently into my face before pronouncing in a very pleased, loud voice,

"We have met before haven't we, I never forget a face, you're the doggie woman aren't you?"

Charles looked faintly shocked. "Doggie woman?"

Percy threw back his head and laughed revealing two rows of perfectly straight white teeth. I hastened to explain to Charles about my little adventure with Flossie and then turned to Percy to congratulate him for recognising me after such a brief encounter.

"I must have looked a complete fright I was so hot and bothered and my hair was all over the place," I laughed, casually turning to glance into the magnificent ornate mirror hanging above the fireplace.

My eyes widened in horror as a ravaged face stared back. Think 'Mortica does Alice Cooper.' My dark hair had gone completely haywire around my face, white except for flushed red checks and black eyeliner that had streaked into two black triangles.

"Oh my God," I shrieked.

To cover up my confusion and embarrassment Percy beckoned to Mrs Hoare and asked her to show me to the nearest bathroom so I could repair the damage.

"Show her into the drawing room when she's ready," he said and then, tenderly pushing a tendril of hair from across my forehead and looking deeply and longingly into my eyes he whispered, "I'm quite sure you are very beautiful."

My heart quickened and I felt like reaching out to run my fingers over his soft perfect lips.

"Chop, chop," said Charles breaking the spell as he took Percy's arm and marched him off. "Make haste and join us as soon as you can."

It took a while to redo my makeup which had suffered serious structural damage. And although I dragged a comb through my hair it still refused to calm down and hung in damp wild curls around my face.

I followed Mrs Hoare to the drawing room as she shuffled along at a snail's pace in worn sheepskin slippers. I took a deep breath to steady my nerves as I entered the room elegantly furnished with antiques. The walls were decorated with faded tapestries and huge cracked oil paintings of cows and horses hung alongside portraits of long dead Hartbornes.

I suddenly became acutely aware that a host of male eyes suddenly seemed to have locked onto my chest with the accuracy of short-range guided missiles. I blushed furiously as I realised that my indrawn breath had accentuated the fact that I wasn't wearing a bra and my erect nipples which hadn't had time to defrost, were starkly outlined beneath my damp satin frock which clung to my curves like a second skin. Feeling flustered I frantically tried to smooth them down with my hands only to arouse them further until they were so rigid and stiff they were positively pornographic.

Percy's father, Sir Walter, was positively drooling in his wheelchair by the fire, his eyes bulged, and his mouth dropped open and a piece of chewed olive fell onto the tartan rug covering his knees.

"My Gad, she's a decent bit of horseflesh," I heard him say. "I demand that she sits next to me at dinner."

Hastily pulling my cardigan together I went over to Delia who was tittering into a glass of sherry.

"Do you think you could flash your tits under Henry's nose, with a bit of luck it might give him a heart attack," she whispered.

I looked over to Henry who was warming his buttocks by the fire as he flirted with a young blond woman with an orange tan.

"I think she must be the new woman who's moved into the restored coach house on the estate," I observed to Delia. "And that middle-aged bloke over there with the leather trousers and the medallion has got to be her husband."

Delia cast a critical eye over him. "He calls himself a business consultant, but I've heard he's an asset stripper. Made all his money in bitcoin."

She immediately christened him the 'Oil Slick,' as we continued to dissect the couple critically for the next few minutes, dragging out their fashion sense and social status like bloodied entrails, poking around for signs of disease. We finally decided they were 'new money,' probably swingers with his 'n' hers towelling bathrobes and a villa in Spain.

I was just about to offer another juicy observation when I suddenly became aware of someone standing at my shoulder. It was Mrs Poole. Gladys the housekeeper has worked at the Hall for as long as anyone can remember, living in a tied cottage on the estate with Cess who works on the land, just as his father and generations of Poole's have done since the year dot.

"Sherry?" asked Gladys.

"Thank you, that would be nice," I said. "Or maybe not, maybe I should stick to soft drinks."

"So, it's a soft drink then?" said Gladys shuffling off.

She brought me a sweet sherry. I looked at Delia and shrugged. "I hate sweet sherry," I said wrinkling my nose as I knocked it back.

"Word's going around there's a family crisis," whispered Delia. "Lady Howgrave mentioned it to Percy before you came in after Gladys had spilt gin all over Sir Walter. She's all at sixes and sevens."

I glanced around the rest of the large spacious room to see Charles' uncle and aunt, Lord and Lady Howgrave deep in conversation with Camilla and Neville Shotley, two big cheeses in the hunting fraternity. I saw Camilla shudder as she caught my glance from across the room. Camilla and Neville treat me with complete disdain just in case they're tainted by association with my family as we are distantly related on my father's side. Camilla's great grandfather Arthur was a cousin of my great grandfather Joel. Their side of the family inherited most of the land, the money and the buck teeth. Our side of the family inherited a few acres, a flair for business, brains and good looks.

I gave her a little wave. Her face momentarily tightened before relaxing into a saccharine smile.

As my eyes scanned the rest of the room, I decided that the chance of any decent talent appearing was negligible until Percy appeared at the door of the drawing room and invited us all to follow him into the dining room. Sitting at the table was the most unutterably and indescribably beautiful man I've ever clapped eyes on.

"I think Michelangelo's David has metamorphosed into flesh and appeared in a vision." I said turning to Delia.

"What was that?" said Charles who had just joined us after chatting to Sir Howgrave about the weekend's Point to Point.

"Err, I was just saying how Michelangelo's David was the most memorable highlight of my holiday in Italy, a masterpiece of classical sculpture whose exquisite lines are only rivalled by Donatello's David in the Bargello."

Charles looked impressed as he sat down next to me at the table. "Didn't know you were an art expert," he said.

"I just dabble," I improvised wildly, changing the subject by commenting that the cutlery was rather attractive. I saw Camilla's eyes narrow in disapproval at the observation which I'm sure she considered to be very vulgar.

"Cow," I thought.

I was joined on my right by Sir Walter who was wheeled to the table by Gladys, while Percy sat at the head flanked by the gorgeous guest who was joined by Delia. She looked across at me and smiled before briefly sucking her index finger in a very suggestive manner. Torturer.

I was told by Charles not to expect haute cuisine as all the meals at the Hall are cooked by Gladys whose repertoire hasn't been updated since the 1960s. The only attraction of a dinner invitation is the wine cellar which is impressive and extensive, lined with fine wine and port from some of the best vintages of the last century.

As the starter was served, Percy introduced the gorgeous guest as Seamus O' Connor, a distant relation and an old student friend from their days at agricultural college in Cirencester. Seamus it appeared hailed from County Kerry in Southern Ireland where he lives in the converted stables in the grounds of the vast family pile, surrounded by thousands of acres of land and tenanted property that has been in the family for generations.

Camilla almost purred with pleasure at the realisation she was seated close to 'old money.' He's definitely an upgrade on Charles I thought as we retired to the drawing room after dinner. I felt him looking at me inscrutably as he started smoking a rollup as thick as a Cuban cigar, despite Camilla's nose twitching like a rabbit in disapproval.

Charles wandered over and placed his arm possessively around my waist. He began to chat to Seamus about Irish history which turned out to be all anecdotal. Seamus listened politely while the smoke from his rollup spiralled up to the ancient fan vaulted ceiling, obscuring his green eyes which narrowed like a cat's as Charles recounted a rather tragic incident when one of his relatives was attempting to kiss the Blarney Stone. "His false teeth fell out and hit an unsuspecting American tourist below," Charles said rather heatedly.

"It was all rather unfortunate. The denture was broken by the impact on the American's head who sued for negligence – not very lucky if you ask me."

"Not a good crack," observed Seamus dryly as Charles launched into a tirade about the latest health and safety diktat, a culture which was driving the country to the brink of ruin. I tried to imagine myself in twenty years' time as his other half and shuddered.

Seamus managed to extricate himself from Charles' diatribe which saw no signs of abating, by claiming he needed to find an ashtray. "Absolutely riveting," he said as he excused himself with a naughty wink in my direction as he turned on his heel.

It wasn't long before the wine and conversation flowed as freely as the fragrant smoke from Seamus' rollup as it drifted across the room.

"Damn fine tobacco, that," remarked Sir Walter sniffing the air. "Smells very sweet. It reminds me of when I was doing my National Service in the Middle East during Suez. We bartered with the locals. Came home with sacks full of frankincense. Used to burn it after dinner. Cracking stuff, you could fart like billy-o and no one would notice."

The Oil Slick threw back his head and roared with laughter as his wife, who'd been introduced as Belinda, managed a tight grin. "I've done a few deals in the Middle East in my time. Easy to make a few bob if you know whose palm to cross with silver," he boasted as he mansplained in his chair. He gave a nod and a wink to Sir Walter, who spluttered into his glass of port. "Sound pretty rum to me," Sir Walter re-joined as Belinda quickly changed the conversation by admiring the curtains. "I hope I didn't offend your delicate ears," said Sir Walter turning to me to avoid her inane observations on the curtains that actually looked as if they'd been ravaged by moths.

"Oh no," I replied smiling. "I'm a journalist and tough as old boots."

"Good," he said as he fixed me with a grateful stare.

He turned to Percy. "Fine woman, don't you think? Glorious, breasts like a brace of plump woodcocks. Decent handful."

Percy blushed. "Reminds me of your mother," reminisced Sir Walter staring into his port. "Fine woman, a bit gamey, but that's how I liked it. Earthy."

His description of Perry's mother was at complete odds with my memory of the late Lady Venetia Albion-Hartborne from when I was a child. A remote, thin, highly strung woman who used to pray very devoutly in church holding onto a string of rosary beads, much to the consternation of the rector who was very 'low church.' "Neurotic," my mother used to call her. She died when Percy was fifteen with wild rumours buzzing on the village grapevine that she'd committed suicide, although the official story was that she died of pneumonia after a lifetime suffering with a weak chest.

Sir Walter's indiscreet recollections seemed to set him off into a deep reverie and within a few minutes his head sank onto his chest and he let out a little snore. Percy beckoned to Gladys to wheel Sir Walter away. "Too much excitement for one evening," he said, giving me a saucy smile, which made Charles grimace.

"I think Rebecca has caught a chill from standing outside in the cold," he said as he rubbed his hands solicitously up and down my back. "I think I'd better take her home." And with that we made our farewells and braved the raging elements to reach the car.

"I don't know about you, but my head feels very strange," I said as we drew up outside my house. Charles, undoing his seat belt, fixed me with a peculiar stare.

"More to do with Seamus's wacky backy," he murmured as put his hand around my face and drew it towards him.

"You are so beddable, it's not true," he said hoarsely as his tongue made its way down the back of my throat.

I pulled back. "The neighbours," I said all flustered.

"Don't torture me," he said roughly as he put his hands on my thighs and slid them up under my dress. I struggled to push them off.

"Relax, relax," he moaned, bending his head and burying it in my lap. I felt his body tremble and for a moment I felt a reciprocal response as his urgency seemed to consume us both. And then the light from the moon shone into the car illuminating the comb-over glued to his head and my desire faded like a flower.

I opened the door and let in a draft of air, fresh after the storm. "I'll give you a bell," he called as I thanked him for a lovely evening and made my escape.

"Nice night?" asked aunty who had spent the evening buying Tupperware boxes off QVC.

"Interesting," I said as I flopped down on the sofa and kicked off my shoes with relief.

"Interesting."

Chapter 8

As soon as I saw Konnie on Monday morning, I knew that she'd had sex with Jake.

She didn't actually say she had, or even mention his name, but I just knew.

"Nice weekend?" she asked cheerily as she went past my desk to go up the stairs to accounts.

"Lovely," I replied.

"Catch you later," she said with a smile as she sashayed up the stairs.

I went into the loo, leant over the sink and felt a hot flush of jealousy consume me until my face felt hot and clammy. I felt a strong urge to be sick. The memory of Jake's warm strong body between my thighs flickered across my mind like horny highlights from an erotic movie.

I looked in the mirror and gave myself a good talking to and told myself not to be silly.

"You always tell Joey that it's important to share," I reminded myself. "Practice what you preach."

And then a little voice inside me said, "Jake's not a flippin' lollipop. Women with ex boyfriends don't go around asking their single friends if they'd like him to give them one, seeing as they're not getting any. Sharing lollipops and sharing ex boyfriends are two entirely different ethical debates."

I was standing with my forehead pressed against the mirror when Moira walked in.

"Feeling peaky dear?" she asked.

"Man trouble," I said bleakly.

"I'm afraid I can't help you with that one," she said kindly. "Although I've always found that a nice cup of tea and a bourbon cures most things. I'll bring you one in a tick." Funny I thought, as I went back to my desk, how a simple kindly gesture can ease the most savage feelings that only a minute before had threatened to engulf you. I was eating my bourbon and drinking my tea when

Keith the editor came over to tell me that I would have to go and cover at the district office in Newton Saucey for the day as it transpired that Colin, the reporter who usually ran it was up on a drink drive charge at the local magistrate's court.

"Let's hope our arch-rival the Newton Saucey News doesn't get a whiff of it or it'll be on their front-page Thursday," said Keith.

I have a huge professional respect for Colin, because despite the fact that he's inebriated most of the time, he's got a really good 'nose' for a story and never misses a trick. He gets most of his scoops in the pubs around Newton Saucey, standing there in his faded suit and lurid shirts, his nicotine stained fingers holding a pint. It's amazing what scandal people tell you when they know you're a reporter, you become privy to the seamy underbelly of society, the flotsam and jetsam swirling around in the social sewers, veneered with a thin layer of respectability that only just manages to keep a lid on it all.

As I began to gather up my stuff to head off, I suddenly realised that I would miss my tête-à-tête with Konnie at lunchtime. I felt torn and started to dither. Did I really want a blow by blow account of her sexual smorgasbord with Jake, or would it be better to leave it and then avoid the subject tomorrow? As if. It felt like having to decide whether or not to have the dog put down. Should I prolong the agony and put off the evil hour or get it over with? And then a thought struck me, how could I not see her when I needed her sex-tactic advice on my looming problems with Mervin, Charles and Ted?

I dialled her extension and invited her round for tea. Job done. I felt so much better.

How could I possibly survive without our girlie chats?

"Men, who needs them?" I thought as I drove over the border to Newton Saucey, through the winding roads that cut through the rolling expanse of wooded hills and lush valleys with hawks and Red Kites swirling overhead, hungry for carrion.

I wandered into the district office, said 'hello' to Judy the receptionist and then went straight to the kitchen to make a cup of tea to help psyche myself up for the day ahead which promised to be major dullesville.com. The office is just a glorified shop front with one reporter's desk and a reception area for people to wander in off the street to put adverts in or to fill in an obituary form. The only redeeming feature of the office is the view of the street from the window and the people going by.

Sometimes they pop in for a chat to tell you the latest bit of news which often comes in handy if you're short of a few column inches. The downside is that you're a sitting target for people like local councillors who bore the pants off you with their latest initiative such as recycling 'putrescence.' That's veggie waste like spud peelings, translated into English.

I hadn't been sat at my desk for very long when I was distracted by the sight of Cess Poole walking past the window with a wheelbarrow full of produce from his vast allotment on his way to the farmers' market. I stood at the window and gaily waved hoping he'd call in and give me the latest gossip update, hot off the press from the Doom and Gloom. But he walked straight past as if he hadn't seen me. The mystery deepens I thought. First Gladys walks round Hartborne Hall like some weird servant out of a Hammer Horror movie and now Cess is acting like he's a zombie from The Dawn of the Dead.

I decided I'd pop across to the farmers' market at lunchtime on the pretext of buying an organic apple to see if I could winkle anything out of him, it wasn't like Cess to be backwards in coming forwards with gossip.

By 11 o clock I was gagging for a chocolate fix—a bourbon biccie may be okay for a slight emotional tremor, but Konnie shagging Jake surely qualified as a seismic mental trauma that justified the consumption of a 'king size' Mars Bar. I nipped out to the newsagent and was back sitting at my desk enjoying a really deep throat chocolate experience when this hunky guy walked in and came straight over to me.

"Is there a reporter I could speak to?" he asked.

I felt a desperate desire to choke as I withdrew the Mars Bar very slowly and laid the moist sticky object on the desk.

Aware that my lips were smeared with chocolate, I wiped my mouth with one hand while sticking out the other to introduce myself. Not a good start I thought. Why couldn't he have come in five minutes earlier when I was busy looking professional writing up a news story?

I hastily invited him to take a seat and asked how I could help, not thinking for one minute that he would have an interesting story to tell. But as it turned out, what he had to say was quite fascinating and I knew almost immediately that it would make a good human interest feature, a humbling, heart-breaking story that I might, if I was canny, be able to flog to the nationals for a tidy sum to put towards buying a new stair carpet.

He introduced himself as Scott Henderson and then began to tell me in a strong Australian twang, the very poignant story of how he was sent to Australia from Ireland as an orphan in the 1960s after being given up for adoption by his birth mother. It was a story about triumphing in the face of adversity, overcoming physical and emotional abuse in an Australian children's home to work his way through school as a way of escape, to a life as a successful entrepreneur. But the early emotional traumas created havoc in his personal life with a string of failed relationships following a disastrous early marriage.

"I'd got everything materially I wanted, but at the back of my mind there was a piece missing in the jigsaw puzzle that told me who I was and where I belonged," he said simply, threading his fingers together so tightly that his knuckles shone white. He went on to explain how he decided to do some research and found a site on the internet with an address for an organisation set up to help migrant children deported from the UK.

"It's taken a long time, whoever gave me up for adoption tried to cover their tracks, but I traced my roots back to Wethershire and my mother."

I asked him if his search had been worthwhile. Lowering his eyes, he simply whispered, "Yes." He was a big man, but I could see that telling his story had been difficult. The hurt ran very deep.

"Do you fancy a cup of tea?" I asked.

He agreed and seemed to visibly relax. And when he smiled, I couldn't help noticing that he was very attractive in a rugged sort of lumberjack way. I looked over to Judy to ask if she wouldn't mind sorting out the tea, the poor woman nodded dumbly, she'd obviously been so moved by Scott's story that her desk was obscured with piles of screwed up tissues.

"I would be glad to," she sniffed as she bustled off, wiping her eyes and vigorously blowing her nose.

As we chatted over a cup of tea, it became apparent that although Scott was keen for the story to be published, he wasn't prepared to reveal the names of his parents. "My mother tells me that Wethershire is riddled with gossips and she's not sure if she could face them, although she's livid that she was deceived about me and wants to see justice done."

'Damn,' I thought. No names, no story. I had to play this one carefully and suggested that he gave it another try.

"Your mother was more sinned against than sinner," I said. "I'm sure she'd get the sympathetic vote, why don't you let me talk to her?"

He visibly stiffened as he declined my invitation. I assumed a nonchalant attitude as I tried every trick in the book to winkle out the information I needed, but it was obvious that Scott was going to keep the vital juicy titbit I needed firmly in its shell, although I could see he was torn.

I reached over and squeezed his hand. "Think about it," I offered, "and ring me next week, there's no pressure."

I nearly punched the air with victory when he promised to go back to his mother to ask her to reconsider.

"I'll call and let you know either way," he said as he stood up to leave the office. His face hardened slightly. "I promise I will do what I can." His fists clenched as he hesitated slightly and then he shook his head and sent me the most inscrutable look before turning on his heel to leave.

It was two o'clock before I had the chance to track down Cess after agreeing with Scott that if he could get his mother to agree, I would do a full-length feature story. I gave him my direct line and extracted a promise that he would let me run with it. I also had the foresight to get his mobile number. As soon as he left the office, I pounced on the half-eaten Mars Bar congealing on my desk and consumed it like a ravenous dog. How fortuitous I thought as I munched, that Colin's court case came up today, otherwise he would have had his grubby little fingers all over the story.

"I'm going out to buy an apple," I said to Judy and rushed off before she could put any more calls through about events to raise funds to stop a village hall from closing down or a steeple falling off a church.

As soon as Cess caught sight of me, he buried his head in a sack of parsnips. After he'd been rummaging for about five minutes, I asked him if he'd dropped anything in there by mistake.

"Dropped your teeth in there, Cess?" I shouted across the trestle table after I remembered how I'd laughed when he'd recounted that years ago his teeth had dropped into a cement mixer and he'd just reached in, got them out and rinsed them off before popping them back into his mouth.

His head slowly emerged, like a tortoise from its shell and then he turned and fixed his eyes on me.

"Oh, it's you," he said ungraciously as he started to hump the bag around his stall. "Everything okay?" I asked nonchalantly as I casually turned over a bunch of carrots.

"Do you want to buy those?" he asked.

"Can do," I said. "Gladys all right? Thought she looked a bit stressed on Saturday night."

Cess stuffed the carrots viciously into a bag. "Stressful time, what with all those high falutin' folks who thinks the sun shines out their arses. Do this, don't do owt, do the hokey cokey and turnabout. Told her to stop it years ago."

"I thought Percy's friend Seamus seemed rather nice," I said in a conciliatory tone.

"What, you mean his fancy man?" Cess replied.

"Really?" I said, my heart sinking like a stone. "Are you sure, I thought they were just old friends from their student days?"

Cess gave me a quizzical look. "Known each other since they were nippers. Mrs Albion-Hartborne, she were an O'Connor. Thick as thieves those two families. Thick as thieves."

He handed me the carrots and as he took my cash he said rather cryptically,

"There's one law for the rich and there's one law for the poor, there ain't no justice to be 'ad," and then he turned his attention back to his sack of parsnips.

I got back to the office to find Colin sitting glumly at his desk.

"So, they didn't lock you up and throw away the key then?" I quipped.

"Twelve months ban and a fine for speeding," he said. He looked a tragic figure sitting there in his best suit fiddling with one of his famous novelty ties.

"Are you sure a tie with roadrunner on the front was a good choice for today?" I asked him as I wandered off to the loo which had a permanent layer of his fag ends floating on the surface.

I heard Judy snigger.

"Anything interesting turn up today?" Colin asked vaguely as I took myself off. "Same old stuff," I said as I waved goodbye. "Nothing that would make the front page of the Sun."

Konnie seemed to have a sort of radiance about her as she sat at the kitchen table while I prepared sausages and mash for Joey and Ashley who was staying for tea while his mum and dad went off to Wharram Percy for a wine tasting evening.

She sat placidly while I gabbled on about the Australian guy's story I'd managed to pinch from under Colin's nose.

"He sounds interesting, was he dishy?" she asked.

"Yeah, he was kinda nice," I said. "A bit wizened from the sun and maybe a little old for me. But anyway, I've got enough men on my plate at the moment, even though none of them are remotely dishy. I mean, two of them are sick bucket standard and one of them is only useful to wheel out when I've got nothing else to do." Konnie sighed and smiled faintly and was just going to say something when I interrupted.

"I mean, the only man who has come anywhere near Egon Ronay standard was that Tor bloke and I blew that by ticking the box of his wiggy friend who looked as if he'd borrowed someone else's teeth."

I told her to sit tight while I went upstairs to get his e-mails off my mobile so I could read extracts from them to her so she could advise me on a reply.

"My dearest flower," I read. "My darling rose petal. You have made me the happiest man in England, nothing, not even winning first prize with my onion sets can compare to knowing you want me as much as I want you. My dearest heart, my one and only, I am all yours, body and soul and I can't wait to claim your body which I have to say is very tasty. I send you all my wildest kisses. Ted."

I motioned to a list of other X-rated e-mails that I daren't read out in case Joey and Ashley overheard the contents which conveyed, in very explicit terms, the bedroom delights in store for me for when we consummate our relationship.

"I bet he only used one hand when he wrote those," said Konnie with a shudder. "Oh, don't even go there," I squealed. "I thought I'd e-mail back and say that there must have been a glitch with the computer software or something, I can't possibly, possibly go to see him."

Konnie gave me a pitying look as if I were a half-wit.

"Of course, you must go to see him dummy," she said.

I looked at her with suspicion. Surely, she didn't think…? I must have looked dumbstruck with shock.

Jabbing her finger to her forehead she asked me to think of one good reason why it might be in my interest to give Ted a visit. Try as I might, I had to concede that I could see no reason to incarcerate myself in a room in close proximity to a repulsive individual who had probably induced a sprained wrist in anticipation of the experiences he assumed we would be sharing during my visit.

"I give up," I said. "Enlighten me."

Speaking very slowly in a voice usually reserved for very small, recalcitrant children or senile old people, she pointed out that Ted had an extremely attractive neighbour who I would like to have it off with.

"You are a genius," I told her and waltzed around the kitchen waving my mobile with Ted's e-mails on it in the air, with the sudden realisation that all was not lost with Tor. And then I suddenly thought about the difficulty I would have to face in keeping the amorous Ted at bay until I could make contact with him and pirouetted to an abrupt halt.

I was just about to put this dilemma to Konnie when the doorbell rang. "Answer that," I shrieked to Joey and Ashley who were glued to the telly in the front room. Straining my neck, I shrieked loudly three more times until my ears popped and then gave up and answered the door myself. Delia swept in followed by Toy Boy.

"Darling, I need a refuge," she said.

As soon as she spotted Konnie at the table, she immediately broached the subject I'd been avoiding all day.

"Darling tell all, are you and Jake an item, or were you naughty and just had your wicked way with him?"

Then, realising I might be traumatised by the thought of the love of my life having sex with one of my best friends, she put her hand over her mouth and her eyes widened. "Don't worry," said Konnie blithely. "Rebecca's all au fait about me and Jake. She's given me her blessing to service her ex."

And then she went on, as girlfriends do, to give a blow-by-blow account of her weekend, which, from what I could gather, was spent mainly in a horizontal position in Jake's bed.

"Good for you, just what the doctor ordered," said Delia.

And then, turning to me, she said that she was also suffering from a common affliction that could only be cured by lying down in a darkened room.

"Any chance of using your spare room?" she asked. "Pretty please?"

I told her they could help themselves so long as they locked the door and did it without sound effects.

Delia blew me a kiss before disappearing up the stairs with Toy Boy in tow. What a day I thought later as I slid between the sheets. One friend has sex with my ex while another has sex in my spare bed. And all I get are smutty e-mails from a wanker in a wig. I had to agree with Cess I thought as I drifted off to sleep. 'There's no justice to be had.'

Chapter 9

Journalists always feel aggrieved when they are labelled with the sobriquet hardboiled hack because it really is most unjustified. But unless you've been one yourself, it's difficult to understand how you can socialise with a rival journalist you consider to be a friend one day and then shaft them the next without a twinge of guilt. And maybe, to be fair, it might be a tad difficult to understand how a journalist can take notes during a harrowing inquest where the state of a putrefying murdered corpse is explained in clinical detail, and then go off for a Big Mac and French fries. But they're just doing their job. Like a fishmonger gutting fish.

So I wasn't surprised when I saw the front page of our rival newspaper, The Newton Saucey News on the internet when I got into work. Their paper hits the streets the day when ours goes to press.

As soon as I saw the headline, I knew that Keith would go completely ape. 'Herald journalist in drink drive shame,' it shrieked. The story, which was execrably written, exploited the absolute privilege enjoyed by court reporters by chucking in every morsel of Colin's sad lonely existence, to a bloodthirsty news-hungry public.

'The court was told,' I read with morbid fascination, 'that the defendant was on his way home after visiting an establishment in Newton Saucey known euphemistically as a 'massage parlour.'

"Anything on the front page we haven't covered?" shouted Keith as he walked in. I printed off the front page of the newspaper and holding the page gingerly by one corner, quickly handed it over to him without a word before beating a hasty retreat.

I'd just reached my desk when I heard Keith's explosion rip across the office.

"What the bloody hell did that sex-starved twerp think he was doing?" he raged in fury, his eyes bulging like a bull frog.

"He said it was for research," I yelled helpfully.

"Research my ass, that guy's a fucking liability. Get me a fag someone now." He disappeared into his small office to ring Colin to give him the bollocking of his life.

"Nice one," said Dick as he scanned the story. "Not often you get a juicy scoop like that fall into your lap."

I waited until the uproar over Colin's exposé had died down before I tried Scott Henderson's mobile. It reverted to an answer phone every time I tried it. I'd no intention of giving up so I dialled it at regular intervals until I heard a familiar Australian twang.

"Hello." His voice was really quite sexy.

"Hi, it's Rebecca from the Broadmarket Herald," I said. "Just catching up. Have you managed to speak to your mum yet and is she happy for me to go ahead with the story?"

I could tell from Scott's guarded tone that something had happened since we had last spoken and that for some reason, he was wildly backtracking.

"It's difficult at the moment," he said guardedly. "I don't think she's ready to go public with it yet. I didn't quite understand the delicacy of her situation regarding my real father, it's rather complicated and could cause a great deal of embarrassment if his identity came out."

My ears were buzzing like two vibrating antennae as I smelt the whiff of a major scandal.

"Fine," I said as casually as I could. "No worries, but I'll keep in touch shall I, maybe meet up for a coffee?"

Scott seemed genuinely pleased. "I'd sincerely like to do that before I head off back home. Call me, maybe next week, I'm sorry about the story, but well it was nice to meet you so maybe it's no matter."

My eyes gleamed. "It was nice to meet you too Scott, I'll be in touch."

I pressed down the receiver and then sat knocking the phone handset thoughtfully against my chin. I've got to play this one very carefully, I thought. The guy's an innocent abroad, that's for sure, but if I play my cards right, this could be a scorcher of a story.

It's not often that I take my work home but the thought of how to get Scott Henderson to reveal his parentage preoccupied me as I drove to Hartborne to pick up Joey from Mum's. Despite being a relic from the 1950s she's given me unfailing support since breaking up with Giles, I don't know what I'd do if she didn't look after Joey every evening after school and take Flossie out for walks.

Her pristine fifteen-year-old Yaris, with only 15,000 miles on the clock, was parked on the drive but there was no sign of either of them.

Anyone who has lived in a small village will know that all your movements are monitored 24 / 7 by a band of neighbours with rubbernecks, so I knew that if I went for a stroll, I'd find someone who would know where they were.

They can't have gone far, I thought as I strolled down the street. It wasn't long before I found out after bumping into Gladys Poole who had just come out of the Doom and Gloom.

"Hi Gladys," I said. "Seen anything of Mum and Joey, they're not at home?" Gladys told me that they were busy decorating the church ready for the harvest festival on Sunday.

"I've been a little busy so your mother offered to do an extra window this year although she's using Cess' vegetables. You know they're highly prized by the old folk if they get them in their harvest parcels."

I was gagging to ask Gladys if she was feeling okay but it was difficult because I hadn't seen her looking so well for ages. In fact, she positively glowed.

"You're looking well," I said cheerfully.

"Never felt better my dear," she said smiling.

And with that she scurried off down the street. The church windows glowed like jewels in the darkness as the light, filtered through the stained glass, was fretted like shards of sparkling glass onto the path, the ancient graves and the massive shadowy yews. A cold wind blew off the fields at the end of the lane where a stile led to fields full of grazing sheep.

The smell of eight hundred years of history assailed me as I opened the oak studded door to see an old and a young head bent closely together as their hands worked to wind long strands of ivy around the smooth oak partitions that separates the nave from the chancel. Every window ledge was heaving with fruit and vegetables while the pulpit was crowned with a frothy necklace of chrysanthemums.

"What do you think mum?" asked Joey as he turned his head and saw me wandering down the aisle.

"It's beautiful," I replied as I bent to touch the smooth rounded skin of a marrow lined up with cauliflowers and cabbages, brightened up here and there with contrasting tomatoes and mandarin oranges.

"I've just seen Gladys," I said to mum. "She seems very chirpy, has she won the lottery?"

She stood up from where she'd been kneeling with Joey and climbed into the pulpit to add some contrasting ivy to the decoration. She began to fill me in on all the Gladys gossip that ranged from wild speculation to the fact that 'words' had been exchanged up at the Hall and that Gladys had handed in her notice after working there for more than fifty years. The shock had set Mrs Hoare's rheumatism off and there had been no one to cook or clean a thing.

"The whole place is in a shambles and Sir Walter refuses to have anyone in and I've heard they're living off Chinese takeaways from Chop Suey's in Newton Saucey.

Apparently, Percy doesn't even know how to open a packet of cornflakes."

She paused for breath and said dramatically, "They say that the shock could kill Sir Walter. But you reap what you sow," she said, casting her eyes around the church.

"He's always seemed a decent sort to me, never done anyone any harm from what I've heard and Percy is so funny and charming and handsome."

Mum leant over the edge of the pulpit.

"Don't forget what the Bible says," she said darkly, wagging her finger at a non-existent congregation. "Man is born in sin and shaped in iniquity."

I laughed gaily. "Well, Percy is certainly shaped in iniquity, just looking at him makes me have naughty thoughts."

Mum looked heavenwards in horror as if a thunderbolt might suddenly shoot through the roof and strike me down and cautioned me to repent of my irreverent remarks immediately.

"Don't forget, we are in God's house and as far as I am aware, Percy is a very abstemious young man, I've certainly never heard of him taking a young lady out," she chided.

Unfortunately, not, I mused as I drove home in the car as Joey chatted on about how he'd been practising a psalm with Granny which they were going to read during the service.

Fresh from my little sojourn in church I was feeling unusually virtuous and started humming little snatches of Amazing Grace, until I turned into our road to see a red Ford Probe parked outside the house with the Big Fat Fossil wedged inside.

"Hell's bells with quadraphonic stereo," I said as I pulled onto the drive. "Why doesn't he do society a favour and go away quietly somewhere and die?"

Joey looked at me. "Is he a Spam Man mum?"

I pretended to look cross. "How do you know about that flappy ears? And, to answer your question, yes, he is, mega spam."

I got out of the car to see Mervin heaving himself out of his obscene phallic symbol, a metal penis extension on wheels. I've always thought that any man who drives a naff car like that has to suffer from premature ejaculation at the very least or else have a very well-developed sense of irony.

Huffing and puffing up the drive he extended his hand and explained that he was, "Just passing by and thought he'd pop in."

I grudgingly invited him in for a cup of tea and then set about cooking the dinner, making sure he didn't get the impression that he was invited to join us. Joey sat staring intently at Mervin across the kitchen table. It was quite obvious to me that Mervin wanted to 'talk about our relationship,' but I steered the conversation to other issues and prattled away about the weather and how autumn seemed to be arriving much later nowadays.

"I've still got Canterbury bells in full flower in my garden," I said. Mervin looked at Joey and said pointedly. "Haven't you got any toys to play with? When I was your age, I spent all my time with my train set."

Joey wrinkled his nose. "Train sets are for nerds. Only nerdy people play with train sets."

Mervin's moustache quivered. "Well, I still play with trains, I've got an enormous train set in my shed, I made all the models myself. It's a very constructive pastime."

Joey stuck his bottom lip out and continued to stare impassively.

"Do you like spam?" he asked.

"Joey," I cautioned.

"As a matter of fact, I am very partial to spam," said Mervin enthusiastically. "In particular spam fritters, with pickled onions and chips."

"Mum says…"

"Joey," I said sharply. "I think we've heard enough from you for now, run along and go and amuse yourself somewhere else."

"Meany," he said as he shot out of the door.

Mervin looked much happier and made some fatuous remark about Joey being a clever kid and then suddenly changed gear and the conversation veered off in a completely different direction.

"I was wondering if you have given any more thought to the conversation we had, you know, about us."

I always find being put on the spot in these situations really difficult. Delia says that if I'm not careful I'll find myself walking past a registry office one day with some man I can't abide and rather than hurt his feelings wander in and find myself married. I decided to be firm.

"Well, to be honest, Mervin, I don't think I'm ready for a relationship—maybe when Joey's left home and gone to university."

Mervin looked gob smacked. "But that's years away. I mean you are a very attractive woman—for your age, but eight years, well, time can be very cruel to a woman."

I took a deep breath and gritted my teeth. "Well, I'm prepared to take that chance." The conversation continued backwards and forwards in the same vein until it was obvious that Mervin was not going to be shaken off.

"And will you be remaining celibate?" he persisted. "I mean, if, you know, you need from time to time sexual intimacy," his voice thickened. "I would be only too happy to oblige." That did it.

"To be quite honest, Mervin, you're not my type." There I'd said it.

Mervin looked amazed. "I don't understand," he spluttered.

"You know, there's no spark," I said clicking my fingers. "You don't push my buttons."

He looked defeated at last. "I'm not sure I push any woman's buttons," he conceded.

"Well, I haven't for a very long time."

He sat there looking crestfallen. There was an awkward silence.

"What do I need to do?" he asked mournfully.

"Umm," I said. "You could, to be honest…" and then I stopped. It was too painful.

"No, go on," said Mervin. "Tell me."

"Well," I said, gesturing with my hands the outline of a very large person. "The lardy bits should really go," and then motioning around my head as if I were polishing a halo, I continued, "And the fuzzy hair. Zip." I sliced my hand backwards over my head.

Mervin instinctively clapped his hand over his mouth when I motioned to his moustache, but I slapped it and then whipped off his glasses. "Much better," I observed.

"Anything else?" he asked in a reedy voice.

I tweaked his jumper. "Man-made fibres are incompatible with a sex machine. Too much nylon inhibits sexual activity. They will all have to be ditched."

I stood back and surveyed him. "Yes, I think that's it. Do all that and your shag rating will rocket."

Mervin's face brightened instantly and then a shadow went over it and he asked how this transformation could take place.

"I wouldn't know what to buy or where to go, I get everything I wear out of catalogues, and before my mother died she did all my clothes shopping for me."

"Don't worry," I said. "I'll enlist the help of Delia and Toy Boy. I'm sure Delia would love to give you a makeover, she's got a good eye for style and Toy Boy will have you toned and waxed in no time." Mervin flinched. "Back, sack and crack," I added for good measure. His face paled. "Only teasing," I joked.

Somehow, I hadn't the heart to refuse him dinner and to be fair, after realising I'd got a 'no entry' sign outside my knickers department he chilled out and seemed almost human. Almost. I walked with him to his car and as he turned to get inside after giving me a hug, I suddenly had a thought.

"By the way Mervin, there's one more thing. The model railway."

Mervin looked horrified. "Don't tell me that's got to go," he said.

"No, but it might be best if you didn't mention it to future prospective girlfriends. I mean you've got a choice, playing tunnels and trains in your shed or tunnels and trains in your bed. It's up to you."

He smiled displaying a rather nice set of teeth and said, "Model railway? What model railway?" And then he slid his key into the lock, turned on his Probe, revved his engine and roared off.

Chapter 10

It seems apposite to me that the word venery has two distinctly different meanings in theory but which bear a relation to each other in practice. It's one of those words that if you spent forever looking for its real meaning or origin would leave you chasing after your own tail in ever decreasing circles.

Everyone on the planet, unless they are a pathological liar or a saint, is driven by venery in one sense of the word. In fact, venery drives everything we do, from a lust for world domination down to why Bob the flirty butcher always gives me the juiciest pork chop or an extra sausage. Sex. Venery, a word derived from the Roman goddess Venus, is the pursuit of sexual gratification, an activity which we shouldn't feel too guilty about indulging in or else we'd become extinct as a human race pretty quick.

But, if you partake of the other sort of venery, derived from an old French word 'venerie', then instead of a desire to reproduce your genes by bonking your brains out, you enjoy nothing more than a desire to kill, by wearing silly clothes and galloping across the countryside on horseback with a pack of hounds in pursuit of a fox.

So it fascinates me that one single word encapsulates both the concept of life and death and contains in itself its own opposite. Weird. It also means, if I got straight to the point instead of going all round the houses and being metaphysical, that it's really odd that the tiny percentage of the population that hunt, contains a disproportionate amount of people who are more prone to indulging in venery of the sexual kind as well as in venery of the hunting kind. People who hunt are either oversexed or they've got too much time on their hands, or, when I think about it, probably both.

I couldn't help this observation when I did my annual daughterly duty by attending the Wethershire Conservative Association dinner with Mum.

All the great and the good of Wethershire 's hunting, shooting and fishing set were assembled at the Newbold Saucey Country Club, including Lord and

Lady Howgrave and Sir Walter. Of course, there was also a varied selection of weirdos that seem to be drawn to local politics like moths to a candle flame. Despite not having one thread of moral fibre in their being, they worm their way onto the MPs candidates list by virtue of the fact that they've posted a few election leaflets, or they are parachuted in from Tory HQ like our local incumbent Sir Granville Bland MP, a former hedge fund manager who was the shadow home secretary's fag at Eton. He thought hedge laying was something traders did in the city. Democracy? You've got to be joking.

The first thing I did when we arrived was to check out the seating arrangements. I found to my dismay that I would be flanked on one side by Basil who fancies himself as a bit of a lothario and on the other, by a formidable blue-rinsed old harridan called Barbara Prendagast, a local town councillor. Sitting opposite, to add to insult to injury, were Camilla and Neville and thankfully, within grimacing range, Delia.

"You won't be naughty dear, will you?" asked mum anxiously as I arrived to pick her up. "Promise me you won't let me down, promise me you won't 'out' yourself as a feminist? I have to think of my position on the fund-raising committee. One has standards to maintain."

I was severely tempted to point out that maintaining standards hasn't been a major preoccupation for many politicians over the last twenty years or so, but I managed to bite my lip.

I listened as mum prattled on in the car as I drove to the Country Club. "You won't believe me when I tell you, but Maureen Bakehouse accused me of slicing the onions the wrong way for the buffet we had at our branch meeting last week. I told her straight that our president Lady Howgrave taught me to cut onions that way and if it was good enough for her, then it was good enough for me. She had no answer to that."

On and on she went hardly pausing for breath, casting aspersions on the domestic incompetence of some poor woman who had taken the tea towels home to wash.

"Stiff as a board, stiff as a board. I had to take them home and do them all again." I decided to halt her mid-flow. "All very interesting stuff but have you heard about any exciting new policies? Solution to end world poverty, the Middle East crisis, trains running on time."

Mum looked miffed. "There's no need to be facetious. I'm just a foot soldier in the battle to win the next election, I don't need to worry my head about all that. I leave all that to our MPs in Westminster."

As soon as I walked through the door I noticed that all the couples seemed to be suffering from parabiosis, like Siamese twins sharing the same circulation of the blood. Wherever a woman's husband went, she was sure to follow and vice versa, they all seemed to be joined at the hip.

Except for Delia and Henry who seemed to be doing their best to avoid each other and Neville who seemed to be avoiding Camilla like the plague.

"Nice to see you," he said as he sidled up to me. "We need new blood here, especially when it's as warm blooded as yours," he raised his eyebrows suggestively. As though catching the scent of a hunt, Basil strolled over and instantly homed in on my chest.

"Lovely to see you here Rebecca, in fact," he said, nudging Neville in the ribs and looking at my chest. "I'd like to see a lot more of you."

He held his hands under his massive vibrating beer gut as they both laughed loudly at his double entendre.

"Fat chance," I said, smiling sweetly as I glanced down at his flab. "I've always thought that the sexiest part of a man's anatomy is between the ears, so that disqualifies both of you."

Before he could reply, his long-suffering wife Doris sidled up to him and gave a wan smile. "Have you got five pounds for a raffle ticket dear?" she asked, holding out her hand like a beggar.

"Oh, I don't know about that," joked Basil as he gave me a wink. "Bit of a spendthrift my wife, I have to keep her on a tight rein."

I felt seriously in need of some fresh air. As I made my escape, I bumped straight into Charles who was bounding up the steps to the entrance.

"What a lovely surprise," he said as he slid his arm possessively around my waist and planted a moist, slobbery kiss on my cheek. All eyes turned to fix on us like super glue as we entered the room together. You could almost hear the gossips' antennae vibrating like a rampant rabbit, one of the most eligible and respectable men in Wethershire in a close encounter with an impoverished single mother. Scandal. Barbara Prendagast's generous bosom heaved in shock while Camilla's lips pursed like a cat's arse. Hilarious. I decided to ham it up. I put my arm behind Charles' back and placed my head lovingly on his shoulder. He gave a sharp intake of breath and squeezed me tighter.

"What the hell are you playing at?" hissed Delia as she made her way to her place at the table.

"I can't resist making the tongues wag, and it will make Mum happy, crank up her snob value," I whispered in an aside.

I smiled sweetly as I sat down, sensing the murmurings of disapproval and a strange whistling sound as the old guard simultaneously drew in a sharp intake of breath through their false teeth. To rank up the tension I waved gaily to Charles who was sitting at the top table. Camilla looked daggers, while the blue rinsed brigade started chattering excitedly like monkeys in the jungle warning each other of oncoming prey.

Bingo.

After the meal came a speech from Sir Granville Bland who played to the house by ranting on remorselessly as if on auto pilot, stringing along a bunch of hoary old sound bites about family values. I'd just about nodded off until I was woken by a blood curdling, foam frothing cheer as he turned his attention to Brexit. Roaring like an American evangelist, he warned that we'd had a lucky escape from the EU's clutches before it had a chance to strangle us with red tape.

Delia's face turned bright pink with mirth when I glanced over at her, raised my eyebrows and mouthed, "kinky." Camilla's eyes narrowed menacingly. I was so relieved when the dinner was over that I jumped up with relief when Charles bounded over and invited me to join him at the top table.

What a huge joke I thought gleefully as I sat sipping a glass of champagne next to Sir Walter in his wheelchair as he looked across at the hoi polloi. I raised my glass at Camilla as she looked at me with barely concealed contempt. "I think a bit of beef went down the wrong way," I said to Lady Howgrave who observed that she was looking a bit bilious. Mum preened like a peacock when Charles suggested she join us and got quite tiddly on champagne.

"Made an honest woman of her yet?" roared Sir Walter to Charles as he looked at me across the table. Charles smiled weakly and replied that he hadn't managed to make me a dishonest woman of me.

"Chaps nowadays, too slow off the mark. Show her who's in charge, man, show her your mettle." Sir Walter roared with laughter at his own joke as he poured copious amounts of brandy down his throat.

"I think Neville and Camilla are having a bit of a tiff," Mum said in a slightly squiffy voice as she observed Camilla hissing at Neville with her scrawny neck arched like a cobra ready to strike, as he stared at Delia's cleavage with his tongue positively drooling into a G&T.

"She's always had a silly high opinion of herself," she continued. "Of course, you have to make allowances, it's anybody's guess who her father is, her mother was a right one." She hiccupped gently as Lady Howgrave's mouth dropped. I decided it was a good time to leave as she started to make a list of possible candidates.

"You need to set your cap at a rich man," Mum said in a sleepy voice as I drove her home.

"Charles Smythe Bothum-Wethem was giving you sheep's eyes all night."

I got back home to find Thelma watching The Chase on catch up with her feet up on the coffee table as she babysat for Joey. She laughed until the tears ran down her face as I regaled her with the events of the evening.

"Camilla was doing her Lady Muck impressions and Sir Walter was just plain mucky," I told her.

"Don't you worry," she said sagely. "He'll get his comeuppance one of these days. As the saying goes, you can't run with the fox and hunt with the hounds forever."

Chapter 11

It's funny; not funny ha ha, but funny kinda weird, that when I've seriously cocked-up, or said something monumentally crass and stupid, I feel as though I will never be able to face the world again, despite consoling myself with the fact that I can distinctly recall the same sort of thing happening in the past. Not only did I survive it, but I can't even recall the incident, yet it doesn't stop me feeling as though I could literally die of shame. My face burns and I feel as though my innards are being rapidly consumed by a particularly virulent strain of the Ebola virus and my body is in imminent danger of being reduced to a few gristly scraps that will eventually dissolve from the heat of extreme embarrassment.

All it took was a phone call to Hartborne Hall. I decided, after being enlightened about Gladys' sharp exit, that it would be nice to offer a little helping hand to Percy and Sir Walter who obviously needed ministering to in their hour of need. The unappetising fact that I'm a crap cook was subsumed by the memory of Percy's tight, neat arse in his jodhpurs and the urge on the night of the dinner to slide my fingers into his soft moist mouth—and worse.

It took a while to summon up the courage. I dillied and dallied and shillied and shallied by clearing up the dinner things, picking up the phone and putting it down, wiping all the work surfaces, picking up the phone and putting it down, flicking through the channels on the telly, picking up the phone and putting it down and talking to myself in the mirror.

"Seize the moment," I said to my reflection. "What have you got to lose?" If I was thinking straight, I would have thought; a peaceful night's sleep, unbitten fingernails, hours of recrimination and resorting to an alternative therapy to Prozac—the consumption of vast quantities of chocolate. But I didn't. I picked up the phone.

"Hello, Hartborne Hall," a familiar sexy voice answered.

"Hi, is that Percy?" I asked nervously, my sixth sense already alerting me to the fact that this was not the cleverest idea I'd ever had.

He acknowledged that it was and so I launched into an incoherent jabber-fest about how my mum Vera, who was the sister of Thelma, had told me while she was decorating the church, that she'd heard that Gladys had left them in the lurch and Mrs Hoare's rheumatism had flared up.

"Who is this?" Percy asked sharply. "And what rumours is this woman Vera spreading about my domestic arrangements?"

I cringed. "It's Rebecca, I came to your house for dinner with Charles last Saturday night. I thought you might need help; I know Sir Walter doesn't like foreign food."

"You're not making any sense," Percy said with irritation. "Please start again. Why should my father need help because he doesn't like foreign food? He's never liked foreign food, he's not likely to change now, you can't teach an old dog new tricks."

I felt seriously ill. "Look, I just thought that if you haven't got a cook, I could cook for you instead, you must be bored of Chinese takeaways by now."

I could tell that Percy was completely exasperated. "I'm not aware that we've advertised a position for a cook?"

My mouth felt as though it was lined with sandpaper. "I don't need a job, I'm a journalist…"

I started to explain, but before I could make myself clear Percy shouted in a shocked voice, "What, God forbid!"

And then he started to interrogate me, and we had the most ridiculous conversation that didn't make the slightest bit of sense.

"So, you see," Percy said. "What happened was a very long time ago and it is nothing but malicious gossip and if you write a word, I'll sue."

"I only offered to cook you lunch on Sunday," I bleated, "I honestly haven't the faintest idea what you're going on about."

Percy coughed and cleared his throat a couple of times. "It seems as if we've been talking at cross purposes. If as you say, you merely want to cook lunch on Sunday, that is very kind of you but really not at all necessary. I have Seamus staying here who can whip up lots of nice things."

"Oh," I said. "I'm sorry if I've offended you."

I heard him exhale. "Thinking about it, I seem to recall Rebecca that you are rather sweet. I'm sorry if I was short with you, please forgive me."

"I forgive you," I said in an almost inaudible whisper.

"Look," he said. "Why don't you and Charlie boy come for lunch on Sunday anyway? Leave it with me and I'll give him a call."

And with that he put down the phone.

I felt shaken by the experience and started to move about the kitchen as if I'd suddenly been afflicted by a bad dose of St Vitus Dance.

"You fool, you fool," I kept repeating to myself out loud as I jigged around the table, covering my face with my hands with the shame of it all. I decided to go and have a lie down. I put a pillow over my head. 'Why don't you listen to reason, woman?' I chastised myself at least a hundred times. 'Delia has told you that Percy's nothing but a big clit teaser'.

I don't listen I reasoned, because I'm like any normal, sexually active woman, I think with my bits. And very nice thoughts they are too I remembered, as I curled up into a ball of sexual frustration. And then suddenly, amidst the morass of indignity and horror, shone a glimmer of light.

'He said that I was rather sweet,' I remembered dreamily and then wandered off into the land of fantasy where all my doubts about the desirable androgynous Seamus whipping up something nice, were jettisoned into infinity. 'Clutching at straws,' Delia would say.

Just then the phone rang. Joey appeared in the doorway.

"Phone, again," he said. Joey's main gripe with me is that I spend too much time 'yapping' on the phone. Every time I answer it, he resorts to emotional blackmail to try and shorten the call. "Neglecter," he says mournfully as his big blue eyes widen to the size of saucers.

I gave him a worried look. "If it's the big Fat Fossil tell him I'm in the bath and I'll call him back."

Joey looked at me on the bed. "But you're not in the bath."

I jumped off the bed and rushed past him flapping him exasperatedly out of my way.

"Hello," I said rather sharply.

"Darling, got a bag on, have we?" I heard Delia drawl.

I looked at Joey who had followed me to the phone.

"You let me think it was Mervin," I said accusingly.

He looked at me pityingly. "O, you deceitful tongue, surely God will bring you down to everlasting ruin."

I told him not to repeat such silly things.

"S' true," he said. "It says so in the Bible, Psalm 52. It means you're going to rot in hell."

I could hear Delia laughing down the phone. "Tell him to go away and say his prayers and ask him to say one for me, goodness only knows I need it."

I was intrigued and asked her what she'd been up to.

"I don't know quite how to say this," she said. "But, well, things have changed."

I asked her what she meant.

"I've got feelings for Toy Boy; I mean real feelings."

I told her to be sensible. "You are walking into dangerous territory Delia, I mean to feel affection is one thing, to have real feelings is suicidal."

Delia said rashly that she didn't care. "I can't face sitting on top of Henry's dick anymore. I refuse. He went mental after I flushed his Viagra down the loo. And if he keeps throwing his dinner around the room anymore, we'll have to get the decorators in."

I warned her that if she wasn't careful Henry might suspect she'd got someone else. "Never," she said. "I mean, he heard that piece of gossip about my vibrating Freelander from Sir Howgrave at Percy's dinner. It never crossed his mind that it might be me. Married women are indifferent to sex you see, we only do it to fulfil our wifely duties. Our husbands satisfy our every need, whereas women like you are just gagging to be shagged by every man in Wethershire ."

I couldn't believe it.

"Oh, yes," said Delia dryly. "Apparently he'd only have to crook his little finger and you'd lift up your skirt like a shot. A single parent you see. A brazen little trollop. You my dear are officially anybody's on the totty market."

"Fleece him," I said. "Take him to the cleaners."

"I intend to," she said.

"By the way," she added. "Before I rang you, I got a phone call from Seamus. He's invited me to lunch at the Hall on Sunday, without Henry. He's very astute, we just gelled somehow."

I felt a rush of excitement and repeated my conversation with Percy, slightly rephrasing huge chunks, and then I told her that I might see her there.

"I hope Charles can't make it," I said. "Because then it would be a nice foursome, with you and Seamus and Percy and me." It seemed too good to be true.

"Hello," Delia said. "What is the weather like up there on planet Zog?"

I admit that lust can addle the brain, but until I have proof beyond reasonable doubt that Percy finds me resistible, I will reserve a smidgen of hope that one day he might give me one. I will cling to his endearment that he thought I was rather sweet and let Delia live on in ignorance.

"You're probably right," I agreed. "But I do think my brain must need rewiring because it sets all my hormones to green when I see men like Percy and Jake that I can't have and then all my signals to red when I'm with the ones that want me."

"Yes, but as you have eloquently pointed out so many times, the ones that want you are complete DUDS. I mean you can't switch on a car with a dud battery, so how can a woman be switched on by a DUD man? Take Toy Boy's cousin, Merv the perv, I mean frankly he's a complete minger."

"Arhh, but not for much longer," I said. "He's agreed to a complete makeover, he's promised to lose the lard, de-fuzz the face and get new trendy gear which means the sweaty armpits issue will be resolved if we get him into natural fibres."

Delia asked if the new-look Mervin would include a personality transplant. I pointed out that if he had a new sleeker, sexier image he might not be such a boring old fart.

"He'll have more to talk about instead of droning on about his ex-wife and anyway, it'll be fun. I suggested that you and Toy Boy would take him in hand," I ventured hopefully.

"Well, you know I like a challenge, but this is like turning Quasimodo into Brad Pitt with the equivalent of sticky-backed plastic. The man's only hope is radical plastic surgery. Mind you," she added, "It will give me an excuse to be with Toy Boy, I can't keep pretending for much longer that I'm visiting his house to give him advice on interior design. His neighbour's daughter's boyfriend is a whipper-in at the hunt. You know what it's like in Wethershire , gossip travels faster than light."

I agreed. I mean, I've heard it on good authority that I've had affairs with at least three married men. The trouble is that all the rumours contain snippets of innocent information, but when put together have no foundation for scandal whatsoever. But hey, when did that stop anyone from spreading porkies as thick as pig shit?

"Talking of premier league DUDs," I said. "I've composed an e-mail to that speed dating Ted, to accept his invitation to go around to his place, on the off chance that I might bump into that dishy Tor."

Delia urged caution. "If I were you, I'd go in reinforced knickers and passion-killer clothes, something to shroud your curves, like a burka."

I told her that as a journalist I'd been in lots of dodgy situations and I could take care of myself. "I'm more Boadicea than Bridget Jones," I pointed out. "Flex that cheese wire." Wince.

I pulled up the draft email on my mobile phone and asked her to tell me if it contained any minutiae of sexual come-hither.

"It goes something like this," I said.

"Dear Ted, I'm sorry I haven't replied to your email earlier, but I have been busy decorating the church for the harvest festival and practicing singing in the choir. It would be nice to visit your garden, but I can only visit during daylight hours because I'm too afraid to drive in the dark. I would prefer to go out and perhaps explore your village and have a drink in a tea shop because I feel it is too forward to spend time alone with a man friend on a first acquaintance. Rebecca."

"Nice one," said Delia approvingly. "You sound like a suitably frigid old spinster. Although you must remember that with some men, the fact you have stepped over the threshold of their house is interpreted as an open invitation to penetrative sex."

I acknowledged that she was absolutely right, but not to worry. "If he makes a move, I'll set fire to his wig. It looks as if it's made out of flammable material, failing that I'll shove his dentures down the back of his throat."

We both howled with laughter, and I promised to give Delia a full report on my progress.

This is all Jake Manderson's fault, I thought after I put down the phone feeling more apprehensive than I cared to admit. His malign influence has plagued me ever since we split up. I'm going to find that Tor and flirt with him full-on and no-one, least of all a toupee-wearing old roué, is going to stand in my way.

Chapter 12

I've always really, really loved catalogues. Really loved them. All my childhood hopes and dreams lay between the pages of Empire Stores. It only takes one whiff of a fresh, new catalogue to take me back to the days when my fate for the year was heralded by the arrival of the latest issue. Only the clothes on offer that season were available, money was too tight to buy clothes outright, if I didn't fancy anything in the catalogue, tough. So, the seasons were marked, not by the arrival of daffodils or the falling of leaves, but by catalogues, swim wear in the spring and boots in the autumn. The excitement, the thrill of drooling over the latest range of jeans has never been surpassed. Of course, there were only two serious contenders on the jean's market to choose from, Levi's or Wrangler's.

Social semiotics were much easier to interpret; we weren't confused by a dizzying selection of designer labels. You were either in and 'hip' or out and 'square.' 'Hip' people wore Levi's or Wrangler's, whereas a 'square' person wore the only alternative; shapeless, sexless, 'Supermarket Heavies.' Adorn your person with these hideous, shapeless jeans and you were instantly disqualified from the human race. Easy. My fat cousin Trevor wore them. He always had green lips from drinking too much limeade. If you so much as sat next to him, you were contaminated by association. An outcast.

Harsh reality boiled down to one inescapable fact. If you hadn't got a pair of Levi's or Wrangler's, you'd never get snogged. No chance. And mini heels, you had to have mini heels, or your life wasn't worth living. Which is why I often felt that mine wasn't. While all the 'in' girls swanned around showing off their hip-hugging jeans, my wardrobe was full of the teenager's scourge, catalogue Crimplene or hand-me-downs.

"But you look lovely darling in your pleated Crimplene suit," Mum used to say earnestly. The hours I sat tight in my bedroom refusing to come out if there was even the remotest possibility that I might have to wear it in a public place populated by fertile males. I'd have licked toilets clean to have owned a pair of

Levi's. Nothing could compare to the indignity of Wendy Parker, the prettiest girl in the school, sniggering down her nose at me togged out in my Crimplene gear and flat, sensible shoes. And Camilla's cast-off duffle coat with horn toggles. It's a wonder I survived.

"All I ever wanted was a pair of Levi's and some elastic roll-ons," I explained to Konnie in the kitchen during our lunch break at work.

"Roll-ons are before my time," she said. "Although I do remember seeing them hanging on my granny's washing line. Looked a bit pervy to me."

I explained to her that they were a rite of passage, an entrance into womanhood that made you go all curvy like an egg timer.

"They must have been designed by a man," observed Konnie. "Imprisoning your bits so they could hardly breathe. It's no wonder there were fewer unwanted pregnancies. By the time you managed to peel them off you'd have gone off the boil. So sexless."

I raised my cup of tea and lisped, "Let's sing a thanksgiving song to the thong, the labia liberator."

"You women have got it all wrong as usual," said Keith, who'd been listening to our conversation as he washed his cup in the sink. "I've got very happy memories about those particular pieces of underwear from when I was a teenage lad. The hours I spent scanning the pages of catalogues looking at women wearing roll-ons. Heady stuff."

Konnie stroked her chin and nodded exaggeratedly. "Explains a lot," she said.

"You don't understand," said Keith flicking her around the head with the tea towel. "It was the nearest we got to porn." He suddenly slapped his forehead with the palm of his hand. "Rebecca, that reminds me, I want you to do some research on that massage parlour that our sexual DIY man Colin allegedly paid a visit to. Dig around a bit. Find any dirt." He rubbed his fingers together under my nose. "See if they offer 'extras' for cash."

"Charming," I said. "What do you want me to do, hang around outside and interview the punters?"

Squeezing a tea bag into his cup he assured me that no, he didn't. "Just use your initiative, it's a great story and we all like a happy ending," he said with a wink as he sauntered off to have a fag.

The things I have to do to earn a living, I thought as I went back to my desk.

I picked up the phone and rang Colin.

"Did you see anything going on untoward when you went to the Newton Saucey Massage parlour to undertake your 'research?'" I said. "Y'know mass orgies or girls with surgically enhanced breasts offering S&M?"

Colin cleared his throat and said indignantly, "Certainly not. I went there because I sustained a rather nasty groin strain playing football and Tiffany the masseuse was extremely dexterous in manipulating my injury."

"I see," I replied, desperately trying not to laugh. "So, it must have come as a shock to learn that the Newton Saucey Massage has a reputation as a knocking shop?"

"I had no idea, no idea," Colin replied. "Tiffany was very professional and gave me her card so she could follow up our session with a home visit. But what with the trial and everything I simply haven't been up to it."

I asked him if he still had it. "I may have it lying around somewhere," he said nonchalantly. "If I find it, I'll let you know."

I wandered over to Keith's desk and there was general hilarity all round when I told everyone about Colin's groin strain and the fact that he wasn't up to a home visit.

"He's up to no good, that's what he's up to," said Keith. "And the only football he's ever played is predicting the scores for his pools coupon. Mucky bugger."

I decided to put the unsavoury subject of the massage parlour to the back of my mind and concentrate on more pleasant thoughts such as the chance of bumping into Tor during my forthcoming visit to Ted. I'm fed up with sleaze, all I ever seem to encounter is sex-crazed sleaze buckets wanting a fondle. They're either married, rejects or trolls, all on permanent standby to whip out their bits at a moment's notice.

It's so rank.

Mind you, however hard I've tried to ignore it, sex seems to have reared its ugly head time after time today. It even came up at the Newbold Saucey Town Council meeting, remarkable seeing as it's usually about as titillating as a lecture on lancing boils. Town council meetings have got to be the nadir of a journalist's existence. As a guardian of the Fourth Estate, it seems a tad undignified to have to endure endless meetings where paltry issues are discussed with all the pomp and solemnity of a UN debate on whether to deploy medium-range ballistic missiles against an aggressor. Town councils are simply a terminus; a place garrulous old people inhabit before their children cart them off to an old people's home.

I arrived to find the usual crew of crusty old worthies, including Cess Poole, gathered round the table in the Town Hall. I sat at the press bench with Tony Talbot from The Newton Saucey News, a pale, thin, unhealthy looking junior recruit who can often be found rummaging through the reduced food items at the supermarket to help make ends meet on his meagre trainee wage. We shared a grimace of sympathy at the ordeal ahead of us as we opened our notebooks.

"I'd just collected my pension from the Post Office," began Barbara Prendagast in a hectoring tone. "When I stepped off the pavement into a huge mound of animal faecal matter. Dog owners should be made to act responsibly and poop the scoop." Chairman and town mayor, Roy Sturgess, peered over the top of his half-moon spectacles and looked in our direction to ask if we had managed to jot down all the relevant information.

"Rebecca and Tony this is a top-line grave issue that needs to be addressed." There was a murmur of agreement.

"I didn't think the cemetery was on this week's agenda," piped up deaf old Lionel Bunce, the local undertaker and the longest serving member on the council. "It's filling up, it will be standing room only if we don't get a move on."

"We were talking about dogs," boomed Roy across the table. "Barbara had an unfortunate incident outside the Post Office."

Lionel looked alarmed. "Accident. Is she dead? I'm sure I saw her earlier on?"

"I'm very much alive, Lionel!" shouted Barbara in the voice of a sergeant major on parade. "We were talking about dog dirt. I vote we move a motion."

Everyone raised their hand except Lionel who wafted his vaguely under his nose, "Sounds extremely unpleasant to me. Is the cleaner in?"

The vote was passed with one abstention which I took to be Lionel's. There was a general sound of muttering and shuffling of papers before the next item on the agenda was aired. I hadn't bothered to look at it as it's usually so tedious the boredom factor kicks in earlier and therefore lasts much longer.

"The next item on the agenda," said Roy, peering closely at the page, "seems to be sex." A buzz went around the room. I noticed Lionel screwing his hearing aid firmly in his ear.

"Yes, it seems that concerns have been raised as to the status of Newton Saucey Massage, situated in Long Passage, an establishment that caters for relaxation, massage and alternative therapy."

He took his glasses off and swung them between his finger and thumb. "Can anyone shed any light on this matter?"

There was a long silence, broken by the odd cough here and there.

He glanced down at his notes. "According to my information, the establishment is run by a Ms Jones who leases the property from a Mr Johnny Dickinson."

Cess Poole raised his finger.

"Ha, Cess, you are familiar with Newton Saucey Massage?" queried Roy with raised eyebrows.

"No, no, I don't take with all that," said Cess blushing a bright shade of puce. "It's just that I've half a mind that Johnny Dickinson has moved into the Old Coach House with his misses at the Albion-Hartborne's place. They've got a lurcher. Pretty sure that's right."

Digger Manners who has also been a permanent fixture on the council since time immemorial, suddenly perked up. "Ideal dogs for ferreting lurchers, beats a terrier any day." His remarks ignited a general debate on lurchers versus terriers as hunting dogs until the mayor brought the meeting to order with his gavel.

"Order, order, the item on the agenda is a suspected house of ill repute, we are not here to talk about dogs and hunting. Any suggestions on how to address this sordid affair?"

A flurry of ideas followed. "I vote as a member of the health and safety committee that we pay a visit for an inspection to make sure that everything's up to scratch," piped up Lionel. Barbara vetoed the idea. She sat there looking so fierce that nobody it seemed dared to disagree.

"I think a letter to Mr Dickinson is in order," she said. "We need to make him aware that his property is allegedly being used to procure sexual services for monetary gain. This sort of establishment has no place in Wethershire . We need to find out who is behind it and root it out."

Tony seemed unmoved by the juicy story that had just fallen into our laps and sat with a deadpan face picking at the frayed cuffs of his jacket and rubbing his acne scars. I hope he doesn't see the potential for a good headline. Town Council in Porn Probe. Nice and meaty. I immediately phoned Delia with the story when I got back home.

She was fascinated. "A porn king. Who would have thought it? A man living off immoral earnings in little old Hartborne. What would your mother say?"

"She'll soon find out," I said. "I'm going to do a story in the paper. I bet it's the only steamy story to come out of Newton Saucey Town Council for years, apart from when Jim Tucker's mountain of pig manure caused a health hazard with that horrible stink and all those flies."

"I'd love to be a fly on the wall to witness all that sleaze," said Delia. "Or maybe it's too horrible to contemplate when you think of certain potential customers like Neville having a hump."

We laughed and imagined the awful scenario of him caught out in the throes of passion. "I wonder if he takes off those silly yellow socks he wears?" giggled Delia. "Skinny hairy legs and his puny body sawing away, it's too awful to contemplate, a right spam wham."

I think I'll give Mr Dickinson a call to see if he's got anything illicit to hide, I decided. I wonder if he'll be wearing his leather trousers? I remember leather trousers when they used to feature heavily in catalogues in the 1980s, high-waisted ankle stranglers that made your bum look massive. If you wore a pair, men automatically assumed you were a tart and available. I must admit I always fancied some but the dry-cleaning costs put me off. I suppose if the crutch got a bit wiffy you could always spruce it up with a dab of shoe polish. Forget Margery's piffly poop scoop story, Newton Saucey Massage could be the best scoop we get all year. And the dirt that it could dig up could be so big it could give quite a few people a heavy dose of emotional diarrhoea. There's nothing like public humiliation to clear the bowels.

Chapter 13

Mucklesbury calls itself a village but it isn't really. It's just a straggly extension of the nearest town that if you didn't know where you were you could be anywhere in Eastern Europe, not that I've ever been there. I almost expected to see large toothless, lined old women appear on the streets carrying dark rye loaves, or appear out of the depressing Soviet-styled buildings designed around a randomly built town centre with a concrete cenotaph in the middle stained with pigeon shit.

Occasionally there appeared here and there amongst the grot, the graceful remnants of a Victorian building defaced by modern plastic single-paned windows that gave the facade a blank, soulless air, while large horizontal gaudy shop fronts distorted the perspective of the street giving the appearance of a shanty town.

I drove up and down the dreary place where any hint of greenery in the front gardens of the houses had been submerged under concrete slabs, or gravel with glimpses of black plastic showing through.

Ted's directions told me to turn left at a junction with a betting shop on the corner. The trouble was there seemed to be a betting shop on every one. Round and round I went until it started to feel like a surreal experience, like I was in a panoramic cinema with an art film showing the futility of meaning, the never-ending cycle of life and the facile achievements of humanity in trying to capture it. Art mirroring life, mirroring art.

It did my head in so in the end I gave up and rang Ted on my mobile and he guided me to his house like a stricken ship into port. As I turned into his road, I saw a row of pretty nineteenth century cottages built in the shadow of a church with a graceful spire. It must have been part of the original small hamlet that had spawned an eclectic collection of houses and shops that swamped the original character, turning the whole place into a faceless wilderness of nonentity.

Ted's house was stuck onto the end of the pretty terrace, double-fronted and carefully plastered with pebbledash with the original windows replaced by modern plastic frames with reproduction glazed lattice. The original slate roof had been swapped for concrete tiles adding to the general appearance of a cheap B&B in Blackpool.

Next door in complete contrast was a pretty terrace with the original sash windows and neat re-pointing between the small bricks. A navy VW Golf was parked outside.

It must belong to Tor I thought. Result. Before knocking on Ted's door, I peeked into the windows of the front room but the view was obscured by a front garden and blinds. I texted Konnie. 'Reconnaissance mission accomplished. Target identified.

Surveillance in operation'.

Suddenly a familiar be-wigged head appeared out of the door of Ted's cottage and before I could take evasive action was enveloped tenderly in a loving hug while one hand generously squeezed my left buttock. Not a good start.

"Hello me darling," Ted said huskily, nuzzling my neck. I stepped back and held him at arm's length on the pretext of looking at him.

"Still the same as ever," I said with a rictus grin, wincing inwardly as I took in the teeth, the wig and the concave chest. 'Even worse in natural light,' I thought grimly. Ted took my arm and guided me into his house. Minutes after he shut the door, I heard a car door slam and glanced out of the window to see the Golf being driven off down the road. Shit.

Ted guided me through to the kitchen where the table was resplendent with the best china teacups and saucers and a plate of French Fancies. The house was spotless, although it had a slightly oniony smell which I later discovered was emanating from a magnificent bunch of leeks hanging up in the conservatory.

Ted pulled back a chair and invited me to sit down while he made the tea.

"Earl Grey, Lapsang Souchong, or Tetley?" he asked. I preferred Tetley any day but felt he'd be disappointed if I did so I opted for Earl Grey.

"Just as I thought," he smiled. "I said to myself, Ted you've got a girl with class coming to see you, so you've got to behave accordingly." As we chatted a gorgeous ginger cat wandered rather haughtily into the room.

"Yes," murmured Ted as he poured hot water into a teapot. "I've always gone for a posh pussy."

"Pardon?" I said.

"Princess, the cat, she's always 'ad airs and graces, she'll only drink out of china, won't you pet?" he said rather hastily as he bent down to tickle her beneath her chin.

He carried the teapot to the table smiling nervously. "Big cat lover," he explained to my deadpan face.

"Something to tickle your fancy?" he said as he held out the plate of cakes which wobbled slightly in his tremulous hand.

I took a pink one. "Lovely house Ted," I lied. "I didn't realise though that Mucklesbury was such a long way from Wethershire . I forget sometimes that I live out in the sticks."

Before I could go any further, Ted launched into a long rambling explanation of the history of Mucklesbury and the surrounding towns which have a long history of coal mining, long since replaced by light industry and high unemployment.

"Nice neighbours?" I asked, when he stopped to sip his tea.

Frustratingly he started at the far end of the row and I had to hear all about the recently widowed Molly whose husband Reg had died a lingering death from emphysema caused by working down the mines, and her struggle to cope on her own had left her with painful psoriasis.

"I take her twice a week down to Aldi to stock-up like, but it'll be a long time before she's able to catch the bus what with the long waiting list at the 'ospital."

I also had a potted history of Joan and Brian and their wayward son Raymond who'd got in with a 'bad lot' and jacked in a decent apprenticeship as a mechanic to go off to Falaraki as a tour rep.

"You should 'ave seen the photos he brought back, it's worse than Sodom and Gomorrah. I can show you them if you like," he said hopefully with a rather lecherous leer.

I hastily declined.

"And what about the house next door with the Golf parked outside," I asked quickly, hoping to cut out at least three life histories before he came to Tor.

"Nice chap, lovely bloke is Tor. Salt of the earth. Not here much though, lives in London most of the time."

My heart froze. "What's he doing here then?" I asked.

He's got a house in Mucklesbury because his ex-partner lives in a nearby village with his daughter Freya and he stays here to spend time with her.

"Never see her otherwise. Bad vibes with his ex, they don't hit it off. She lives up at Monkstonhill in a swanky 'ouse, skittish thing she is. Thin as a bloody rake, ex model, not my sort, no flesh on 'er bones. Not like you," he said looking at me appreciatively. "I like a bit of meat with me two veg."

He tapped his knee. "Why don't you come and sit here and let Ted give you a cuddle, no point you being over there and me being over 'ere."

Thankfully, Princess mistook the invitation for her and jumped up and started to make herself comfortable.

"Leave her there," I said before Ted could push her off. "I wouldn't want to disturb her; she obviously feels left out."

Ted gave her a black look, but she obviously had no intention of budging and curled up, digging her claws into his trousers for safe measure. The absurdity of my situation suddenly struck me and I had to struggle to subdue a rising panic that threatened to make me either cry hysterically or dissolve into a fit of giggles. Why do I always have to take the difficult route in life, I asked myself as I doggedly ploughed on trying to extract as much information from Ted about Tor without raising his suspicions. It didn't take long to realise that although he looks a bit half-baked, he is in fact a very sharp cookie.

"Didn't you meet Tor at the speed-dating evening?" he asked. "If you were so interested, why didn't you ask him then?"

I reminded him that we only got three minutes and denied vehemently that I was interested after he asked me outright if I fancied him. Luckily, I'm a practiced liar, a vital qualification for a journalist.

"Did you tick his box?" Ted asked inquisitively as if he were a lawyer interrogating a prosecution witness in a trial at the Old Bailey.

"No," I said honestly.

"I told him that you'd taken a shine to me and that we'd been e-mailing each other."

He said you weren't his type. "Too clever by 'alf, that's what he said."

It's only male pride I reasoned, a typical symptom of male inadequacy, as my blood started to boil like molten lava as I tried to feign disinterest.

"Really, well I thought he was a bit wet, I wouldn't want to be with a man who only fancied dim women," I retaliated.

I felt it was time to change the conversation in case I heard anything else I didn't want to hear, so I asked if I could see the garden. Ted jumped up, immediately unseating a disgruntled Princess and came around the table solicitously taking my arm as we embarked on a guided tour of his pride and joy.

Our first stop was the conservatory which housed the massive leeks and various cactus plants and succulents. The garden was truly beautiful with gnarled old apple trees in a small orchard, a hawthorn hedge, flower beds, a vegetable patch and well-established trees and shrubs. The plot ran to at least half-an-acre and every piece was cultivated to perfection. I loved it.

I turned to Ted.

"You're a genius," I said with sincerity. "It's nice to know there are these hidden places that have been cared for over the generations as a harbour for wildlife. It's really lovely." I felt quite moved.

"Not for much longer," Ted said. "I've sold half the plot to a local builder for an executive 'ouse. No choice, see, I needed to pay off the wife. I'll have a bit over for a holiday. Thought I might join young Raymond for a bit of sunshine."

I surveyed the plot where the small orchard stood with free-range hens pecking around a hen house. 'Is nothing sacred?' I thought sadly.

Ted, seeing my downcast face put a comforting arm around me. "Cheer up. I tell you what, come with me to Falaraki, for a bit of sea, sun and sex, all expenses paid of course."

I thanked him profusely but made the excuse that I never went anywhere on holiday without Joey.

I tried to gently move away but his grip tightened around my waist but before I could escape, he rashly tried to slip one hand beneath my jumper.

I instinctively leapt from his grasp as if I'd been electrocuted. "Just checking to see if you were feeling chilly," he wheedled.

"I'm boiling," I said as I marched across the lawn with the sudden feeling that I was being watched. I looked up to the back of Tor's house and saw him clearly looking out from one of the top windows. I stopped and stared and then slowly raised my hand in acknowledgement. My heart started beating fast with excitement. Ted came stumping up behind me suggesting grumpily that it was time to go in. He took me into the sitting room while he went to make a fresh brew. I looked around the room decorated in pink; pink carpet, pink dralon three-piece-suite, pink striped wallpaper with a contrasting floral dado and pink curtains. Even the skirting boards were painted pink.

Ted came in with a tray and saw me looking around. "The wife had lots of faults but she's got exquisite taste, I'll give her that," he said as he placed the tray on a small table draped with a lace cloth.

As he started to pour the tea, there was a knock on the back door. Putting the teapot down he told me to stay put. I could hear voices; one was unmistakably Tor's. I listened at the door.

"I thought I'd return these shears that you kindly lent to me Ted. I've just come across them; I'd forgotten I had them."

Ted said 'thanks,' adding that he couldn't stop for a chat because he was entertaining. "I've got a visitor," he said. "Must go."

Deciding to take my chance I walked through to the kitchen catching a glimpse of Tor standing in the door looking drop-dead gorgeous.

"Hello," I said smiling.

"Hello to you too," said Tor with a sexy, lazy smile that reached to his eyes and made me go weak at the knees.

Ted took one look at me and said abruptly, "Call back later if you've got anything else to tell me, the tea's getting cold." And slammed the door. "I thought I told you to stay where you were?" he said in a wheedling tone worthy of Uriah Heap.

I crossed my legs saying I was desperate for the loo and couldn't wait— "Weak bladder," I said as I motioned to my nether regions. He ushered me to the loo which had a toilet roll cover made from a plastic lady wearing a pink frilly nylon dress. It joined a kaleidoscope of other pink object d'art that seemed to swirl around in a whirlpool and tangle my mind into a slipstream of consciousness as my visit went by in a blur. All I could think about was drowning in Tor's smiley eyes. I watched Ted's lips move as he did his best to entertain and as he chattered away I realised he was all mouth and no trousers and I wasn't in any danger of being ravished against my will. I woke out of my revere when he offered to give me a tour of the house which was decorated in the same lurid style as the sitting room except for the back bedroom which he hadn't got around to desecrating with DIY.

The plain walls, bare floorboards and original fireplace were all that was left to give testimony to the elegance and restrained taste of an earlier age. The room was simply furnished with a few examples of early English oak and a beautiful chair made from elm. Three early Fenton Ware jugs were lined up on the windowsill and a fabulous example of a Claris Cliffe vase, stuffed full of biros, stood on a beautiful nineteenth century bureau.

"This is the junk room," Ted said dismissively. "The stuff belonged to my grandma, haven't the heart to chuck it out. Reminds me of when I were a lad."

I explained that far from being junk, the furniture and pottery could net him a small fortune. His eyes lit up at the news.

"I used to say to the wife we should take it to the Antiques Road Show, but we never got round to it; thought nobody would be interested," he said incredulously, hardly able to take it all in.

He was well chuffed by the time I left, he only managed a half-hearted pass at the door as he was so taken up with the idea of flogging his grandma's heirlooms so he could take off to see young Raymond earlier than expected.

As I staggered off with two plastic bags full of vegetables from his garden, I took one last look at Tor's house and noted the number.

I'm going to write to him I thought as I drove home, I've been celibate long enough. If I don't get a man soon, my knickers will spontaneously combust and I'll be a candidate for Marcel Duchamp's Mona Lisa with the caption 'she's got a hot ass.'

That's me all right I thought, as flames of lust licked along my thighs with the memory of Tor as I sped through the dreary suburbs back to the lush and verdant fields of Wethershire .

Chapter 14

I'm sure it would save the NHS millions of pounds if a scientist could come up with a mathematical formula to explain the dynamics of intuition. I mean my intuition is razor sharp in identifying people I want to avoid at parties, like the smug married bores who drone on and on about house prices and school fees, or the party lech who keeps making excuses to brush past me so he can rub his crotch against my bum.

But the other sort of intuition, the sort that alerts me to whether someone fancies me or not, can flicker on and off like a faulty switch and drives me insane with indecision.

I've already eaten a packet of indigestion tablets to ease painful windy flatulence caused by the nervous strain of whether to trust my intuition or not over the issue of Tor. It goes without saying that any agonising dilemma like this can only be eased by an increased intake of carbohydrates.

I know that Tor fancies me. I think. I thought I knew instinctively in the spilt second that we exchanged glances on Ted's doorstep. Within minutes of his eyes meeting mine, I felt a warm deep tingly feeling suffuse my nether regions where it stirred around doing naughty things to my bits.

If only I could freeze-frame that moment and take it home to analyse it at leisure, turning it over and over in my hands like an antique Grecian urn to see if it was genuine or not, I would feel happier. But all I have to deal with is a fleeting moment, a 'feeling'.

Added to that is the tiny little germ of self-doubt that divides and multiples as soon as it is given fertile ground to feed on. It consumes my head until it fries with the certainty that it was all a fanciful illusion, shadows in a cave illuminated by my vanity and overactive imagination.

The kitchen was a fire hazard by the time I'd written a note to send to Tor after I finally decided that I could not afford to indulge in the luxury of intellectual introspection if I wanted, well, sex basically. And lots of it. I stood knee-deep amongst the rejected scribblings that I'd spent hours composing, reading aloud the version that I felt struck a balance between a friendly enquiry about how he was and a subtle hint that I was available for 'extras'.

I was in full flow when Joey wandered into the kitchen to ask me who I was talking to.

"Nobody, just thinking out loud," I said as I hastily scooped up armfuls of discarded paper off the floor.

"Are you trying to get a man?" he asked casually. "Dad's got a new friend called Fiona. She cooks things for posh people and says, 'okay yah' all the time." He wandered off.

I was in a ferment of curiosity as I meandered after him trying to sound dead casual as I asked him how old she was, if she was pretty, had any children or ever stayed the night.

"Dunno," he said.

I knew it was fruitless to push for further information. It's as much use as trying to phone up a call centre to make an enquiry about your mortgage statement. Before you know where you are, you've been transferred to six different departments who all deny responsibility for your account and by the time you've put the phone down your head is spinning and you're no nearer to finding an answer. It takes time, cunning, patience and if all else fails, a considerable degree of grovelling. I decided to bide my time.

"You'd better go and polish your halo if you want to be ready to read your lesson in church with Granny," I called to his receding back as he climbed up the stairs.

I was looking forward to the harvest festival because afterwards I was going to have lunch at the Hall where I could gaze with adoration upon the divine Percy. Unfortunately, Charles cancelled a previous engagement so that he could make it, but I decided not to let that spoil my enjoyment.

The church was packed as we made our way down the aisle to a pew where my mum and Aunty Thelma had saved us a seat. It was a jolly service with children from the Sunday school acting out the parable of the sower under the proud gaze of their parents. A procession, led by an earnest looking little girl wearing a hairband, wandered off to sow imaginary seeds around the church, where some we were told fell on stony ground and others were caught up and strangled by weeds which represented the cares and pleasures of this world. I instinctively looked at Percy who was sitting in the family pew in front of the organ. He looked decidedly strained. My eyes scanned over the familiar faces sitting in their regular pews as the procession moved to circle the font. Suddenly my eyes were distracted by a big rugged looking man sitting between Gladys and Cess. I had to look twice before I could place him. It was Scott Henderson.

My mind was so distracted by the sight of him that I found myself singing the wrong words to the hymns and my voice went up a scale when everyone else's went down and then I put a fiver in the collection by mistake. Joey gave me an agonised look when I unthinkingly clapped after he read the lesson with mum.

"You are so embarrassing," he hissed as he sat down. The minute the organist struck up with Purcell's Trumpet Voluntary to mark the end of the service I nudged Joey to move sharpish, but we were jammed in by mum praying like a penitent at the end of the pew.

She was kneeling down for so long I thought she'd nodded off and by the time she finally heaved herself upright the isles were as jammed as Tesco's on a Christmas Eve.

"Did you see that man sitting with Gladys and Cess?" I asked aunty Thelma as I tried to elbow my way through the throng. "Do you know who he is?"

I should have known that aunty Thelma would be up to speed on the latest movements going on in Hartborne. My mum has one of the longest rubbernecks in the village. Not much gets past her.

"Well, according to your mother he's a family friend from Australia," she informed me. "He's staying for a few weeks in the Horse and Groom."

She looked at me and gave me a knowing smile, "I thought you seemed distracted during the service, obviously your mind wasn't focussed on higher things. I must admit dear that if I were thirty years younger, I would be tempted. Shall I ask Gladys to introduce you?"

She looked quite startled when I vehemently declined the offer. If Gladys invited him to meet me then my cover would be blown and he would run a mile, I thought. I needed to catch him off-guard.

"Concentrating on Charles are we?" she said as he suddenly homed into view.

"Yes," I lied. "I wouldn't want him to think I was interested in someone else now would I?"

She looked quite disappointed; I know she doesn't think very highly of him. She thinks I'd run rings round him and get bored and lead him such a merry dance the poor man would give in and let me get away with it and I'd end up despising him. Too right.

"You've always been a handful, ever since you were a little girl," she's always telling me. "Your poor mother was way out of her depth from the moment you were born."

As soon as Charles presented himself in front of us, I introduced him to Aunty Thelma and beetled off. I was determined to ask Scott why he was with Gladys and Cess. I managed to make good progress weaving my way in and out of the crowds, but I was stymied by the rector standing at the door shaking hands with everyone as they passed.

He insisted on holding my hand longer than was necessary so I couldn't escape before he'd asked me how I was, how nice it was to see me in church and how he hoped to see me there again before Christmas. I found myself promising to help sing carols in the choir so I could extricate myself and continue my quest for Scott. I searched high and low but there was no sign of him. I finally had to concede defeat.

I got back to find Charles being obsequiously charming to Aunty Thelma who I could tell wasn't having any of it. I'd arranged for Joey to have lunch with her and mum, and as I said goodbye, I exhorted him to behave himself.

"I'll behave, if you behave," he said back smartly.

We arrived at the Hall at the same time as Delia who pulled up so hard in her Freelander that the wheels made the gravel spew up everywhere. She looked flushed.

"Didn't see you and Henry in church," I said.

"We've had a massive row," she said fiercely, seeming not to care that Charles was present.

"You see," she said turning to him directly. "Although I'm a fifty-year-old woman it appears that it's unseemly for me to go out unaccompanied. Like a dog without any road sense. Henry seems to think I might forget my manners or something. Silly me."

Her face tightened. "He can rot in hell for all I care."

Charles was thoroughly embarrassed. He comes from a social class where you're born with a stiff upper lip. Discussing relationships is like going to the loo in public. One doesn't. Intense emotional agony is only allowed if your dog dies or one of your horses loses a race. Seriously.

His face blanched. "Quite," he gasped loosening his collar.

I could tell that Percy was not himself as we made our way to the drawing room after being let into the Hall by Thomas the stable hand. I'd heard that Percy was prone to histrionics but even I thought his behaviour was a bit OTT. We found him lying across a chaise longue looking like the poet Thomas Chatterton, with a ghostly complexion to match. One arm was draped dramatically over the back while the other was held poetically over his forehead. Seamus was hovering around trying to persuade him to have a pint of Guinness to steady his nerves.

"Oh, go away," Percy was saying, flapping his hand at him as though he were an annoying fly. "The damage is done, you don't understand, an oaf, an oaf, a hulking great oaf."

As soon as he spotted us out of the corner of his eye, his whole demeanour changed, as he bounded over towards us and invited us all to sit down and have a drink. "Seamus is the chef today," he told us and then said rather facetiously. "Off you go and make us something nice with the help of your young kitchen assistant, Thomas."

"I intend to do just that," Seamus said with a smile.

After he'd gone, Percy amused everyone with a hilarious account of our earlier telephone conversation, I pleaded with him to stop but he carried on and was so funny that even I had to laugh.

Once he'd finished, he arched his back and rubbed the back of his neck with his hand.

"I feel so damned stressed," he said. "Any of you lot good at giving a massage?" Charles looked horrified and Delia just looked over at me. "I'm sure Rebecca would love to give you one," she smiled.

Percy laughed. "Darling, I'm not sure I'd go that far, but who knows?" And then he summoned me to stand behind him to give his neck and shoulders a good rub.

"Harder, harder," he moaned, as my hands moved rhythmically beneath the collar of his shirt. I felt flushed and overcome with a desire to bend down and kiss his neck beneath the soft tendrils of his wavy hair.

Charles sat there looking crosser and crosser. "You're nothing but a tease," he exclaimed to Percy as he began to undo the front buttons of his shirt.

"You're not jealous, are you?" Percy asked as he grabbed my hands and started to move them over his chest. My hair spilled over his shoulders and he closed his eyes and began to play with it as my hands greedily explored his exposed chest and beautifully taut stomach that has a delicious ridge of soft hair running down from his belly button to his trouser tops. As I traced it with my fingers, I suddenly became aware of Seamus standing at the door.

"Sorry to interrupt such a tender scene but lunch is served," he said in a voice suppressing an emotion I couldn't quite identify.

Percy lazily opened his eyes and kissed the palms of my hands before letting them go.

"It'd better be worth it," he said as he languidly buttoned up his shirt.

Charles was very attentive throughout the meal and emboldened by Percy's brazen behaviour began to take wild liberties. I crossed my legs very firmly after I felt his hand underneath the table sliding above, below and between my thighs while he whispered snippets of John Donne in my ear, "Come madam, come."

I whispered back unpoetically, "You're asking for a slap," but it only seemed to inflame him further. I squirmed and looked imploringly at Delia, but she was totally engrossed with talking to Seamus. I turned to Percy.

"Is Sir Walter ill?" I enquired as I felt Charles' shoeless foot starting to stroke my calf.

Percy said that Sir Walter was out visiting at Lord and Lady Howgrave's house and that he was as well as could be expected.

"Something wrong then Percy?" asked Charles.

"No, no," said Percy hastily. "It's just that he's not getting any younger and he doesn't help himself getting worked up over things, he'll have another stroke if he's not careful."

"I wouldn't mind having a stroke," said Charles looking directly at my chest.

"Neither would I," said Percy looking disconcertingly in the direction of Thomas as he retreated to the kitchen after putting a big bowl of fruit salad on the table.

Suddenly, for the second time in two days, I felt struck by a flash of intuition. It felt extremely uncomfortable. The scales fell from my eyes. Charles fancies me and I fancy Percy and Percy fancies Seamus and they both fancy Thomas and Delia is in deep doggy doo because she's in love with Toy Boy. It all slotted into place. I think. We're all either completely fucked or I'm going mad I decided before dismissing my intuition as wild speculation. You're imagining things I consoled myself, the idea's too fanciful for words.

Chapter 15

This week's been like a white-knuckle rollercoaster ride on the emotional equivalent of Nemesis without any brakes. For a start, I feel as if I've been involved in a stint of work experience to learn what it's like to be a man. As in permanently horny. And secondly, it's Konnie's birthday tomorrow and she's invited me to a little soiree at her house to celebrate. With Jake. Apparently, she's in lurve.

And that doesn't take into account the peripheral issues such as my mixed emotions over Percy which torture me in the knickers department and the mysterious Fiona who could, for all I know, become Giles' wife and by definition Joey's stepmother.

What if she's really nice?

My first problem started when my bits started to go all zizzy the minute I posted my letter to Tor. I suppose posting a letter has a sexual resonance, what with the big wide red slit and the act of slipping the hand inside to make a deposit in the hope of entering into a dialogue or relationship of some kind.

I feel as if I've just sat at work all week like a big blob with wet pants, secreting masses of pheromones and dribbling all over my computer. It's made me appreciate how hard it must be for a man, quite literally I suppose, to think, talk and walk all at the same time and maintain a basic level of equilibrium, what with all that testosterone sloshing around.

"How are you?" asked Konnie solicitously as I sat there at my computer twirling my hair and tying it into elaborate knots.

"Sex starved," I replied.

"You need to get out more," she said. "Which is just as well because I'm having a bit of a birthday 'do' at my house on Saturday and of course you are invited. Special guest," she smiled.

"Right," I replied, twirling my hair more vigorously than ever. "Sounds cool." I think it's really self-defeating to feel sorry for yourself and I rarely indulge, but on this occasion, I felt I deserved it. I launched into a full-scale self-flagellation exercise. Who would have thought it I tortured myself, that when I met Konnie, she would end up, by a wild coincidence, falling for the secret lover that I was besotted with and used to bore her rigid about between tutorials? I bet she gets a really nice birthday shag, I continued, digging the knife deeper, as I stared mournfully at my computer monitor. "Are you going to sit there all day like an imbecile or are you going to actually get some work done?"

I lifted my head and turned around to give Keith a feeble smile.

"Slave driver," I replied and then, stretching like a cat, I decided I needed a bit of exercise, so I embarked on a trip to the loo. I made a detour on the way back via the kitchen to make a cup of tea and then I felt I needed some fresh air, so I nipped out to get a bar of chocolate from the newsagents. I still couldn't settle when I returned, and I sat there squirming in my chair.

I felt a desire to jump up and down, preferably on a naked reclining male with a pertinent part of his anatomy at right angles to his body. I remembered the ridge of fine hair on Percy's flat belly and imagined tracing it all the way down beneath his trousers. Phew.

My fantasy was rudely interrupted by the phone ringing.

"Broadmarket Herald, Rebecca speaking," I drawled as I poked at a bit of toffee that had got glued to my back teeth.

"Hi," drawled a familiar Australian voice. "Scott here. Just keeping a promise, I made last week to give you a call."

I sat bolt upright, all thoughts of Percy's private parts evaporating in an instant.

"Great to hear from you," I said. "Are you still okay to meet up?"

He confirmed that he was, so we arranged a venue at a coffee shop a couple of days later when I'd got a quiet afternoon after the paper had gone to press. I was jubilant when I put down the phone, so I sauntered over to Keith to tell him I was on to a hot story.

"I'm pleased to hear it, can't afford to have you mooning about the place staring into space, a bloody Martian could have landed on your desk this morning and you wouldn't have noticed."

I managed to blag my way through the rest of the day by dealing with all the easy on-diary stuff and copying and pasting press releases verbatim even if they were completely shite. All my motivation and drive seemed to be lurking around in my pants while my imagination and creativity seemed to be floating about somewhere outside my head. I found Konnie popping aspirin and vitamin pills at lunchtime in a right panic thinking that she might be going down with a virus that's doing the rounds.

"Got any bromide in your bag?" I asked.

The next day wasn't any better. I woke up, turned over and groaned. What I would give for a decent seeing to I thought as I started the whole ghastly ritual of tearing round like a blue arsed fly to get to work to earn a pittance to keep body and soul together. Oh, and the odd item of clothing that a single girl needs as a sex substitute.

I mean if you haven't got a man's todger available then a new pair of shoes comes close in the orgasmic stakes. First the anticipation as you take the box out of the shiny bag, then the foreplay as you lift the lid to gaze greedily and stroke them and then the orgasmic shudder as you slip your foot inside. Toe-curlingly awesome. I decided to throw caution to the wind and wore my mini skirt and black ankle boots to work.

The impact was instant. Moira's mouth dropped as I wandered into reception and when I swanned into the office Dick did a double take, eying me up and down appreciatively as he walked past carrying a big box. "Nice," he murmured before bumping into a chair.

The contents of the box went flying and I left him frantically scrabbling around on the floor on his hands and knees picking everything up. Result. I sat at my desk and flexed my fingers before starting work. I slowly made my way through a pile of envelopes that all contained very worthy, but very boring letters or circulars. Then, at the bottom of the pile, I came across a small letter marked Private & Confidential. Interesting. I opened it with curiosity to find, not a letter, but a business card inscribed with the name of a man who could sort out my horny hormones in an instant. Tor. I immediately abandoned my desk to rush upstairs to Konnie's office. I was breathless with excitement. I waved the card under her nose before giving it a big theatrical kiss.

"I've been delivered from the temptation of succumbing to the sexual advances of a DUD," I squeaked, to the confusion of the rest of the office.

"Let me see, let me see," Konnie said reaching out to snatch the card.

"Well, he's obviously keen. This is a card offering sexual services. Forget the 'Artist by Design,' the only designs he's got in his head are the ones on how to get his hands on your body."

I felt exultant as I explained to Konnie that I had also sent Tor a letter and how our correspondence would have crossed in the post.

"It's amazing that in the short time we saw each other at Ted's we both instinctively knew we had the hots for each other and decided to do the same thing. Wow." Konnie said she saw the hand of fate at work and suggested it would be a good idea to invite Tor to her party as my partner. What a brainwave. Tor's as dishy as Jake any day and it will rile Jake no end to see I've got someone else. Not that he wants me. He's just a big fat mangy dog-in-a-manger who would prefer all his ex-girlfriends to pine away to a shadow of their former selves without him to worship and adore.

"His ego wouldn't fit into a supermassive black hole," I thought as I made my way back dreamily to my desk to write Tor's details into my contacts book.

I found it even more difficult to concentrate with the imminent prospect of getting my bits out of storage and I wondered, if I was given the chance, whether I would trade in five days of my life to be at Konnie's party sooner. Interesting concept I thought as I wandered over to the photocopier.

"Is your skirt legal?" asked Keith as he lifted his head up from reading proofs.

"You should be oblivious to the fact I'm wearing a short skirt," I replied. "You're married."

"I didn't know getting married made you go blind," he said.

I leant over the photocopier and put my chin on my hand as my mind became flooded with fantasies of Tor. The sooner Saturday arrives the better, I mused. In this mood, I'm dangerous.

I decided to wear my mini skirt for my meeting with Scott in case I needed added ammunition to get the low-down on his birth mother. I didn't plan to go as far as a full-blown Sharon Stone, but it's amazing how easy it is to turn a man's head to jelly just by crossing and uncrossing your legs. Pathetic really. But handy.

I'd arranged to meet him in Newton Saucey at around 4 o'clock so that I could surprise Joey by picking him up earlier from Mum's. I felt full of confidence as I marched into the coffee shop in my mini skirt and armed with a hunch that he was none other than Gladys' secret love child.

"You look happy, had a good day?" asked Scott as I walked over to where he sat waiting in a corner of the cafe.

"I'm a happy person," I replied cheerfully as I scanned the menu.

After the waitress had brought me a pot of tea, I cupped my face in my hands and asked him how his new-found hometown in a small corner of rural England compared to the wide open spaces of his adopted country.

"I like the rain," he said. "And the mists in the morning, the rugged moors and the small patchwork fields and the antiquity. That's smart. But the people," he shrugged, "are almost feudal, kinda quaint and amusing if yer just visiting, but for an Australian and a Republican like me, a bit hard to swallow."

"So, you don't rate the King then?" I asked smiling.

"I'm sure he's a very nice guy, but," he took a deep breath and spoke so earnestly that it led me to feel his opinion couldn't be entirely objective. "The British upper classes, they seem to think they can live outside the rules, do what they like and damn the consequences. They hide their gutter morals behind airs and graces, etiquette, whatever it is you call it. It stinks like dingo shit."

He shut up quickly and began to break a piece of cake on his plate into crumbs.

"Sounds like you speak from personal experience," I said.

"I never said that," he said sharply. "I said remember, that I didn't want to talk about my birth mother."

I never asked if it was to do with your birth mother I thought with quiet interest.

We looked at each other steadily in the eye.

"Is she upper class then?" I ventured daringly, knowing I had to be pushy or I wouldn't get the story.

"No," and as I've already said, "the subject's off limits."

I assumed an air of puzzlement. "So, what are we here for then, if we can't talk about your mother?"

Scott looked embarrassed and seemed suddenly tongue-tied. I tried not to smile as I sat looking at this big, strong rugged Australian macho man, lost for words. I decided not to help him out. The silence continued until he stutteringly said, "I thought it might be, well, you know, nice to get to know, you know, you," he blushed furiously.

"Oh," I said completely flummoxed.

This is going to make it difficult I realised instantly. If I lose my professional detachment, then I might never get to the truth. And for a journalist to get so close and not dig up the story is like a bloodhound standing over a patch of ground sniffing a juicy bone and leaving it buried. Impossible.

"I told my editor I was out of the office getting a good story," I said. "What shall I say when I get back?"

Scott held up his hands, "You're the journalist. You can come up with a better story than me."

"How about, Gladys Poole is your mother," I said in a cool, clinical, professional tone. I felt a momentary twinge of guilt as I saw his face blanch.

"How did you know that?" he said fiercely, leaning across the table. "Tell me, tell me how you knew?"

"It's called doing my job," I said, my heart beating fast.

"I thought you were different, but I was wrong," he said woodenly. "I thought," he paused. "What the hell!" He threw his napkin on the table and motioned to the waitress to bring the bill.

"You thought what?" I asked with curiosity.

"I thought we were the same, you and me." I looked at him questioningly.

"You might be able to pull the wool over other people's eyes," he said. "But you don't fool me. You've got the saddest eyes I've ever seen."

I instinctively lowered them and studied my hands. He stood up.

"Are you going to talk to Gladys, find out what dirt you can dig up. Find out who my father is and drag Gladys' name through the mud?" I sat still, not saying anything.

"Lost for words now are we, the clever journalist?"

I felt aware of him standing there. "Look at me," he said. I looked.

"Don't cross me, Rebecca Pearce. I'm not a man to be crossed." I looked away.

He moved his hand towards me as if to stroke my face, but he let it drop before it reached me.

"Don't do this to us," he whispered hoarsely. And then he left.

"Don't do what?" I thought as I felt my world turn upside down.

Chapter 16

There is a turning point in everyone's life, such as Oedipus' fateful meeting on the road to Boeotia, the Apostle Paul's epiphany on the road to Damascus and Lot's lucky escape when he legged it out of Sodom and Gomorrah after a tip off from God it was D-Day.

Okay, my life's crossroad might be a teensy weensy less dramatic in comparison, but it seems as if it comes pretty close at the moment. I don't know which way to turn and if that's not bad enough, I'm plagued with the irritating notion that I don't really have a choice, as in Providence and all that palaver and I feel powerless, trapped in a philosophical straitjacket of indecision.

One thing that has hit home is the need to be well-armed against the slings and arrows of outrageous fortune that life might throw at me over the weekend, as in kissy-kissy Konnie and Jake and a potential new love interest.

I decided there was really only one strategic option to boost my weakened defences, flex the credit card in the sales.

I'd just made up my mind to go on a shopping orgy when Delia phoned to say she was going to pick up Toy Boy to help him continue his transformation of Mervin from polyester troll to designer babe.

"He's already got Mervin to shift the hair and zap the moustache and he's decked him out in designer glasses and trainers. Apparently, he looks almost human. Hard to believe, I know, but miracles do happen," said Delia.

I suggested she invite him along to Konnie's party to see if the makeover had any impact on the opposite sex.

"We could do some research, you know, watch to see if the look of horror that usually crosses a woman's face is when she's confronted with Mervin, is no more."

"I think that might be too optimistic at present," Delia said in the sort of solemn voice used by a doctor giving unwelcome news to their patient. "The best we can hope for at the moment is indifference, we've got to take account of the lard remember."

I warned her that if Mervin came along to Konnie's party it might be advisable to distance herself from him or the other guests might get the impression that the two of them were an item.

"It will consign your credibility to the dead zone," I said.

"That won't be a problem," Delia replied in a tone I knew spelled trouble. "I'm taking Toy Boy and I don't care if people put two and two together. I intend to brazen it out."

I implored her to see reason and pointed out the dire consequences if Henry found out that she was seeing another man – a younger and more virile one at that – the proverbial would hit the fan like ripe manure. But she was adamant and said that she'd wasted too much of her life pandering to Henry's rages and putting up with his infidelities.

"He won't notice anyway," she insisted. "He's spending all his free time in that wretched pub the Doom and Gloom. He gets one of the farmhands to drive him over there and stands at the bar drooling over the new barmaid. She can have him for all I care."

I hope Delia's right about Henry I thought as we ended the call. But I have my serious reservations. For Henry's type, there's one rule for men and one for women, as in men can do all they damn well please while women should do as they're damn well told. I wouldn't like to be in Delia's shoes, even though they are Jimmy Choos.

I was duly picked up by Toy Boy in his Audi TT with Delia sitting in the passenger seat stroking his inner thigh. I clambered in the back and we roared off to Leeds to meet up with Mervin in a wine bar. The most noticeable thing about Mervin was that he wasn't noticeable. My eye wasn't instantly drawn to some human excrescence standing out like a sore thumb.

No, he just looked, well, almost like a regular guy. Fat, but normal.

"Merv mate," said Toy Boy slapping him on the back as we joined him at the bar.

I was seriously impressed with Mervin's new image. It's amazing how trendy gear can change your perception of a person from nerdy to normal overnight. Cruel, I know, but true. His new short, frizz free haircut with a faint wedge and titanium framed glasses made him look like a different person, transformed from a train spotter to a sort of lefty intellectual. It was only his clothes between his neck and ankles that hinted that all was not as it seemed.

But it was progress. All he has to do now is lose the weight. I wonder if you can lose it from your ears? I felt slightly disconcerted while we were having a drink as I got the impression he thought his wardrobe revamp qualified him for a second chance in the relationship stakes.

"We make a good foursome, don't we?" He gave me a leery look over the rim of his wine glass. "We'll have to do this again sometime."

"I'd wait until you get a bevy of new girls to choose from. I'll just wait at the back of the queue," I said before looking at my watch and making my excuses to escape.

We agreed to split up, with Delia and Toy Boy heading off in their quest to kit out Mervin in some party gear while I went off in the opposite direction to find a bargain, including some naughty underwear for a potential horizontal jogging session with Tor.

I cruised around the shopping centre, salivating at the fifty per cent discount posters in the shop windows, designed to lure shoppers inside to part with their hard-earned cash. I drooled over the gorgeous frocks in the designer boutiques but became philosophical when I realised that the flimsy, floral, skimpy strappy scraps were incompatible with my rear end. Does my bum look big in this? I mused. Let's put it this way. Why wait for an eclipse of the sun when my backside could block out the sun for the entire northern hemisphere. Depressed or what?

After about an hour, I felt distinctly wobbly around the edges after being gripped by rising hysteria at the ghastly realisation that everything was either too big, too small, too young, or simply hideous.

I feverishly decided to retreat to a coffee shop to muster forces for a counterattack by replenishing my energy with a latte and double chocolate chip cookie. Not a good idea.

My credit card was gagging for a fix by 4 pm as the deadline loomed to meet Delia and Toy Boy for my lift back home. I felt like indulging in a bout of biblical breast beating, wailing and gnashing of teeth – and pulling my hair out by the roots.

I summoned up my energy to climb the escalators for the last time. It felt like scaling the south face of Everest. With the countdown to 5.30 ticking away, I threw caution to the wind and bought a sexy designer bra with an eye-watering price tag and blew a hundred quid on a red patterned skirt, flowery cardie and a jazzy t-shirt. As soon as I put in the credit card pin, I realised I'd got nothing to go with them.

"Nothing for it but another trip to the sales in the New Year," said Delia laughing, as she caught sight of my crestfallen face as I recounted my shopping frenzy fiasco in the car as Toy Boy drove us home.

As soon as I got in, I slung the bra on the bed, shoved my other unfortunate purchases to the back of the wardrobe then raided the fridge. I found three low calorie ready meals, buy two get one free. Ate two. I need to get a grip if I'm going to score with Tor. I berated myself as I swallowed the last mouthful and again as I surveyed my hirsute legs in the bath. Should I go for the full Monty and get my legs waxed from top to bottom or go for half hairy half smooth?

All this agonising flowed from the moment Tor's business card landed on my desk and culminated with a stomach-churning nervousness when I called his number. It felt almost as bad as when I have to do a 'death knock,' turning up unannounced on some unfortunate person's doorstep to ask how they feel about the fact their nearest and dearest has just been horribly mangled to death in a pile-up or been savagely murdered by a serial killer.

I started to speak gibberish the minute he answered his mobile and must have said 'what' and 'pardon' half a dozen times before I managed to calm down enough to have a normal conversation.

I assured him that I didn't think him too forward for sending me his card and no, his actions wouldn't jeopardise a burgeoning romantic relationship with Ted.

"I must admit I was rather surprised when Ted told me that you and he were an email match. I was under the impression that you didn't really take to him," he said very tactfully.

I hastened to explain how I'd mistaken Ted's name for his, omitting the fact that it was because I was totally traumatised by Konnie's ardour for Jake and told him that I'd only gone to see Ted on the off chance of seeing him.

"Is that too awful?" I asked.

"Even if it was, I'm glad you did. It was nice to see you, really nice."

There was an embarrassed silence. "You must have a good memory to remember the newspaper where I work," I said to fill the silence. "And you're a good fibber. You said you only had a slab for a garden. It's actually quite big and full of lovely plants."

"I didn't want you to want me for my garden," Tor said laughing.

"So, what do you want me for?" I ventured rather provocatively.

"Why don't we meet up and I'll show you." he replied.

By the end of the call he'd accepted an invitation to Konnie's party. "Bingo," I said turning to her as she'd been hovering in the background while I made the call. "My days as a celibate are numbered."

I experienced a sense of déjà vu when I opened the door to Tor when he arrived to take me to the party. The last time I'd opened the door to a potential lover I'd found a wimpy, balding nervous toff standing on the threshold, but now I beheld a vision of more than six foot of pure, primed, rippling handsome muscle holding a bunch of flowers.

"Why bother with the party?" I thought as my knees buckled under the glare of Tor's lazy, sexy smile.

"Hi," he said, bending to kiss me on the cheek. "You smell nice."

I invited him in, and we chatted while I found a vase for the flowers. We circled each other, smiling nervously as we chatted idly about the long journey from Mucklesbury and how he didn't realise Wethershire was so far out in the sticks.

He asked after Joey and I told him that he was staying with Giles overnight.

"Giles drops him off around lunchtime," I said as our eyes met over the top of the bouquet. Tor smiled wickedly.

I lowered my eyes demurely and turned to arrange the flowers. He came and stood so close to me that I could sense the electricity between us as I picked up a beautiful lily to inhale its fragrance.

"It's so beautiful," I said as I stroked the petals, trying hard to suppress a desire to turn to him and beg him to ravish me.

I heard him draw in his breath and as I picked up the flowers to put them in the vase. I felt his hand take them from me to stick them in any-old-how while his other hand circled my waist. The next minute we were snogging each other's faces off.

"Where's this party?" Tor whispered as he reached out to untie my silk wraparound dress while his eyes looked suggestively at the ceiling.

Somewhere in the depths of my befuddled brain flashed the name Jake, followed by the word's retribution and vengeance. The words, slapper and desperate also sprang to mind if I agreed to go upstairs.

I pretended to take his words at face value and told him it was in Broadmarket and if we didn't get a move on, we'd be late. He looked me deep in the eyes and asked me if I was sure I wanted to go and when I said I did; he held my face in his hands and kissed me gently on the forehead. His tenderness moved me more than his passion and I was tempted to change my mind but resisted and so we turned up at the party that was already in full swing. Delia arrived soon after, accompanied by Toy Boy and Mervin who looked great in a navy blue polo shirt and dark trousers, cool black shoes and a trendy watch on his wrist. Nice one.

"You've done wonders with Mervin," I said to Toy Boy, who as usual looked dead sexy in jeans and a t-shirt. He smiled revealing gleaming white teeth set in pristine pink gums. It's no wonder Delia doesn't need HRT I thought as I looked as his pert little arse which she was stroking fondly.

Konnie was in her element hanging on to Jake's arm as she introduced him to all her guests.

"And this is Tor," she said when she reached us. "And Rebecca, you know Jake of course in the biblical sense. They were an item, years ago," she explained to Tor.

"But he's mine now."

As they moved on to greet the other guests, Tor looked at me quizzically. "Do you mind?" he asked, and I was able to answer quite truthfully and thankfully, 'no'.

He put his arm around my waist and stroked my stomach with his other hand. I couldn't resist looking over to Jake who I noticed wasn't indifferent to the fact I had a new lover. "Serves him right," I thought as I stared straight back at him.

It must have been obvious to anyone that Tor and I had the desperate hots for each other. We couldn't resist touching each other up and if I wandered off to talk to someone it wasn't long before I felt his arm snake around me.

"It seems as if I've got a rival," said Mervin who waltzed over accompanied by a big buxom wench with massive thighs on show beneath a tight, white leatherette mini skirt.

"This is Rebecca, we had a slight 'thing' going on once," Mervin explained to the girl, before smiling dismissively.

I opened my mouth to object but tactfully decided to keep schtum. It seemed ungracious to point out that Mervin was practically a sad sex pest in his previous incarnation as a polyester troll.

"Lucky you," I said to the girl who I later found out was called Paula who he'd met on Plenty of Fish the night before.

I helped myself to a couple of G&Ts from the booze on the kitchen table as I wasn't driving and didn't touch the nibbles as I was too excited about being with Tor. A fatal combination. Added to that was the memory of the disquieting conversation I'd had with Scott Henderson which had touched a raw nerve that refused to go away.

"What does he know about me, I thought as I sipped my third G&T. I'm not unhappy. Am I?"

I felt confused which made me feel as if I needed a cuddle, so I wandered over to Tor who was chatting to Delia and Toy Boy.

"I was just asking Tor to let you know that we're off now," said Delia casting meaningful glances in the direction of the kitchen. "I've just had a nice chat with Moira who works with you at The Herald. It seems that her friend Beryl who she's brought along, is Lord and Lady Howgrave's housekeeper. She knows Henry from the hunt. Small world isn't it?"

I explained to an intrigued Tor in a slightly tipsy whisper, the intricacies of Delia's complicated love life.

"It's understandable really," I explained. "You see her husband is a farmer and, in his heyday, shagged anything that moved. But Delia's a reconstructed woman now and isn't standing for it anymore, so she's traded him in for a younger model. He's no good to her now anyway because his willy doesn't work."

Tor replied that he understood perfectly. "Why would a woman want a man who couldn't give her pleasure?" he asked provocatively.

"Absolutely," I agreed.

He rubbed his hands from my shoulders down to my hips and back again and then looked me in the eye.

"Why don't we go somewhere quieter?" he said.

"Why not," I agreed. It seemed a perfectly sensible suggestion to me.

Before I know what was happening, I found myself flat on my back on top of a pile of coats on Konnie's double bed.

"I feel like a teenager," I giggled as Tor lay down beside me.

"So, you do," he moaned as we started on a kiss that deepened into a hot steamy sesh.

I happily let Tor untie the ribbons on my dress. "I want to look at you," he said hoarsely as I sat astride him.

"Worth every penny," I thought as he pushed back my dress to reveal my new sexy bra.

Just then, the door burst open and Mervin staggered into the room with Paula's arms circling his neck and her thighs straddled around his waist.

I turned to see Mervin who stared open mouthed at my chest. He emitted a deep groan and let go of the unfortunate Paula who slid to the ground in an undignified heap.

"Any room on there for us?" he panted as his hands moved instinctively to his trouser belt.

Tor and I were out of there quick sharp. We laughed about it when we got home, all the way upstairs in fact and into my bed.

"I haven't thanked you for the letter that you sent to me, you beautiful, uncomplicated, naughty girl," Tor whispered in my ear in the morning.

"That's very remiss of you," I said as I stretched out with naked abandon beneath the sheets. "You'd better remedy that at once." So, he did.

Chapter 17

It's taken years of soul searching and self-inflicted slaps to stop denying myself the occasional indiscretion for fear of divine retribution. "Vengeance is mine, I will repay, says the Lord," was guaranteed to strike terror into the heart as my gums worked guiltily on forbidden chewing gum in Sunday School. And my childhood was positively plagued by a fear of the Bogie Man.

"If you don't behave the Bogie Man will come and get you," was the dreaded well-worn phrase dredged up by Mum when I was being naughty, which was often. And the ominous sounding death rattle of the exhaust on the rag-and-bone man's pick-up truck would make my little heart race so fast that I felt dizzy with fear. Everyone knew that the rag-and-bone man didn't just collect unwanted junk, they took away very naughty little girls and boiled down their bones to make glue.

I would fling myself, prostrate with fear onto my bed as he passed by and dream of my own funeral, where my poor, battered, pitiful body, salvaged from his lair, would be laid out in a coffin for all to see. I derived a strange sense of satisfaction from the idea. "Mum will be sorry then," I would think, almost wishing it would happen so she would have to endure a lifetime of self-recrimination for cruelly making me do as I was told. I must have been a right melodramatic little pain in the ass.

Nowadays of course children scoff at the idea of a Bogie Man. Parents don't have any recourse to a useful ogre who will conveniently gobble up their wicked children if they don't eat their greens.

"Yeah right," Joey says, stroking an imaginary beard, whenever I try to reincarnate the Bogie Man to scare him into submission after a knee-trembling telling-off session falls flat. Kids today are just too sophisticated for their own good. Self-flagellation was a popular hobby for my generation, everyone was at it. Even if you were into sex, drugs and rock and roll you signed up as a follower of Mahatma Gandhi and gave your sandals away to tramps. Self, self, self, that's all kids think about these days.

Having said all that, I suspect that today will be a 'making up for being a bad parent day.' It's impossible to do what I did last night and not pay a penance. Having wild passionate sex with a virtual stranger ranks high on the scale of bad; if the Bogie Man were alive and well, I'd definitely be a Prit Stick.

However much I try and justify it by reminding myself that I selflessly abstained from sex for years because I hadn't met Mr Right, it doesn't seem to wash. I'm not actually sure I'd know Mr Right if he introduced himself with a calling card. Let's face it, I just felt hot and horny and a bit bewildered thanks to a cryptic remark from an Australian guy and Tor, by sheer coincidence, passed beneath my nose at that particular point in time on life's conveyor belt. Thank God it wasn't Ted. Only joking! Having said that his latest e-mails are no joke. A lovelorn swain forsooth. I wish he'd just pack his wig and bugger off to Falaraki and drown his sorrows with a goldfish bowl full of Red Bull and vodka. When will men understand that when a woman says, "I'm not ready for a relationship," it really means, "push off I'm not remotely interested?" No doubt when hell freezes over.

Anyway, sacrifice for sins number one today came when I suggested to Joey that we could walk to Mum's this afternoon for tea and she could drive us back if it rained. Joey loves the walk from our village to Hartborne, but I hate Mum's driving, it gives me the willies. "An inch is as good as a mile," she'll say breezily as she narrowly avoids a head-on collision with a combine harvester. Why can't she be one of those infuriating old people that drive so maddeningly slowly that your car almost stalls in first gear as you judder along behind them?

Flossie did a slight stress wee with excitement when she realised she was getting an extra walk, pulling on her lead with such force that Joey practically had to run all the way there except for an embarrassing interlude with another dog. We'd reached about halfway to the village where the road reaches the top of a steep hill, when I saw Gladys approaching in the opposite direction with Scott Henderson and her beloved whippet trotting at his heels.

Now one of the problems when you adopt a rescue dog is an inability to spot canine psychopathic urges. How was I to know when I fell in love with Flossie on account of her cute wonky ears, that she would turn savage if she took a dislike to another dog?

My heart sank as soon I spotted Gladys's whippet. A well know trigger for Flossie's wrath. Within seconds, there was a frenzy of growling and flying fur as they lunged at each other in a rabid attack.

"God's strewth," Scott shouted as he whacked haphazardly at the pair of them to no avail. Joey vainly tried to drag Flossie away, but the whippet, unrestrained by a leash, merely followed. I must admit I was impressed when Scott risked, if not life, a limb, when he shoved his arms between the two dogs, grabbing hold of the whippet and lifting it, snarling and snapping into the air. Gritting his teeth, he clamped its legs together, though it didn't stop the most horrible bloodcurdling howls as the dogs continued to snarl at one another which made holding a civilised conversation difficult.

"Scott said he met you in Newton Saucey recently," Gladys shouted above the din.

"That's right," I said feeling wildly embarrassed as Scott shot me a vicious glance. Her next remark was completely drowned out as Scott joined in the general howling after the whippet made a bid for freedom by sinking its teeth into the arm of his jacket.

"Better go!" yelled Gladys as she whipped a dog lead out of her pocket and attached it to the whippet's collar. "I think it's going to rain soon anyway," she continued as she looked up at the darkening sky.

"Oh no," I replied as I made to follow Joey along the road, looking back to wave a conciliatory goodbye to Scott. He went to raise his hand then, obviously thinking the better of it, shoved it back into his pocket, walking off, head bent down into the wind.

"Be like that," I thought, as I marched off, although I couldn't help wishing that things between us were on friendlier terms.

Mum was all sweetness and light when we arrived as she hovered at the front door with the teapot.

She spent the afternoon blathering on about inconsequential gossip and the forthcoming Hunt Ball at the Newton Saucey Country Club, the social highlight of the rural calendar. Anybody who's anybody goes there, acting like a magnet for unattached women. It's a cattle market for people where mothers parade their daughters like heifers at an auction. It's almost painful to watch as big-boned country girls hang around in herds with their hands crossed demurely over their childbearing hips, holding little evening bags.

Celebrity makeover queens would be in their element. Surely there can be fewer places on earth where so many ghastly frocks are on display at any one time. I'd lay my life on the line to bet that the saying, 'you can't make a silk purse out of a sow's ear,' was coined by someone at a hunt ball.

"I've bought you a ticket," Mum suddenly interjected as she glanced out of the window as the sound of thunder rumbled in the distance. "You need to find a man to take care of you, although I simply cannot understand," she sniffed, "Why Charles Smythe Bothum-Wethem won't do. Stringing him along like a lovelorn puppy. Poor chap." Her eyes narrowed and she gave me her old Bogie Man stare of old. "I feel a distinct sense of froideur from Lady Howgrave. Your father would turn in his grave with the shame of it."

We'll all be in our graves soon I thought wildly as mum drove us home like a Formula One racing driver navigating the track at Le Mans. I gripped my seat belt instinctively holding my breath as we hurtled along the rain lashed road in her Yaris.

"Mum says you're a bad driver Granny," Joey piped up from the back seat as she wrenched the wheel around narrowly avoiding a pheasant straying across the road.

"She says you're a menace."

"Nonsense," Mum replied as she navigated a sharp bend on the wrong side of the road. "I've got an unblemished driving record, apart from one or two, or maybe three minor bumps." She turned to give Joey a reassuring smile just as the unmistakable shape of Percy's delicious derriere homed into view as he cantered down the road on his hunter.

"Look out," I screeched as the horse reared up and then bolted like a bullet from a gun as we whizzed past like the clappers. I looked with horror out of the back window as the horse followed us down the road at a gallop with Percy clinging onto the bridle like grim death. I cringed with embarrassment as mum slowed down at the village junction to see the whites of Percy's eyes staring with terror into the rear-view mirror before he finally managed to rein his mount to a precipitous halt.

"You mad old bag," he yelled as he struck his crop on the side window. "You nearly had me killed. This is ten thousand pounds' worth of horseflesh you crazy old crone."

With that, he turned his horse and galloped off up the road back to Hartborne.

"Well," said Mum with a sharp intake of breath as she pulled up outside my house.

"That was most uncalled for, how very rude."

I was so stymied with the acute embarrassment of Percy calling my mother, albeit justifiably, a mad old bag, that I forgot to do what I always do without fail when I get home. Check my answer phone. It's absolutely unheard of seeing that the phone is my social lifeline. When was the last time I walked into the house without picking it up to check my messages? Never. I was just trying to square my recent near-death experience with my impulse to salve my conscience for shagging Tor by walking to Hartborne when Joey walked into the kitchen to drop another moral bombshell.

"Who's Tor?" he asked.

I was so completely taken off guard that I stammered without thinking, "It's a heap of stones darling, rocks, you know, on mountains."

"Well, you've just had a phone message from a talking rock then, saying thanks for last night you were wild, can't wait 'till next time."

I feigned shock, "Really, how weird, must be a wrong number."

"He said, thanks for last night, Rebecca, you were wild," Joey replied doggedly.

"Even weirder," I said. "Strange coincidence."

Joey wandered off upstairs unconvinced. The minute he was out of sight I pounced on the phone to find I had two messages.

"Hi, thanks for last night Rebecca you were wild, can't wait 'till next time, speak to you soon, Tor."

My toes curled with mortification as I deleted the message and waited for the next one.

"Hi Rebecca, Tor again, I'll call back later."

"Shiiiiiit!" I hissed through clenched teeth. Self, self, self, that's all you think about, I thought as I lay and cradled Joey on his bed as he drifted off to sleep. It's got to stop. A selfish shag and four people could have been killed. I could never have forgiven myself. "That's because you would have been dead dummy," a small voice in the back of my head whispered. The sound of the phone ringing suddenly interrupted my tortured musings.

"Hi, Tor here, how are you, what have you been up to?"

The allure of stoicism and abstinence dissipated almost immediately. I vainly tried to be strong. "I've been contemplating the infinite in the face of an unusual set of circumstances that could have ended in tragedy." I explained the sequence of events, tracing it back to our carnal encounter the night before. Tor seemed bemused. "Is it fun punishing yourself? I must say I've never tried it. I apologise if what we shared was so reprehensible."

My knickers flashed an urgent message to my brain which quickly translated into a firm reassurance that I'd loved every minute of it. "So, so sexy," I breathed, instinctively stroking the inside of my thighs.

"So, you can come over to see me on Saturday then, I'll stay over in Mucklesbury 'specially?"

I agreed instantly. By the time I'd put down the phone I felt as hot as hell. "That's where you'll end up if you're not careful," a little voice wormed into my brain.

"Oh, shut up," I said to myself, as I lay down on the bed and indulged in a much needed minge massage. Sod the Bogey Man. A girl's got to do what a girl's got to do. It's only natural after all.

Chapter 18

"It's odd isn't it?" I asked Moira, as I handed over my two quid for the work's lottery syndicate. "That while most people secretly believe that one day their winning numbers will deliver, they dismiss health scares such as the clap by bonking away like mad without a condom thinking, 'it won't happen to me'."

She agreed. "Yes, it is rather. Apparently, it's best not to buy a lottery ticket too early in the week because it increases your chance of being run over by a bus. I always buy mine on a Saturday afternoon."

"Eh?" I said, as she wandered off.

"I think she means that if you buy your ticket early, statistically you stand more chance of being run over by a bus, then buying a winning ticket," explained Dick.

The idea crossed my mind after I went over to Mucklesbury and saw Tor last night. I mean, I don't mind baggage that's kind of hand luggage size, but I think we're talking industrial sized crates here. I just knew there had to be a catch somewhere. I suspect a relationship with Tor could be too much like hard work. He might be drop dead gorgeous, kind, solvent, blah, de blah, de blah, but he suffers from an affliction that crippled all of Shakespeare's heroes, a fatal flaw. He's boring.

It comes in the shape of his ex-partner Rita, a mad succubus of a woman. No doubt there's a law that's been passed that forbids casting aspersions on the clinically insane, so I will be polite as I can and say, that compared to Rita, Rochester's Bertha was as meek and inoffensive as an angel.

The first inkling that there might be a teensy-weensy problem manifested itself when the front door opened before I'd even had the chance to knock.

"Who the fuck are you?" asked this rather startlingly beautiful wraithlike woman with wild violet eyes.

"Nice to meet you too," I said holding out a bottle of wine feeling a right nit.

Thankfully Tor came into view, although he was all of a dither.

"Rita if you don't mind, I've got a visitor, if you want to come back tomorrow, we can discuss things then." He showed her the door.

"How dare you bring your floozies to this house, how dare you?" She turned to me, "If you have any sense of dignity you will leave now."

I might just do that I thought, as I clocked Tor's agonised expression.

"Rita, please stop it," he cried as she turned dramatically and waltzed off down the small passage to the back of the house. Tor held my face between his hands, kissed it quickly and then held up his finger and told me to wait. "Don't move, stay right there, I'll be right back," he said.

I waited patiently, flinching now and then as I heard the occasional crash of crockery, rubbing my hands up and down my arms to keep warm in the chilly night air as the rioting continued. Suddenly all went deathly quiet.

"Hello," I called. The silence was broken by the sound of savage sobbing. A dishevelled Rita suddenly appeared from the gloaming and rushed past like a whirling dervish into the street, Tor followed closely behind.

"Rita," he called urgently. "Don't be such a bloody fool." He wiped his hand across his brow and shook his head wearily as she leapt into a white Mercedes and tore off down the street like a bat out of hell.

"Finished?" I enquired politely.

"I'm so sorry," he said solicitously as he drew me by the hand into the house. "I can explain."

It turns out that Rita is in denial, she cannot accept that there is life after Tor. Not that she wants him, it's just that she doesn't want anyone else to have him either. Just in case Freya takes a shine to them.

"She doesn't like rivals you see. She has to be centre stage, number one," he said bitterly. He looked at me with agony. "She's had numerous lovers. Paraded them in front of me, but she goes nuts if I so much as looked at anyone else." His voice faltered, "Forgive me?"

Before I had a chance to answer, there was a knock at the door. Tor stiffened.

"Wait here," he said.

"Fine," I said. "Don't mind me. I just hope you're insured."

I heard faint mutterings, "Is everything all right, I heard a commotion?" a man's voice enquired, I relaxed. The voice started to get nearer and louder, I tensed.

"Here we go again," I thought as a familiar bewigged head suddenly popped round the door.

"I saw Rebecca's car and it's just as I suspected," said Ted in an accusatory tone.

"You've stolen my woman."

He rushed towards me and grabbed my hands. "I knew it. I knew there must be something keeping us apart. Betrayer," he said turning to Tor. "Beast!"

I sighed, "Is there any chance of a cup of tea around here?"

Tor, grateful for something to do, tiptoed over the broken pieces of crockery littering the floor to fill the kettle.

"Had a row?" asked Ted hopefully as he surveyed the scene. I explained that Rita had got a bit upset. "Cracked," said Ted pointing to his head. "Completely cracked, he'll never shake her off."

Attempting to change the subject, I asked Ted politely if he'd booked his flight to Falaraki.

"I've been waiting to see if I was going to be accompanied by an attractive companion," he said, looking daggers at Tor.

Tor sat down at the kitchen table with a look of exhaustion and plonked three mugs of tea in the middle of it. "Any gin?" asked Ted. Tor, looking distracted, started to drum his fingers on the table. "No." A long silence ensued, only broken by the sound of Ted slurping his tea through his dentures.

Tor finally broke the silence. "Rebecca's travelled a long way tonight Ted and hasn't got much time, so let's deal with the issue shall we, like responsible adults, we don't want to fall out now do we?"

"Dunno, depends," said Ted, shrugging his shoulders.

Exasperated, Tor asked Ted to spell out his terms and conditions quite clearly.

"Don't let's beat about the bush," he said, just as I swallowed a mouthful of tea. Well, I couldn't help but see the funny side of his remark and tried really hard to suppress a laugh, but it's difficult mid-swallow so to speak, I did my best but felt as if I'd swallowed a crisp sideways.

"Now look what you've gone and done," said Ted as regurgitated tea poured forth like a geyser. He jumped up to pat my back and surreptitiously wipe drips of tea off the front of my sweater.

Tor rushed to get a dishcloth and demanded that Ted stand clear. Ted snatched it.

"It's my girl, I'll do the wiping thank you," he said waspishly.

To calm matters, I assured them that I was quite capable of wiping myself down. I took the cloth from Ted.

"I'm very flattered that you care so much Ted," I said. "But Tor and I are an item now, it's official."

He stood there mulling this titbit of information over, gurning like a cow chewing the cud.

"How about a job share like, one week on, one week off?"

"Forget it," said Tor.

A look of defeat crossed Ted's face as he sank forlornly onto a chair.

He put his head in his hands and shook it from side to side.

"I'm 'artbroken," he said, his voice tinged with pathos as he gave his head an extra vigorous shake to emphasise his pain. A bad move. His wig fell onto the floor like a ripe scab to reveal a glabrous shiny pate with not a wisp of hair in sight.

Quick as a flash, I rushed over and picked it up and wedged it back on without a word. Unfortunately, it went back on a bit skew-whiff. Ted stood up and readjusted it with quiet dignity.

"I'm going now," he said. "But I've been 'urt and betrayed and like an 'orse, I never forget."

"An elephant," corrected Tor. "An elephant never forgets."

"Me neither," said Ted turning on his heel, disappearing down the passage.

Tor sat down on the chair just vacated by Ted and put his head in his hands and shook his head in a fair imitation of his predecessor. I tweaked his hair. "I hope this is glued on properly, I mean we don't want it falling off at an inappropriate moment, do we?"

Tor looked up and smiling weakly, took my hand.

"Do you really want to," he asked. "After all that nonsense?"

I straddled his knees and gave him a kiss and a cuddle. "Umm," I said slowly, opening his shirt buttons. "I think I could be tempted."

He pushed his hands beneath my skirt and discovered my stockings and suspenders.

"Naughty, naughty, girl," he breathed.

I slipped off his knee and led the way upstairs, I went to go into the first room I came to, but the door was locked.

"Not in there," said Tor, as he led me to another room with a large ornate Victorian bed. "But here, and here and here," he murmured, as he lay me on the bed and kissed my eyes, my mouth, the nape of my neck and the small of my back as he pulled down my skirt.

"It was awesome," I explained to Delia, on the phone the next day. "How did I manage to abstain for so long? A sexual Sahara without an oasis, except for the occasional bout of tonsil tennis."

She said that she understood completely. "My bits are permanently switched to max now, and I often think, how on earth did I manage all these years without having a man half my age and twice the revs? With Henry, all I got was a couple of humps and a fart and then he'd collapse on his back with his mouth hanging open like a corpse."

"That reminds me," I said. "I haven't told you about the Grim Rita yet have I?"

"Tell me all," she said. "I'm agog."

I went into intricate detail about last night's farcical evening and how, despite the fact that Rita is obviously slightly unhinged, she is very beautiful, very manipulative and has got Tor's balls in a vice. "I think she must have implanted a couple of microchips in them when he was asleep and she's operating them via remote control. She presses jump and he jumps."

Delia listened intently, offering the occasional, "never," or "you don't say." before offering her summing up.

"It's doomed, darling. The man is aptly named. He's between a rock and a hard place. Tell her to get lost and he loses his child, or dance to her tune. You're not the kind of woman to play second fiddle to a cracked record. Believe me, I've been there, got the t-shirt."

I told her I'd got just the solution. "Send Henry out to buy your lottery ticket on a Sunday morning. According to Moira, if you do that it's highly likely you'll get flattened by a bus."

Delia laughed when I explained how Moira had got her statistics in a twist.

"But just think if it were true," Delia said. "Especially if the ticket was a winner. A double jackpot if ever there was one. If only."

Chapter 19

Women have been blamed for every woe that has befallen mankind throughout history. Eve's desire for wisdom led her to succumb to the serpent's temptations while Pandora was so overcome with feminine curiosity that she couldn't resist opening a box from which flowed every imaginable evil that destroyed all the peace and harmony in the world.

This 'fiction' has led me to the conclusion that the origin of the well-worn phrase, 'she asked for it,' can be traced right back through time to the beginning of our so-called post-lapsarian world where surely a male author, or legislator, apportioned blame for society's cock-ups to women, thereby providing a handy justification for men's misdeeds ever since. I think the phrase 'men think with their dicks,' is a darn sight closer to the truth and acknowledges the latent power women have over men which makes them want to subdue us.

"Are you in your anti-men mood by any chance?" asked Konnie after I'd finished a particularly vicious diatribe against the weaker male sex, as we sat at my kitchen table for a post-party catch-up, delayed due to the fact that Konnie and Jake had spent some 'quality time' together in Paris.

"Just pointing out the anomalies between historical fact and the fiction peddled about women in all religious and mythological texts," I replied.

"Tor not phoned?" she asked, assuming the tone of solicitous concern you use when you ask someone if they've passed an exam which you suspect they're too thick to pass.

"Constantly," I answered. "I'm not surprised though; we're dynamite in bed together. I've been over to his place and he's been to mine since the party. And we met halfway for a drink last night and ended up having a shag in a lay-by." I smothered a yawn. "I'm knackered."

"So, what's the problem then?" asked Konnie. "Is your relationship just a series of carnal encounters or is it something more?"

"Is there something more?" I replied.

"You are in your anti-men mood," she said decisively.

"Maybe you're right," I admitted. "There is a certain ambiguity about the way I feel about men. I mean, they do provide a useful service but…."

My mobile buzzed with a text message. It read, Miz u. C u soon. Lust T.

"See what I mean?" I said, showing Konnie the message.

"I've only known him a short while and he's already invading my personal space. What more does he want? Discourse as well as intercourse? It freaks me out." I tossed my mobile phone from hand-to-hand as if it was a piece of burning hot metal before dropping it into my handbag.

"He can't be right for you, he's obviously not the 'one'," said Konnie in a sagacious tone. "You see, as soon as I met Jake, I just knew we were right for each other. There hasn't been a moment's doubt since. I love him and he loves me, it's as clear as eggs is eggs."

My brow furrowed and I deployed an irritating habit I've got when I'm flummoxed of rubbing my forefinger up and down my front teeth, as I tried to get my head around the conundrum Konnie had just presented to me.

"I don't want to sound pedantic," I said slowly. "But, when I met Jake, I felt exactly the same way as you do now. But, by the time we'd finished, I'd come to the unwelcome conclusion that the only person Jake loves is himself. He obviously wasn't the 'one' for me because he's now the 'one' for you? Are you sure your theory is infallible?" I was desperate to know. After all, if there's an easy solution that I haven't fathomed yet that could determine instantly whether someone's right for me or not, it wouldn't half come in handy. I'd save a fortune on my phone bill for a start. "And what does it mean," I continued doggedly. "When you say, 'as clear as eggs is eggs,' surely an egg is only an egg because society arrives at meaning through consensus? An egg could just as easily be a table and Jake could secretly be in love with Sabrina."

"Ahh, but Jake isn't in love with Sabrina, never has been, he only went off with her because you buggered him about," Konnie replied in a triumphant tone, as if that exposed some serious flaws in my logic.

I was intrigued. "So, if he didn't love her, did he ever love me? Was I the 'one' for him?" I needed to know.

Konnie prevaricated. "Well, I think he did care about you, a bit. Maybe more than a bit. But the fact is, it didn't work out for you and it's working out for me."

She gave me a hard stare and wagged her finger at me as if I were a naughty schoolgirl, "I'm just a straightforward mathematician." She held two fingers up like a V sign. "One and one makes two, okay? Vis-à-vis my relationship with Jake, it's quite simple. Jake loves me and I love him. Period. The Arts have got it all wrong. Abstract thought proves nothing. It just screws you up."

Undeterred, I was determined to get closer to the truth. "So, has Jake ever told you that he loves you?"

Konnie smiled. "He says he doesn't need to."

"That's because he thinks politically," I said. "Politicians are incapable of telling the truth. It's a well-known fact. They always leave themselves with an escape route. Jake could always say, "I never said that I loved you," couldn't he? And that would be the truth, wouldn't it?"

Konnie looked very confused and a bit worried and said in a slightly huffy voice, "Words don't mean anything, it's actions that count; that's what Jake says, and I think he's right." And then, slightly undermining her argument she asked if Jake had ever said that he loved me.

"No," I lied. "Never."

"Well, that proves it then," said Konnie brightly. "Because I know that he did."

I hadn't the heart to tell her that it proved absolutely nothing and that, by a slip of the tongue, she'd betrayed the fact that Jake had in fact loved me. Why didn't I believe it at the time?

"I'm glad that you are both so happy," I said quite honestly before standing up and waving my arms in an expansive gesture and saying with dramatic delivery, "I'm glad, because it's helped me to move on, to find, the 'one'."

I performed a theatrical bow and we both fell about laughing so loudly that we didn't hear a knock on the front door. It wasn't until Joey appeared in the kitchen followed by Scott Henderson that we realised we had a visitor.

"I hope I'm not intruding," Scott said nervously, pointing in the direction of the door.

"Shall I come back another time?"

I gestured to a chair. "Please join us, the more the merrier."

Sitting on the edge of his chair he explained to me that Gladys had told him where I lived and had assured him that I wouldn't mind if he called by.

"She told me that you could be completely trusted," he said to me earnestly. "So I thought that I'd call round and apologise for my earlier outburst in Newton Saucey, I was a bit out of order but, strewth, it's been stressful these last few months."

Konnie interrupted. "Does anybody mind filling me in on all this intrigue? And hey, it would be nice to be introduced. I'm Konnie by the way," she finished as she held out her hand.

"This is Scott from Australia," I interjected. "We met in in the Newton Saucey office when I was covering for Colin. Scott's got a really good story to tell but it's a bit sensitive, could open up a nasty can of worms that might ruin a few Wethershire reputations."

Scott's face brightened. "That's what I've come to talk to you about. I've changed my mind."

"Whoopee," I said as I put a mug of tea down in front of him.

He held up one hand. "Not so fast. Gladys wants me to tell the story of my birth, how she was forced to put me up for adoption and then tricked into thinking I was going to a good home. But no mention of my father."

His face broke into a smile, "Gladys says she that she wants the truth to be told and that she's proud of me and wants the world to know that she's my mother."

"Tell me, tell, me, tell me," Konnie said imploringly. "Update me on what Rebecca's already told me. I'm bursting to know."

I cautioned her and Joey, who was sitting in the dog basket with Flossie, that if Scott repeated his story, they mustn't breathe a word of it to anyone.

"It's an exclusive," I explained. "I don't want that Newton Saucey News rag of a newspaper to get wind of it, they wouldn't do the story justice. And I don't want Colin to steal it." I pointed my hands at my chest and said fiercely, "It's my story. It belongs to me."

I was surprised at the vehemence of my tone and dismissed a quizzical glance from Scott with a toss of my head. He smiled enigmatically before turning to Konnie to outline the tragic story of his unhappy start in life and the subsequent cruelty he endured. Konnie's eyes filled with tears as he laboured on with his history, sometimes stopping to gather his thoughts, or to rub his hands wearily across his eyes as he recalled painful memories that obviously still had the power to wound him.

"I decided it would be a good thing to tell my story, to expose the injustice that had been done to me and to thousands of other children. I felt it would be a cathartic experience, to tell my story from the beginning, finding my home country, the place where I was born, and my mother. I didn't appreciate that the truth of my story could upset the tissue of lies woven by my father."

His hands clenched into fists and he quickly stood up and turned his back to us, moved by a visible fury. I instinctively moved across to him and placed my hands on the back of his shoulders. I could feel his whole body trembling. I pressed him closer to me and then looked earnestly at Konnie who moved to hold his hands in hers.

"Hey," she said softly as she stroked his clenched knuckles. "What goes around comes around, that's what you have to believe. Bitterness is bad. Let it go. Allow yourself to be happy. You deserve it."

Scott visibly relaxed. "God strewth, you're right you know," he said. He turned to place his arms around us both. "Know what I'm going to do? I'm going to take both of you out to dinner. That's if you'll let me."

We both agreed instantly and spent the next few minutes deciding on the best place to eat.

"Have you got a partner that you'd like to bring?" Scott asked Konnie. "We could make it a foursome. Would you mind that?" he asked turning to me. "Or would that be out-of-order, I mean, if you're already taken." He stared intently into my face. Konnie opened her mouth, but before she had time to speak, I quickly assured him that I was still available.

"Still languishing on the shelf I'm afraid. My heart's for sale, no reasonable offer refused."

He looked pleased and said that he was glad that he'd called round and would contact me the next day to arrange a time with Gladys to relate their story. Joey showed him to the door and then wandered off to watch TV.

As soon as Joey was out of sight, Konnie let rip with outraged indignation. "You two-timing harlot," she hissed. "How could you lie in Scott's face like that? Your thighs are still warm from another man and yet you blatantly masqueraded as a single woman. My heart's for sale, no reasonable offer refused," she mimicked. "What would Tor say to that?"

She plonked herself down on her chair obviously shaken by my ruthless duplicity.

"What the eye doesn't see the heart doesn't grieve over," I said nonchalantly. "Just because Tor's having sex with me doesn't mean he owns me. And after all, having dinner with someone hardly ranks as two timing does it? Anyway, it's business. If Scott thought I had a boyfriend, he wouldn't be so co-operative."

She looked me in the eye and asked me how I knew that Scott fancied me. "Is there anything you're not telling me? And be honest, don't you feel any shame at all exploiting your sexuality to further your career?"

I looked shocked. "Good God, no." I raised my eyebrows. "Aunty Konnie's got no need to worry. Nothing's happened between us, there's been no exchange of bodily fluids. It's only flirting. He just said that we're very alike, or some such rot." I shrugged dismissively. "I can't see any harm in it."

"He's very attractive," said Konnie.

"Is he?" I asked. "Well, it's too late now and anyway, he'll be going back to Australia soon and as Jake and Sabrina's relationship proved, it's difficult to maintain any romance when there's twelve thousand miles between you. Phone sex may be fun, but I imagine you could tire of it very quickly."

"It's a shame you don't see Scott in a romantic light," Konnie said as she left. "He could do with some loving."

I was preoccupied with her remarks as I put an unusually clingy Joey to bed after reading him his favourite story, the Little Mermaid. His arms went around my neck as I kissed him goodnight.

"You are my real mummy, aren't you?" he whispered in my ear.

"Course I am, silly," I said. "I distinctly remember giving birth to you unless my memory's playing tricks. It's not something you forget easily you know. I mean, you have this huge bump for a tummy that's hard to ignore and then a horrible pain and before you know what's happened you get a snotty little ten-year-old who doesn't tidy his bedroom."

Joey didn't laugh. "Gladys gave her baby away and it made that man really sad. How do I know you didn't get me from someone else?"

I knew that Joey as a country boy understood about the mechanics of reproduction, so I somehow managed in a fumbling, stuttering kind of way to reassure him that he was one hundred per cent legit.

However hard we try to fool ourselves I thought later, as I picked up my mobile to text Tor, we need to be sure of who we are and where we come from.

'Miz u 2. Look 4 ward 2 C ing u. Lust R.' I read the message I'd written and asked myself if it was true. Who knows? I thought as I pressed send. I certainly don't.

Chapter 20

Things are starting to come to a head with the Newton Saucey Massage story. We haven't got enough facts to publish yet without Johnny Dickinson suing the pants off us, but things have popped up unexpectedly which leaves me with the feeling that it won't be long before everything's exposed. It seems that all the clues are there, but we haven't been pressing the right buttons.

"We've been approaching this from the wrong end," said Keith. "We need to stop shilly-shallying around and actually get down to the nitty gritty. Really give it some balls."

He says that the main thrust has got to come from the bottom, and he's told Colin to get his finger out because he wants to see some action.

"First of all, we need to prove who really owns the bloody place and then we've got to actually get hard evidence it's being used as a knocking shop."

Colin said he was certainly up for undertaking more research, but he wasn't prepared to get caught with his trousers down – "speaking metaphorically," he said hastily when Keith raised his eyebrows.

I said that I'd been really getting my knickers in a twist with frustration over the whole affair and I couldn't see us making any progress unless we followed up the only real lead we had with Colin and his groin strain.

"You are a genius," said Keith, as he raised his arms heavenward, punching the air in excitement. "Colin, get on the blower with that Tiffany bird, and see if you can extract some juicy titbits while she manipulates your groin injury. No funny business mind, but you can put it on expenses, claim under miscellaneous."

Colin shifted in his seat, crossed and uncrossed his legs and then rubbed his slightly sweaty forehead with his hankie before admitting he was already acquainted with the lady in question.

"I have to confess I have already taken advantage of Tiffany's particular expertise. But it's gone no further than that," he expostulated as he looked at

Keith's quizzical expression. "It was purely professional, not an encounter of a carnal nature," he added, mopping his brow.

"So, you say," Keith said drily as he reached for his fags.

"It's true," Colin replied, his voice going up an octave. "I couldn't afford her rates even if I wanted to, what with the driving ban and the fine. I'm going to be living off baked beans for months."

He stopped suddenly and looked furtively at the door as if he was about to make a sharp exit.

"Ha-ha!" Keith exclaimed. "Hoisted with your own petard." Colin squirmed like a worm.

Keith pointed his fag at Colin's chest as if he was about to skewer him like an insect. His eyes narrowed. Colin tipped back in his chair and held his arms defensively in front of his chest as if he was being interrogated by the Gestapo. "The reference was only oblique," Colin flustered. "It was open to interpretation."

"You mean to say you've hidden this nugget under your belt all this time?" Keith said. Colin gibbered. Keith put his fag in his mouth and reached for his matches. "I'm going out for a fag. I want results and sharpish. Out. Now."

Colin scuttled off like a beetle. Keith's eyes went heavenward. "Give me strength he muttered, " under his breath as he turned on his heel.

Konnie and Dick were in stitches when I regaled them with Colin's confession at lunchtime. "He said he'd got to rush off to the Broadmarket Magistrate's Court because he'd got a hot story about the Newton Saucey's Tenants Association versus Wethershire County Council over blocked drains. He says it's going to create a big stink," Dick said.

"That's bullshit," I laughed. "It's because he got a flea in his ear from Keith, that story is positively glacial compared to his hot groin strain saga. Can't wait for the sequel!"

I moseyed back to my desk after promising to provide an update on any further salacious hot gossip, to write up some nibs before going off for the afternoon on a mega skive expedition to interview Scott and Gladys and blag a free fancy frock for the ball.

The saying that necessity is the mother of invention has an element of truth. Faced with the fact I can't afford to fork out for a ball gown after my fateful forage in the sales, I came up with a priceless alternative. If stingy politician's wives and Z-list celebs can borrow a designer dress for a night out, then why can't I?

I gave Keith such an expert arse licking that he practically handed me the phone to ring up the best designer shop in Broadmarket to ask Lorraine the owner to lend me a frock in exchange for writing about it on the women's page. Rob the photographer will cover the ball, so I'll get him to take a few snaps. I don't feel guilty seeing as Keith owes me one. My orphan story has got to be one of the best scoops the Broadmarket Herald has had for years. Scott rang and offered to bring Gladys to the office for the interview, but I suggested that, on compassionate grounds it might be better to do it at her place away from prying eyes. It means I'll be home an hour earlier.

I set off for 'Minted', designer gowns and accessories and decided to park my clapped out old Skoda downwind of the boutique so as not to lower the tone. I opened the shop door to be assailed by the scent of money, a heady mixture of warm vanilla and honey, combined with the smell of wool and silk and lilies. "I wouldn't mind a bit of this," I thought, as my feet sank into the deep pile carpet.

"Can I help you?" asked a smartly dressed shop assistant as she glanced in my direction. Her tone suggested I must have wandered into the wrong shop by mistake, making me feel like something the cat had dragged in.

"Here to see Lorraine," I stuttered. "From the Broadmarket Herald."

She held up one perfectly manicured finger. "I see, wait here please," and glided off.

There was a flurry of activity and mutterings at the back of the shop and then the proprietor Lorraine came out, posing briefly in the doorway as if she was making an entrance on the red carpet at a film premiere to a scrum of paparazzi.

"Darling," she said effusively as she let go of the doorjamb, hurtling towards me on five inch heels with her arms outstretched, before air kissing me either side of my face—mwah mwah—with trout pout lips so puffed up with filler they looked like fat fish fillets.

"Let me take your coat," she said as she held it gingerly between her finger and thumb as though it were flea ridden after giving the chain store label a cursory glance as she hung it up.

"Now let me look at you," she said, twirling me round and round until I felt dizzy. I twirled to a stop and felt like a side of beef hanging in a butcher's shop window as she held me at arm's length, surveying me with her head on one side.

"You really need a tan to show any dress off and a good exfoliate and what about your hair?"

"Hair?" I asked in a puzzled tone.

"Up or down?" she said. "Or maybe some extensions?" She held up a lank strand and critically examined my split ends as she informed me in censorious tones that it needed nourishing.

"Nourish, nourish, nourish. There's no excuse for neglect," she said wagging her finger at me as if I were a simpleton. "Now if my dress is to look its best, I insist that Rikki in the salon next-door gives you a complimentary makeover to go with the feature. He can work miracles if he has to."

I felt about two foot tall as she turned to rifle through a rack of glamourous silk dresses. She picked out a selection and then ushered me into a changing room resplendent with a mock Louis XIV chair and curtains tasselled in pink silk.

"If this is how the other half live, count me in," I decided as I slipped a silky satin black dress over my head. I was just struggling to pull up the zip when I heard Lorraine welcome a new customer.

"Belinda darling, you look wonderful, those hair extensions, so envious and the tan, was it the Maldives or the Caribbean, I lose track?"

I instantly recognised Belinda from the dinner at Hartborne Hall as I came out of the changing room.

"Hi," I said to Belinda, turning to Lorraine to explain how we were acquainted. I sensed a distinct shift in her opinion of me as she smiled most solicitously as I was potentially elevated to the top drawer of Wethershire 's society.

"Are you and Charles Smythe Bothum-Wethem an item?" Belinda enquired, not sure if she could admit to such a close acquaintance at this early stage.

"No, and not likely to be either, he's not my type," I replied in an offhand voice as I adjusted the straps of the frock to accommodate my bosom. Wrong answer I realised, as the pair exchanged glances, instantly relegating me back to the bottom draw.

I shuffled over to a full length mirror to check myself out.

Not bad I thought.

Both women turned to examine me critically.

"Dreadful," said Lorraine. "It doesn't hang right. Versace would turn in his grave." And it seemed that the gospel according to Lorraine meant that the scarlet taffeta drained my complexion, the blue silk with diamante straps was too girlie, the green shantung too formal, the black and silver too tight and I hadn't got the complexion for the gold off-the-shoulder number.

Lorraine turned to Belinda and explained the reason for my weary expression as she rejected yet another dress as being too sophisticated. Charming.

"Rebecca's here from The Broadmarket Herald to help profile Minted at the Hunt Ball. It's a cash cow, the cream of Wethershire society will be there and as a stakeholder, sponsoring the nibbles I've got to get it just right."

Belinda looked slightly piqued that Lorraine had suddenly elevated herself to the upper echelons of the Wethershire county set and responded with a wave of her perfectly manicured nail extensions.

"I was informally approached by one of Johnny's top clients, big in the hunting fraternity. He suggested that we could offer our services, but as our business is so reliant on recommendation, we wanted to keep our exclusivity."

I wonder if her nails are retractable, I thought as Lorraine adopted a fixed wide smile showcasing her porcelain veneers.

"I've suggested that Rikki could give Rebecca a makeover, include it in the coverage, after all many of my customers feature in the top 200 rich list."

"Deuce," I thought as I dragged on yet another dress.

"Good idea!" Belinda gushed. "Rikki's so wonderful, I called him at the weekend minutes before Maxine's dinner party and said, 'Rikki darling, it's an emergency I've chipped my nail extension.' I was absolutely traumatised. He said, 'Belinda, I'm with you,' and flew over and mended it in a jiffy. It cost me an arm and a leg but imagine, Maxine would have seized on my imperfection and made a meal of it."

Lorraine just held up her hand and beckoned me back into the changing room when I emerged in a diaphanous pink chiffon. You've got to raise your game love I thought as I trudged backwards and forwards while the one-upmanship battle raged as Belinda wandered around in white crutch-strangler jeans that were so low-slung they were positively indecent. I listened with awe as they discussed their recent clothes purchases with price tags that ran into telephone number digits, interspersed with a demolition job on the absent Maxine.

"Everyone knows that her husband only earns a hundred thou," said Belinda dismissively. "But the way she carries on you'd think he earned top whack. It's pocket money to most of my intimate circle."

"I know, her clothes are so last season," Lorraine replied with incredulity. "I saw her in the health spa recently in last year's velour."

"No," Jenny breathed. "How sad," in a voice usually reserved for someone recently bereaved.

I was nearly in tears, born of frustration and boredom when I trudged out in in a brown shiny Lycra number.

"Almost, but not quite," said Lorraine.

"I'd love it, but it would drown me," said Belinda.

"Meow," I muttered as I struggled into a burgundy bustier and fan tailed skirt that made me look all tits and bum. Never, in a million years I thought, as I looked at myself in the mirror, I look like a high-class hooker.

"Yes! Now we're talking," said Lorraine. "It's got oomph."

I was too tired to object as Lorraine took the dress and teamed it up with long black gloves and a sparkly evening bag.

"Now, you will be careful when you wear this won't you?" she said, as she wrapped everything up in layer upon layer of tissue. My protestations to guard everything with my life were interrupted by her phone ringing.

"Maxine, darling one, how are you?" She handed me a glossy bag before turning her back on Belinda to admire her reflection in a mirror on the wall in front of her as she spoke all lovey-dovey down the phone as if Maxine was her BFF.

"Ciao," I said to Belinda smiling sweetly, as she stood slightly open mouthed with one hand on her hip. "Maybe see you around at Hartborne Hall."

I left the shop with relief to head for Hartborne village and Gladys' humble cottage which couldn't have been more of a contrast to the pampered world of Minted.

"She's around the back," said Cess when I pulled into the muddy yard where he was loading hay bales into the back of a Land Rover.

I wandered to the back of the cottage which stands on a windy ridge above Hartborne with spectacular views of the Wethershire landscape with fields knitted together with ancient hedges and the moors dotted with sheep.

I spied Gladys cutting a cabbage in Cess's famous vegetable patch where Scott was turning over the soil, wearing his shirt sleeves rolled up to reveal well-developed biceps. It looked like a tableau from a Jean François Millet painting as the late autumn sun sank slowly in the west.

Scott looked up as he became aware that I was watching him. His slow smile did funny things to my equilibrium. How's that, I wondered when I'm deeply in lust with Tor?

We went into the cottage just as Cess was lifting a big black kettle off the Aga to pour water into a brown teapot. We settled in front of the inglenook where a log fire burned brightly. "Here you go son," Cess said to Scott as he handed over a mug of tea. Gladys looked at me and smiled. "He's one in a million," she said looking at Cess, as she went on to recall her harsh childhood where single mothers could only bury their dead babies in un-consecrated ground. She was quite matter-of-fact when she talked of a missed opportunity to go to grammar school after her mother died of diphtheria.

"I had to go into service to help support the family and father wouldn't talk to me about sex, so I was completely ignorant. I had no idea how to get pregnant, but I thought I was in love, we were both so young." She sighed. "When I realised," she stopped and looked into the fire, before continuing in a tremulous whisper, "I knew it was out of the question to keep our baby. But I never knew they would send him so far away. So, I came home to Wethershire and Cess was here for me, no questions asked. He's more of a man then ever Scott's father was."

I felt reluctant to leave after I'd finished my interview. It was such a wholesome scene as Scott touched his mother's hand which she caught and held lovingly against her face, that I felt as pure as a vestal virgin when I left, cleansed of all impurities. It lasted all of five minutes when I got home. As soon as I stepped over the threshold, Delia rang to ask if I'd managed to blag a dress for the ball. I recounted my experience with Lorraine and Belinda and the absent Maxine with forensic detail including the misapprehension I was an item with Charles.

Delia asked if I'd heard from him as he would definitely be at the ball. "He keeps sending saucy texts," I explained. "With an equine theme, but I've managed to stall him, for now."

Delia, laughed and prophesised there would be a price to pay for egging him on at the Conservative Association 'do.' "You'll never get shot of him unless you spell it out," she said. "He's under the illusion he's God's gift to women thanks to his pedigree so he'll hang on like a dog humping your leg."

Delia has an intimate knowledge of Charles's social circle as Henry can match Charles in the cash stakes with land and property all over the place. But

137

she loathes all the pretention and howled with laughter at the antics of the social climbing Belinda and her designer jeans with crack exposure.

"Was it her front crack?" asked Delia.

"No, her back crack," I replied. "A good inch."

"Well," Delia said philosophically. "If I showed my crack in public small children could get lost in there. But hey, who cares, big bums are beautiful."

"And biceps," I said impulsively. "Big biceps are beautiful."

"Anyone's in particular?" Delia asked.

"No," I lied. "Big biceps are cool but big brains are better. As I always say, the sexiest part of the man is between the ears."

"Okay, now I know you're lying," Delia said.

Chapter 21

"My life is but a theatre of calamity," I said to Aunty Thelma over the garden hedge, as you do when everything goes shit-shaped and floats off down life's u-bend without permission.

"I must say you do look very peaky and pinched," Aunty Thelma replied in a concerned voice. "If I were you, I'd have an early night."

"Peaky and pinched?" I gasped. "I can't afford to look peaky and pinched it's the Hunt Ball."

"It's no good getting yourself worked up in a tizzy over it. As mother used to say, you die if you worry and you die if you don't."

"Well, that cheered me up no end," I thought as I trudged back indoors.

"Flossie's guffed," said Joey.

I glared at Flossie who sat in her basket looking sheepish.

"Don't you start," I said as I wafted a tea towel to disperse the whiff.

I couldn't help asking myself, how it is that days and weeks can pass by in a haze of uneventful nothingness and then, when it's vital that nothing goes wrong, everything does?

It started in the morning with a call from Tor. I was in bed.

"Just ringing to thank you for last night," he said. "You are one hell of a sexy woman."

I told him that he'd called at an opportune moment and offered to give him an encore over the phone.

"Remind me," I whispered. "Remind me why you think I'm such a sexy woman."

Tor laughed softly. "I will if you promise to give me an action reply tonight, in my bed."

I laughed back softly and reminded him that I couldn't see him because I was going to the Hunt Ball.

He reminded me sharply that he thought he'd expressed his profound hatred of the hunting set.

"So?" I asked perplexed.

"So, I told you that it's tantamount to murder, a macabre and outdated sport that's an outrage in any civilised society."

"So," I asked again.

"So why are you going?" he asked in an incredulous voice.

"Because it's a laugh and I've got this really nice evening dress to wear and Delia's going. And besides, they don't actually kill anything."

I could almost hear his head shaking in disbelief. "I abhor this whole issue with every fibre of my being, yet you still wish to associate with these offensive people, people with blood on their hands, despite what they claim. Vermin." His voice trembled with suppressed emotion.

I told him that I liked intense men, that his intensity turned me on. "Why don't you remind me how intense you were last night?" I asked seductively.

He was outraged. I yawned. He accused me of insensitivity, cruelty, selfishness and bigotry. "You are warped, bourgeois," he snapped.

I pointed out in a bored voice that going to a hunt ball was hardly a crime against humanity. "Just chill," I said.

"If you care anything about me at all you won't go," he said in an anguished voice.

"If you care anything about me at all you wouldn't stop me," I replied. Where have I heard all this before, I thought as I terminated the call in a fit of irritation and rolled over for five more minutes' kip. Jake. That's where. Konnie said she couldn't possibly go the ball because it wasn't Jake's scene.

That's the trouble with relationships, compromise.

I mulled over this relationship dilemma later on as I split logs for the wood burner. I was splitting a particularly phallic looking one when the axe slipped, and the stupid log fell on my foot. Agony. How can I wear my black strappy shoes when my toes clash because they look as if they are inflamed with gout?

And worse, I've got a massive zit. It positively glows in the dark. How can a woman my age still get the wretched things and why does it have to appear now?

It must be stress, unless my hormones have gone haywire since I've rebooted my bits. The next bombshell came when Delia phoned to warn me to brace myself because Toy Boy would be at the ball.

"Are you mad?" I asked with a squeak.

"No worries, he's going with Mervin. Mervin wants to check out some posh totty now he's a shadow of his former self. See if he can snare himself an heiress."

I asked her if she would be able to refrain from gravitating towards Toy Boy. "Seeing all those country wenches will be like steel shavings drawn to him like a magnet. How will you feel when they get their sticky mitts on him – and what if Henry smells a rat?"

She said she'd thought it through, and she didn't care.

"After all, I may as well get used to it. You know Henry is on borrowed time. Look on this as a dress rehearsal."

I felt full of foreboding and asked her if she'd learnt her lines as she might have to put in an Oscar winning performance at short notice.

"I've practised it so many times in my head that I could say them in my sleep. Fuck off you philandering old goat and get used to a taste of your own medicine."

I told her it sounded pretty X-rated and then updated her about my own little drama that paled into insignificance compared to hers, a village pantomime overshadowed by a Hollywood blockbuster.

"I've got a bloated foot and my chin looks like Mount Etna. It could erupt at any moment. Oh, and I told Tor to sod off because he ordered me not to go to the ball because he's anti-hunting."

I gave her a verbatim account of our conversation.

"Tyrant," Delia said with conviction. "Before you know where you are, you'll have to ask his permission to pee. Unless." She paused.

"Unless what?" I asked.

"Unless he's jealous. You tell him he's fantastic in bed and then say you're buggering off to a party alone and then to add insult to injury, ask him to talk you through an orgasm. You sound just like a man darling."

She's right I thought, as I frantically ended the call and rang Tor's number. No answer. I left a grovelling message and then experienced a slight spasm of nervousness.

"You've gone and blown it," a little voice echoed in my brain. "Big time."

I reached for some medication in the shape of a Mars Bar which I devoured in three mouthfuls.

"You're a pig," said Joey, as I cut another one in half and practically inhaled it. I told him I needed it for my low blood sugar.

"Your zit's pulsating," he observed. "It's going to give birth to an alien at any moment."

I picked up a kitchen knife and studied my reflection in the blade. Horrible. I was overcome with sick apprehension and a queasy feeling in my stomach. 'Tor baby call,' I pleaded to my mobile, but it remained resolutely silent. All day. A torture chamber. Every possible response to my remark started to whirl around my head like dirty laundry in a washing machine. Every permutation went through a vicious cycle from a rinse and spin, meaning he was out and his mobile was switched off, to a boil wash which could only mean one thing, he'd popped out for a pint of milk and been cruelly mown down by a car as he walked, distracted by my rejection into its path.

My guts started to contract with so much pain I thought I'd got irritable bowel syndrome. I staggered to my bed to lie down clutching the phone. It rang. I answered it, reaching for it like a drowning woman clutching at a piece of driftwood. It was mum, my heart sank like a stone.

"I've just been talking to Thelma and we couldn't remember if either of us said we would have Joey while you went to be touched up by this Rikki person for the ball.

Anyway, we'd both forgotten that it's Luncheon Club and Barbara Prendergast is doing a talk on Foot Care, bunions. She was a chiropodist for many years you know."

My mind drifted off into a zen zone as she reminisced about Barbara's clinic at the Wethershire Cottage Hospital. "She'd gouge it out like Gorgonzola from your father's toenails. Smelly feet run in the family."

The significance of what she was saying suddenly shot through my brain like a spike and I fell to earth with a crash. I looked at my watch and realised with horror that while I'd been sitting cacking my pants about Tor, I had put myself in mortal danger of missing my 'make over' with Rikki as the minutes drifted softly by like feathers in the wind.

"Sorry, must stop you there," I said to Mum as she rabbited on in gory detail about the symptom's dad suffered with his in-growing toenails. "I've got to see a man about a zit."

"Joey," I screeched as I grabbed my coat. "It's an emergency, stop whatever you are doing and come along this instant. Now."

As any parent knows, children have very little concept of time. Time for them is something that expands to fit whatever they are doing.

"Won't be a minute," Joey's voice drifted down the stairs.

"I'll be in the car," I yelled as I swept out. Five minutes passed. No Joey. I drummed my fingers on the steering wheel and then hooted the horn, twice. Then I flung open the door and swept back in. I searched high and low until I found him under his duvet playing chess by torchlight.

"It was nearly checkmate," he tried to explain to my stony face as I drove to Broadmarket like a maniac. My lips worked incoherently. "I was in Colditz. I carved the pieces out of bone."

As we pulled up outside Rikki's salon, I warned Joey not to touch anything, fidget, or wander off. "Just behave like a model child and don't let the side down." He looked mutinous. "Okay, the nag switch is off," I said as I gave myself one last look in the driving mirror. It reflected back my weary, zit infested face with my lanky hair which I hadn't bothered to wash, hanging down in rat's tails.

"Rebecca, if you could just look this way. Lovely."

I turned in disbelief as I got out of the car to find Rob, the Broadmarket Herald photographer, sticking a camera right in my face. Click, click, click, it went. "Don't!" I wailed, putting my hands in front of the camera lens. "I look like a complete dog."

"That's what it's all about love," he explained as he snapped away. "Before and after shots. I must say you are looking a bit washed out, make the most of it."

With that he shoved his camera back into his bag and said he had to rush because he needed to get to Newton Saucey to take pictures of Sir Granville Bland MP planting a tree. Mortification or what? I nearly died of shame. I sidled into the salon feeling like a complete imposter as immaculate women with flawless complexions and coiffured hair glided past. Rikki pitched up and ushered me into a beauty room, chatting all the while as he gesticulated with his hands to illustrate every nuance.

"Oh," he said, as his hands flew to his face. "I have to say darling that I can't perform miracles although I'll give it my best shot."

He paused and adjusted his man bun before flexing his fingers in front of him like a surgeon just about to perform lifesaving surgery.

"What do you think?" he said to Joey, "Can we transform her into a glamour puss?"

Joey looked doubtful but nodded eagerly. "Go on, I've never seen a miracle."

Rikki set to work. I felt as if I was on a conveyor belt as he summoned a variety of beauty consultants while he stage-managed operations with a theatrical flourish.

Joey was fascinated. For the first five minutes. And then came his regular mantra.

"I'm bored. I'm bored," he said as I was having a facial. "I'm bored," he said as I was having an aromatherapy massage. "I'm bored," he said when I underwent the electronic face lift and again as my hair was washed, highlighted and styled.

"Is he always this bored?" asked Chanel, the beautician as she attached extensions to my stubby fingernails.

"I'm afraid so," I admitted as I caught sight of him out of the corner of my eye wriggling his finger into a stack of nail polish displayed pyramid style on a glass shelf.

I tensed convulsively before turning to him to give a telling off in a strangled high falsetto voice. "I thought the nag switch was off," he said.

"It's back on again." I gave him an evil stare.

"Have you got children?" I asked Chanel to distract her attention.

"No, I don't want any," she replied as she gave Joey a sideling glance. It spoke volumes. This child should have ASBO stamped across his forehead to let the public know that he's an anti-social behaviour order misfit. If only she knew.

Everyone is smitten by smugness before they have children. 'Mine will never behave like that,' people say with conviction. You soon learn. You get beaten into submission by the time they are six months old.

"How's progress?" said Rikki as he waltzed in to see how I was getting on.

"Her zit's disappeared," said Joey grudgingly.

Rikki stared at me. "So, it has. Well, I say, aren't we clever? She's been restored to her former glory with a little bit of Polyfilla and a touch of gloss paint. I could almost fancy you myself," he said with a laugh and a camp wave of his hand.

"Come along," he said, "putting his hand under my arm and guiding me to the nearest full length mirror."

"Who's a pretty girl then?"

Wow. "Is that really me?" I asked. I felt quite shy. The transformation was quite amazing. My reflection threw back a beautifully made-up woman with a spray-on tan and lustrous hair piled high in a tumble of curls on top of her head. I felt like a million dollars.

My confidence was at an all-time high by the time I got home. But the minute I walked through the door I remembered my ill-fated conversation with Tor. My confidence plummeted. I picked up the phone with trepidation. I'd got a new message. "HI. It's Tor returning your call. I'm glad you've seen the light; I'll expect you at eight."

Shit. That was then. This was now. I looked too beautiful to waste myself on a night with Tor. He'd only muss up my hairdo.

"I'll ring him later," I thought as I admired my reflection in the hall mirror. He still wants me. He can wait.

My confidence had recovered to an all-time high by the time I put on my evening dress. It was off the scale by the time three men had propositioned me at the ball before I'd even had time to down my first glass of pink champagne. Admittedly they were all practically gaga, but they were obscenely rich.

I felt invincible by my third glass although I was suddenly brought face to face with reality by the sound of my mobile ringing in my bag.

"Who's that?" I asked.

"Tor Franklin. I think we met once. I thought we quite liked each other. I was obviously mistaken."

I looked at my watch. It was nine o clock. "I didn't get your message," I lied wilfully as my befuddled brain tried to function coherently.

"What message?" he asked ominously.

"Can we talk about it later?" I wheedled. "I'm busy right now."

"I'm sorry I bothered you," he said in a sarcastic tone. "Forgive me, I thought we were having a relationship?"

Relationship, I thought. I hate that word. Relationship, relationship, relationship. If I hear that word one more bloody time, I'll scream.

"We'll talk about it later," I said as I caught sight of Mervin and Toy Boy circulating the room with a frumpy woman with no neck wearing a horror frock, hanging onto Mervin's every word. I was intrigued.

"Sorry, Tor," I said in a tipsy tone, "I really do have to go now, I've got to see a man about a dog. I'll call."

"Don't bother," he said woodenly.

Well. I thought, that's brought the curtain down very unpoetically on this little episode strutted and fretted out on the stage of my life. A tale told by a stupid idiot, signifying nothing. So, what's new there then?

Chapter 22

I was late for work and missed Konnie when I got in so messaged her from my personal email and flagged it urgent. "Stop press: Delia and Henry saga reached a climax. Delia safe and well and living with Gareth. PS: I had a simultaneous orgasm after the Hunt Ball. See me at lunchtime for graphic details."

She messaged back. "Was it internal or external? And who is Gareth?"

"Internal. And Gareth is Toy Boy."

She replied. "Jammy sod."

It was difficult to concentrate on work with the memory of the Hunt Ball seared into my memory. I'd felt gutted after I'd finished my phone conversation with Tor. Gutted.

I couldn't work out how, in the space of a few hours, I had reverted to singleton status from a full steam ahead, potentially for the rest of my life relationship. The only solution I could think of at the time was to replace him. Immediately. When you hit your forties, you can't afford the luxury of grieving for a lost love. Wallowing in anguish might provide an endless stream of amusing anecdotes after you've recovered your senses, 'I lost a stone in a month and stayed in every night reading Eat, Pray, Love, but at my age, time is sex and no sex is boring, especially when you're riven with lovelorn angst. A real libido killer.

"Hey, Rebecca," shouted Keith, breaking into my reverie. "I'm not sure where these pictures of you at the Hunt Ball should go."

Full of curiosity I innocently wandered over to his desk where a crowd of people were standing round laughing at something on his computer screen.

For a split second, I wondered who the picture was of a slightly pi-eyed woman sitting on a rather handsome man's knee.

"Oh, my gawd," I gasped as I gabbled on about pink champagne and the sudden seismic termination of a love affair to rival Wuthering Heights.

"Never," said Keith wryly.

"Who's the gentleman with his face in your chest?" asked Moira.

I scrutinised the picture and realised to my horror that it was Scott Henderson. How on earth did his nose get in there?

Thankfully, Rob had managed to capture a few early shots of me when I arrived at the ball. And looking pretty gorgeous, though I say it myself. It's a shame my finances won't stretch to a facial a month; I'm getting to the age when every little bit helps. And now I've experienced the youth busting benefits of a beauty parlour I'm hooked, craving for the instant fix. From dog to diva.

"Was it Scott Henderson who gave you the you know what?" said Konnie nudging me in the ribs as we went to make a cup of tea. "And what's with the termination of a seismic relationship, did you give Tor the old heave ho?"

Before I had time to elaborate, Keith popped his head round the kitchen door looking for me. "Barbara Prendergast on the blower, something about a successful talk on bunions."

I looked at Konnie and mouthed, "I'll tell you later."

The minute I got rid of Barbara, I tossed off another message to Konnie outlining the fateful phone call with Tor captioned, 'internal memo'.

I explained that I must have looked really glum as I scanned the bar for any potential trouser talent as a temporary stopgap for Tor. "You're looking very sad for someone so gorgeous," a voice said over my shoulder. I turned to see Percy looking really dishy in a DJ.

"Everyone's in a couple," I replied glumly. "Except me."

He smiled. "And me."

He held out his hand. "Fancy a dance?"

I couldn't believe my luck as he took my hand and escorted me to the dance floor.

"No Sheamus here tonight?" I asked him, shouting in his ear.

He shook his head. "He's had to go back to Ireland. Business." He looked deep in my eyes and smiled.

I'd have wet my pants if I'd been wearing any, but I'd got a bare bum to eliminate VPL. Anyway, he promised to give me another boogie on the dancefloor as we were called into dinner.

I found myself placed at a table with Henry and Delia, Camilla and Neville and two single women plus Mervin and Toy Boy, danger zone or what?

Toy Boy was placed next to this plain looking woman with no neck called Henrietta who seemed to have taken a shine to Mervin, while Mervin sat next to this pretty blonde girl called Tara with dazzlingly white teeth and a stunning figure, who'd taken a shine to Toy Boy.

I thought Mervin must be going blind because he asked Toy Boy if he wouldn't mind changing places. Within two ticks, Toy Boy was sitting next to Tara and Mervin next to Henrietta, who it turned out is the niece of Lord and Lady Howgrave and Charles' cousin.

Tara immediately started flirted outrageously with Toy Boy. It turned out she earns a living as a lifestyle blogger, with a little bit of help from a trust fund. She kept asking Toy Boy to pose for a snap to post on her Instagram page. She claimed she has 150,000 followers. I could tell Delia was well narked.

Camilla could hardly contain her fury. "It's so common," she kept muttering to Neville under her breath, as if she expected him to do something. His scraggy head seemed to sink into his shirt collar like a tortoise into its shell as he tried to ignore her and engage in conversation with Henry.

Meanwhile, Mervin was getting intimately acquainted with Henrietta. "I help my uncle," she explained in a cut glass accent, "with his correspondence. I'm his PA." Matters took a turn for the worse when Henry decided it was his turn to enjoy the attentions of Tara and invited her to take a photo of him and Neville, "a rose between two thorns," he said as corny as hell.

He was all over her like a rash as she held up her selfie stick while Delia viciously hacked at the piece of venison on her plate that was as tough as boiled leather.

"Having trouble with that old girl?" Henry asked Delia, as he turned and winked at Tara, joking that he preferred younger and more tender flesh before giving her a right old squeeze. Delia calmly put down her knife and fork, wiped her mouth on her napkin and made her move.

"Well, at least, we agree on something at last," she said, moving over to the chair vacated next to Toy Boy and sliding her arm across his shoulder. "How about a photo of the two of us together Tara?"

The atmosphere was electric as the spark between Toy Boy and Delia ignited as they smiled and flirted with each other outrageously. Camilla smirked. Henry lowered his head and started to paw the ground like an angry bull ready to charge.

"That's quite enough of that," he snarled to Toy Boy. "You can put my wife down now."

"I don't think so," Delia relied brazenly, coining another well-worn phrase. "As the saying goes, what's sauce for the goose is sauce for the gander."

Henry's eyes started to bulge.

Delia stood up tall, put one hand on her hip and delivered the line she had practiced for so long. My vagina instinctively clenched.

"I've absolutely had enough of you Henry, so fuck off you philandering old goat and get used to a taste of your own medicine."

With that, she yanked Toy Boy off his chair, picked up her evening bag and marched out without a backward glance.

"Good on you. girl," hollered Tara, fist pumping the air. "I've videoed the whole thing, I'll upload it onto my YouTube channel."

Henry seemed to fold into a defeated heap on his chair. He loosened his tie and gasped to Neville, "Fetch me a treble whisky on the rocks." He swallowed it in two gulps.

People at the adjoining tables soon picked up on the significance of the action. The news flew around the room like starlings chattering on a telegraph wire. The maître de frantically motioned to the DJ to play some music so he obliged with 'I will survive,' by Gloria Gaynor, to a round of applause. I sent the email off with a flourish to Konnie.

"That is epic," she responded. "Totally epic."

"How's page ten coming on?" asked Dick.

"Fine," I said quickly as I dashed off a few column inches and then went for a loo break.

As soon as I got back to my desk, I fired off another email.

It was all so excruciatingly embarrassing. Henry asked me outright if I'd known about Toy Boy, so fearing for my life, I vehemently denied all knowledge and then made an excuse to go to the bar for a drink. When I got back, he'd scarpered to everyone's great relief.

I wasn't totally bladdered by the time the dinner was finished but I was well-oiled as I'd been knocking back the champers to steady my nerves. I wobbled off to find solace from the whole seismic events with Percy who was chatting to Charles. "You don't mind do you old chap?" he asked Percy. "If I take Rebecca for a dance?"

Percy, like the gentleman he is, insisted that Charles gave me a whirl. Charles took my arm and hauled me off to the dancefloor asking why I hadn't answered his text messages and saying he needed to speak to me urgently and could we go somewhere quiet.

The last thing I needed after the torture of Tor was a conversation about 'us,' so I did the best I could to shake him off after a couple of dances as he was really cramping my style big time. I made an excuse to escape to the loo. I wanted to go anyway to see if there was any truth in the rumours that hunt balls are total sex fests with the loos turning into shagging stations. I was sorry to find they were stuffed full of farting old matrons and ditzy things throwing up in the sink, so I abandoned my research and decided to find Percy again. On my way back I found Mervin and Henrietta smooching on the dancefloor.

"God, she must be desperate," I said as I found Percy at the bar.

"At least they can smooch in public," he said dryly, before grabbing me around the waist and inviting me to dance with a theatrical flourish before we boogied as if our lives depended on it. I thought I'd died and gone to heaven.

I quickly sent off the email to Konnie as Dick came up behind my desk.

"How's it going?" he asked.

"Great," I replied, deciding to spend the next half an hour on actual work before he got me sussed. I made a few phone calls and wrote up a few obits.

Thirsty after all my hard graft, I went to make a cuppa and then nonchalantly went back to my desk to click on Konnie's message.

"Rebecca," it read. "Percy is GAY. If it wasn't Charles who gave you the orgasm who was it? Please. The suspense is killing me."

I emailed back. "No, it wasn't Charles although he insisted, he take over from Percy on the dancefloor and kept gabbling in my ear about wanting to talk to me so I pretended I couldn't hear because of the noise."

After a particularly vigorous jiving session to an upbeat 50s number, I began to feel really dizzy as Charles kept spinning me around. I wailed as I lost my grip and ricocheted off the dancefloor before going over on my shoe on account of a swollen foot, long story, landing straight into the arms of Scott Henderson.

"Hello possum," I said. "Strewth, what are you doing here?" I can't remember much of the next bit except that he bought me a drink and I started to wildly flirt to shake off Charles. I vaguely remember him laughing and pulling me down onto his knee and I suppose in the general hilarity his face somehow landed on my chest. Who knows? I wish I did. Anyway, by this time I really was bursting for another pee from laughing so much, so I staggered off to the loos again. This time I did see some action. I was sitting on the bog with my dress over my knees and my head between my legs when I heard a faint groaning noise emanating from the next cubicle. Intrigued, I stood on the loo seat and sneaked a peek over the dividing wall to see Tara showing Thomas the stable hand the ropes. They were at it hammer and tongues if you get the gist.

I'm going to tell Percy, I decided as I wandered back to the bar, passing Mervin and Henrietta snogging like mad on a sofa. "How can Mervin be necking that woman I thought, when she's got no neck?"

I found Percy propping up the bar. "Percy," I said as I wrapped my arms lovingly around his shoulder. "Come here and listen to Rebecca." He bent his head to listen as I imparted my information very slowly. "Really," he said. "Well, boys will be boys."

I hiccupped and turned to see Scott Henderson walking purposefully up to the bar.

"Would you like lift home?" he said. I meekly nodded as the floor started to sway alarmingly. He gave Percy the filthiest look before he lifted me bodily like a baby and marched with me from the room.

"I want to see if Percy's all right," I whimpered as he carried on walking.

"Don't worry he's a survivor, believe me. He'll come out smelling of roses, smother the dung heap that's his family."

"What do you make of that?" I asked Konnie as I fired off the email so I could write a few nibs to allay Dick's suspicions I was shirking.

"I don't give a damn," came her reply. "Just tell me who gave you the orgasm. Was it Scott?"

I sent her a holding statement, "Patience, patience, all will be revealed in my next email. Read all about it, read all about it, 'Drunk Journalist Hits the Bulls Eye!"

I managed to write up a few newsy court stories and make a few more phone calls and when Dick went for his tea break sent Konnie the denouement to my story.

I didn't realise when Scott insisted on driving me home that Gladys and Cess would be in the car. And when I say car, I mean Land Rover. Scott had to practically manhandle me into the passenger seat as I wailed, "I can't get up there, I'm not a flaming sheepdog."

I sat as still and quiet as a I could with my feet resting on a bag of animal feed, in an attempt to focus on the road ahead as it swayed alarmingly in front on me. "Shush," I kept hissing as Scott engaged in what seemed like a very loud conversation with Cess and Gladys. Feeling no desire to take part, I rummaged around in my bag for my mobile phone to see if I'd got any messages.

I'd got three. And they were all from Tor.

"Rebecca, I'm sorry I was so hasty in telling you not to bother with me, please call, whatever time you get this message, I'll be waiting". The two other calls were similar, but more urgent. I pressed return but frustratingly my battery decided to die and the phone went dead. 'Shit,' I kept saying over and over again as I stabbed at the phone.

As soon as we'd dropped Gladys and Cess off, Scott snatched the phone and put it back in my handbag.

"Behave like a lady," he said.

"How can I," I asked petulantly, wriggling around to get comfortable, "in this scrap heap?"

Scott tried to move the bags of animal feed. "Look," he said in an exasperated voice. "Where do you want to put your legs?"

I gave an enormous hiccup before replying with the most honest answer my befuddled brain could give. "Round your neck," I said with a flirty smile.

Scott's face turned from one of shock to delight. "Okay lady, if that's what you want, what are we waiting for?"

I laughed and moved my hand to stroke his thigh and his very responsive crotch as he drove erratically down the lane from Hartborne to home.

As soon as he pulled up outside the house, he turned to me and groaned and gathered me into his arms. "I can hardly wait," he said as his hands ran all over my chest.

"Me neither," I said as I ran my hands over his rugged face and through his hair.

Our lips were only minutes from locking when my door was wrenched open and I saw Tor standing there with a look like thunder on his face.

"We need to talk," he said. "Now." Then he unceremoniously pulled me down from the passenger seat. Scott got out and there ensued an unholy row, but it ended with me insisting that I speak with Tor alone.

I owe him that at least, reasoned the only rational brain cell left in working order.

As soon as we got into the house, Tor grabbed me and we started kissing passionately. "I thought we were going to talk," I said as soon as I came up for air.

"Later," he breathed as he ripped open the laces on my bustier.

Before I knew it, we were up the stairs and on the bed. I felt absolutely rampant as he gave me such a good seeing to. Who needs foreplay? I felt delirious.

I don't know quite how it happened, but I was in the famous 'girls on top' position and thinking about how excited Scott was in the Land Rover, if you know what I mean, and everything just exploded, whoosh, it was unbelievable. Tor was euphoric and he finished me off good and proper. It was wild.

"I love you," he said as he climaxed, "so much."

And I felt confused and cried and he thinks it's because I love him too. So he's invited me to meet Freya, the other love of his life. Maybe I do love him, maybe I don't.

"What do you think?"

Konnie emailed back almost instantly.

"You don't love him. You should have come sooner with Scott. Meet me for lunch in five."

I emailed back. "Well, I sort of did come with Scott. See you asap." Then added. "Please delete all previous emails to avoid detection and rewrite them and adjust this story accordingly. The sender of this email takes no responsibility for its content."

Chapter 23

The rumblings from Fielding's Farm were becoming audible in the nearby villages and towns long before Delia dropped her bombshell at the ball. Almost everyone it seems had heard snippets about a scandal brewing that promised to be really meaty, but no one was in full possession of the facts.

Not that this stopped people from speculating about it. Rumours were spreading thick and fast about flying plates, slamming doors and a violent midnight row that forced Delia to flee for her life to Scotland to seek refuge with her mother. The fact that her mother used to live in Tunbridge Wells and has been dead for over twenty years has been dismissed as irrelevant.

The first whispers that all was not in harmony in the Fielding household were apparently leaked by a disgruntled tenant living in a tied cottage who'd been evicted for rent arrears. Then there was the awful mix-up at the chemist. Apparently, Henry was apoplectic when he realised that Mrs Hoare had mistaken his Viagra prescription for her rheumatism pills and had wandered off with it right under his nose before anyone realised the mistake.

There was an awful hoo-hah. By the time he caught up with her, all the ladies who travel on the village bus had inspected the rouge prescription after Mrs Hoare complained she couldn't open the lid because it was too stiff. Henry insists there are five tablets missing but no one will own up to anything.

The whole thing's been a gift to the local wags. When Henry walks into the Doom and Gloom, everyone whispers, "Watch out, here comes Willy Wonker." It's killed his credibility with the barmaid. It's amazing really how rumours seem to spread indiscriminately, picking up any piece of idle chitchat or wild speculation like fluff from an old coat that's later deposited in a random, scurrilous heap. I caught a rancid whiff of it while I was minding my own business standing at the checkout at the Newton Saucey supermarket.

"You don't say," I heard a large florid woman wearing baggy jodhpurs and muddy riding boots exclaim to Madge, the checkout operator.

"Heard it on good authority," replied Madge in an audible whisper as she leant forward to impart further dirt. Clutching a cabbage with one hand, she used her index finger to emphasise every interjection. "He's no more than a teenager, a lad, believe me, it's a tragedy. A woman her age."

I pricked up my ears. "Of course, I know Henry well," said the jodhpur woman. "He's got a marvellous seat, a fearless huntsman. They do say he likes the odd tipple though."

"Wouldn't you?" said Madge as she passed endless tins of Meaty Chum over the scanner.

"Word has it that her and the lad were at one of those parties where anything goes, threesomes, the lot. There's a woman called Moira." She leant over the counter and mouthed, "A dominatrix," then drew her finger around her throat and hissed, "wears a dog collar, with studs, you name it, the works."

I was bristling with indignation. "She's something to do with the Broadmarket Herald, isn't she?" said the jodhpur woman. "Is she the editor?"

"I don't know about that but her picture's in the paper every week. Another cover-up you can guarantee it. Scandalous that's what I say, I've never believed what I read in the papers. This confirms it. Absolute filth."

I'd heard enough. I pushed myself forward, incoherent with rage. "If I think what you're saying is true, then it's all lies. The women you refer to are bosom friends of mine and I love them both very dearly."

Madge exchanged a knowing look with the jodhpur woman. "Really," she said in a snide tone of voice. "You don't say." They both smirked. "That'll be £49.32p, Mrs Barnet."

I glared at them both as Mrs Barnet paid for her groceries. She turned to look at me as if I was something that had just dropped out of a dog's bottom, before saying in a snooty tone to Madge, "You know what they say, you should always judge people by the company they keep. Say no more."

They're double trouble like the witches in Macbeth I muttered as I drove home, wildly grinding the gears and driving far too fast. Casting spells in a cauldron, a hells-broth of bile. It dawned on me when I got out of the car that I'd left my umbrella on the counter. Damn, that's the fault of the mudslinging Madge, I thought as I put the shopping away, banging all the cupboard doors shut in frustration. Why do I always rise to the bait and allow her venomous antenna to burrow into my brain to distort my rational lobes into a zizz of static so I can't think straight?

I decided to try out some yoga breathing techniques to calm me down and summon up the vital life force to energise the chakras in my glands, but instead, I wobbled over like a Weeble and hit my head on the kitchen table.

It's not working I decided peevishly, dismissing it all as mumbo jumbo as I went to take a big bag of loo rolls upstairs to the bathroom. Just as I walked past the front door the bell rang. I opened it to find Charles standing on the doorstep.

"Hi, not an inconvenient time to call is it?" he asked, glancing at the loo rolls.

"No, no," I said hastily as I chucked them up the stairs. "Just putting the shopping away. Come in." Typical, I thought. Why couldn't I have been holding something classy like smoked salmon or trendy like quinoa instead of arse wipes?

I led him into the kitchen and apologised for the mess and told him straight that I couldn't promise to be good company because I was in a foul mood.

"People are pissing me off," I explained. "Do you find that sometimes? You know, they really get on your tits bigtime?"

Charles tactfully agreed and suggested I might feel better if I had a glass of wine, if I had a bottle spare. I motioned to the wine rack explaining that it would be the hair of the dog for me as my head was still recovering from the aftermath of the ball.

I cleared a heap of tat off the kitchen table along with a pile of ironing, and a large marrow that Joey brought home from aunty Thelma's that's been mouldering there for over a week because I've got no idea how to cook it.

"That's what I wanted to catch up with you about, what I was trying to tell you at the ball," said Charles as he poured out the wine.

I was saved from any potential embarrassing conversation with the sound of the doorbell ringing again. I'd just got up to open it when the phone rang. Charles kindly agreed to open the door as I answered the call, it was my mother.

"You do remember it's Sunday don't you dear?" she said. "You haven't forgotten you're coming over for tea, have you?"

I was just about to assure her that I hadn't when Delia walked in followed by Gareth.

"Look Mum, I might be late, could you phone Giles and ask him to drop Joey off with you and I'll see you later on? Someone's just dropped by."

"Better company than your old Mum, are they?" she said feebly.

"It's Charles Smythe Bothum-Wethem," I said.

157

Her voice perked up instantly. "Take as long as you like dear, no rush. Oh, and by the way, have you heard about your friend Delia? I told you she was a bit of a Tartar.

I understand she's taken a young lover and Henry's confiscated her car keys and confined her to the house. Can you believe it?"

I took a deep breath to steady my nerves. "Hardly," I said coldly. "Since she's just walked through the door. But hey, why let the truth get in the way of a good story?"

"How are you?" I asked Delia as I put down the phone and gave her a big hug. "Mum's just informed me that Henry has confiscated your car keys and you are now languishing in the cellars of Fielding's Farm."

Delia laughed. "Let them think what they like, I don't care." She kissed Gareth before raising her arms in the air and doing a pirouette around the room, "I'm free, free," she cried. "Liberated from the shackles of a dyspeptic dinosaur." She plonked herself down next to Gareth and accepted a glass of wine from Charles.

I regaled her with the story, hot off the newswire at the supermarket. "Madge has got it on good authority that you and Gareth have been indulging in a threesome, with Moira as a dominatrix wearing a studded dog collar. The Wethershire Chinese whispers have obviously embroidered a sexed-up version of Konnie's party as it rolls along picking up grime, it can only have come from Moira's friend Beryl."

"What party?" asked Charles with interest, sitting bolt upright. "Did I miss something?"

"It was a private affair, very bijou, a few intimate friends," I blustered as it was obvious he hadn't been invited. "Just a few nibbles, very laid back."

Delia caught my eye and quipped, "You know what they say about holes and digging."

Charles looked confused, so to divert his attention I asked Delia and Gareth about their plan of action. "Do you think Henry will take this lying down?"

"No doubt he will," said Delia. "With any willing woman who fancies filling my shoes. I'm sure there will be a veritable harem and he might even score with the barmaid at the Doom and Gloom now there's a vacancy at Fielding's Farm."

Charles looked shocked. "I cannot believe that Henry would be so foolish," he said. "There's one thing to have a fling with a floozie but, for one's wife, well." He stuttered to a halt and sat looking uncomfortable as he rubbed his hands between his knees.

"Charles, you are such a darling," said Delia, as she leant over and stroked his knee.

He smiled and puffed out his chest like a pigeon. "If I had any doubts about leaving Henry, which I haven't, you remind me so eloquently why I did."

With that, she stood up, announced that they were off and swept majestically from the room. "Henry will be on the warpath like some prehistoric caveman wielding a club to drag his wife back to his lair, so we had better get going. I definitely need to lay low somewhere for a while," she said, casting a naughty wink at Gareth as they waved goodbye at the door.

Charles is an old relic and needs to be consigned to the relationship dusty bin, I decided. It was time to go in for the kill, bite the bullet and tell him about Tor. I braced myself.

His chest was looking distinctly concave when I went to sit next to him on the sofa.

"Did I say something wrong?" he asked, looking bewildered. I let out a deep sigh and tried to marshal my thoughts to tell him in the politest and most coherent way possible that he was a raging misogynist. "Stop," he said, holding up his hand, maybe fearful of what I might say. "I know you possibly think that I'm an old fuddy-duddy, but you see, you have to remember my destiny. Let's not forget that," he said with a beatific smile.

"You've lost me," I said. "And before you go on, there's something I need to tell you."

"I've started so I'll finish," he said pompously. "It's very important what I have to say, what I have been trying to say to you in fact, for over a week." He wagged his finger at me as if I were a naughty schoolgirl.

It was quiet except for the drumming of soft rain falling against the windowpanes and the sound of birds twittering under the eaves. Despite the rain, it was humid, and the atmosphere was somnolent and heavy. I started to feel quite drowsy after the late night and the wine.

"Do you know a lady called Tiffany?" asked Charles.

I suddenly felt as if I was drowning under water where a bomb had gone off and I had gone deaf with the blast, with only the muted sounds of voices floating somewhere above me.

"Rebecca, Rebecca," said Charles, clicking his fingers in front of my face. "And a rather seedy individual called Colin, are you acquainted with him at all?" I nodded my head dumbly as I surfaced to a world that had shifted on its axis.

"Well, it seems that between them they have conspired to unseat our sitting MP, Sir Granville Bland. It is most unfortunate, most unfortunate, particularly now when the country needs stability and leadership. Tiffany sold the story to one of those nasty tabloid newspapers and it's due to hit the stands any day now."

His back stiffened. "It's at times like these we all need to make sacrifices for the sake of the greater good." He turned and grasping both of my hands in his said with dramatic delivery. "I'm sorry Rebecca, but it's over."

"What's over?" I asked.

"You and me," he said, as if I was a dimwit.

"And Henry makes three," I replied. "I have absolutely no idea what you are talking about."

"That's what makes you so adorable and funny and sexy." He kissed my hands as if in a benediction. He explained that as Sir Grenville would be standing down to 'spend more time with his family,' he had been anointed to take his seat at the forthcoming by-election.

"I will need to find a wife, and with your personal circumstances, and," he coughed, "slightly unpredictable," he coughed again, "demeanour that I fear could lead to disobedience and discord, it just won't do old girl. I'm afraid it's goodbye from me."

To say that I was gobsmacked, speechless, was the understatement of the century. Here I was, sitting with a gold plated DUD with the hide of a rhino, and his unshakeable upper crust confidence that we were in some sort of relationship. Despite me treating him like he was something stuck to the bottom of my shoe. Delusional or what?

My brain did a rapid calculation. I could either humiliate him now with a few home truths or show magnanimity and keep him as a warm and friendly contact to further my career. No contest. I decided to be gracious, not out of altruism, but self-interest.

He deserved it.

"I totally understand," I said giving his hand a squeeze. "I imagine Barbara Prendergast would be aghast. A Tory wife who doesn't know how to slice an onion!"

He laughed heartily and asked if he could have one last squeeze as he was 'extraordinarily fond of me.' Conveniently forgetting about Tor, I duly obliged and then asked for further info on what had led to Sir Granville coming unstuck, as we snuggled together like old pals.

"Well, between you and me," he said conspiratorially "He's partial to the odd spank. I can quite understand having been to public school, but it is rather unwise, although she wasn't a local gal and had no idea who he was until she met that reprobate friend of yours. We tried to keep a lid on it but unfortunately, it's all been caught on video. Grandville's wife is standing by him and no doubt when everything's blown over, he will eventually end up in the Lords with a nice sinecure."

He drained his wine glass and reluctantly rose to leave, explaining that he had an election strategy meeting at the Newton Saucey Country Club. He embraced me in a tight hug on the doorstep and just as he turned to leave, asked me as an afterthought what it was I wanted to tell him.

"It was nothing important," I said casually deciding there was nothing to gain from telling him I'd been having orgasmic sex with another guy almost the whole time we'd been in our 'relationship'.

Let sleeping dogs lie, I thought as I air kissed him goodbye and then grabbed the car keys to go to Mum's for tea.

I felt absolutely exhausted as I drove to Hartborne. The emotional trauma of the ball and the whiff of betrayal and duplicity that seemed to swirl around like a toxic cloud was sapping my energy. I grudgingly acknowledged I was looking forward to Mum's timeless ritual with her tea and scones as I knocked on the front door.

"Oh, hello my dear," Mum said in a rather startled voice. "I thought you were entertaining Charles Smythe Bothum-Wethem."

I instantly worked out the reason for her slightly nervous tone as I spied Giles with a petite fair haired woman sitting close together on the sofa.

I summoned up my last vestiges of energy as Mum ingratiatingly introduced me to Giles's lady friend Fin.

There followed an embarrassing round of handshakes and introductions.

"Fin's parents live in the Cores Region in France," said Mum. "In a château."

I made an appreciative comment as I accepted a cup of tea.

"Nice," I said.

"Fin said I can go there for a holiday," said Joey excitedly. "They've got battlements and a vineyard and a lake where you can swim with a pontoon to dive off."

I smiled. "Lovely."

Fin was pretty, slim, younger than me and looked pleasant and expensively dressed.

Giles stared at her with adoration. Joey obviously approved.

"And they've got dogs, four of them."

"Great," I said, almost speechless with emotional exhaustion.

"How's Charles?" hissed Mum as I stood on the doorstep to leave. "Any progress?"

"Yes," I replied. "He blew me out. I'm not the right material for a Tory wife. Not quite subservient enough to qualify."

"Well, I did warn you," said Mum. "You should know which side your bread's buttered. Leave it any longer and you'll miss the boat. You mark my words."

It might not be a bad idea to miss the boat I mused, as I lay in bed that night trying to get some sleep as I dreamt about the plight of the beautiful, tragic Ophelia and the lonely Lady of Shalott as she floated down to Camelot.

Chapter 24

Colin's glum face finally appeared on the screen. We were on Zoom with Keith as Colin's drink driving conviction means he has to catch the bus to the Broadmarket office for meetings. It goes on such a circuitous route around all the villages it takes forever. If it turns up at all.

It took Colin a while to realise the microphone was set to mute, much to Keith's irritation, as he sat there mouthing away, looking like a goldfish that's a bit green around the gills.

"So, what's the crack with Tiffany?" said Keith impatiently, as Colin finally pressed the unmute button. Colin cleared his throat. "Well, I can't put my finger on it exactly, but I suspect she's hiding something." He went on to explain that when Tiffany arrived at his house to give him a 'session' her eye was caught by a picture in our rival paper, The Newton Saucy News, lying on the kitchen table. She pointed to a picture of Sir Granville Bland MP handing out prizes at a school assembly and said, "Oh look, there's my Mr Naughty Boy".

"She clammed up after reading the story and I couldn't winkle anything out of her after that."

"This is dynamite," said Keith, rocking back in his chair. "We have hit the jackpot. Let's just hope she doesn't go and flog the story to a national." Colin blanched. "She may have broached the subject," he said, nervously fiddling with his Micky Mouse tie, just as the barmaid from the Doom and Gloom flitted across the screen and deposited a pint next to his laptop. The screen went blank. "He's got a bloody nerve," said Keith. "Just wait 'til I catch up with him."

I was itching to catch up with Delia. She's giving an impromptu party before she scuttles off to Ireland with Gareth. Seamus has offered them sanctuary on his family estate until the furore over the scandal of her split with Henry subsides.

"Don't worry, I won't be gone for ever darling," she told me over the phone. "But Henry's temper is molten, and I can't relax for one minute thinking he's prowling around. It kills the libido. Poor Gareth is stiff with fear except where it counts."

Well, if Gareth is stiff with fear, then rigor mortis will be setting in for Colin, after I updated Keith on my cosy little chat with Charles. He's on the warpath now for the Oil Slick to see if he can nail him for a follow up story. The fragrant Belinda would definitely be persona non grata in Minted that's for sure.

I filled Delia in on the scandal and offered her consolation. "Your story will be relegated to mere tittle tattle compared to Sir Granville Bland getting the bum's rush from the local Tory association and Charles' elevation to prospective local parliamentary candidate. And it looks as if the Oil Slick might be coming unstuck too."

Delia lapped it up. "That's three old farts getting their comeuppance. Let's party!"

Unfortunately, the aftereffects of old farts created a right pong at Delia's party where I had to go solo as Tor couldn't make it because he had to baby-sit Freya. Again. He says Rita throws a tantrum if he says he can't and then tortures him mercilessly by saying he's an unfit father and threatens to withdraw access rights. I won't worry about it. Yet. I can't let my life be dictated to by the whim of some distant, vindictive stranger. It's so scary to think how easy it is to get embroiled in a relationship that's manacled by serious baggage that's nothing to do with you. I just want to be wildly indulged and adored. Slanging matches and willy-wobbling incandescent domestic rows is major yawnsville territory as far as I'm concerned.

Which reminds me of Jake. When we were together, he was the willy-wobbling champion of the world. I can see him now, gnashing his teeth at some heinous crime I'd committed, waving his arms around like a windmill in a hurricane. Any idle throwaway remark could provoke a violent willy-wobbling session. "God, I bet that reality celeb had liposuction to get that thigh gap."

It was enough to set him off on a mental rampage about women's solidarity, fat is a feminist issue and body fascism. His liberal credentials are so predictable and unoriginal it's as if he wrote the bloody script.

"I've got the point," I'd say wearily. "You can put your eyes back in now."

He'd brood for days which was a complete waste of time because I'd never repent. As a matter of principle. Even when I knew I was wrong.

I could tell he was 'off' by the way he was spoiling for a fight at the party when he scoffed openly at Gareth's Aga as if having one was a social affectation. I couldn't resist.

"You've been reading too many Aga sagas," I said. "Just because Gareth owns an Aga doesn't necessarily mean he conforms to a certain social stereotype. Unlike you."

Jake's eyes narrowed and his temples began to twitch as he ground his teeth in an attempt to contain his temper. "That's one hundred and fifty per cent bollocks and you know it," he snapped. I took the bait and we were off. Vicious barbs started flying thick and fast as we fired insults at each other like verbal smart bombs. Konnie, caught in the firing line, vainly tried to stop us but we were deaf to reason. "Now you two, let's call a truce, shall we?" as she wafted a white napkin between us.

We both turned to her simultaneously like two rabid Rottweilers and snapped, "never," before turning back to snarl at each other.

Delia intervened. "No arguing at my party," she said pushing us apart. "We are celebrating the toppling of a despot and I will not allow any dissent." She laughed at the irony of her statement before swanning off.

"Asshole," I mouthed at Jake quietly before popping a canapé into my mouth.

"Jealous," he whispered, smiling sweetly, moments before raising his glass of beer. "Will you two stop it?" Konnie said emotionally and then dramatically flung down the napkin she'd waved between us, before running from the room. "Now look what you've done," Jake shouted, following after her.

"What I've done?" I yelled back. "Speak for yourself." I seethed with rage at the jealous jibe – so not true, well almost.

Miffed, I decided to send a text to Tor. "You might not want me." I thought, as I frantically rummaged around in my handbag for my mobile, "But I know a man who does."

I peered into the murky depths, poking around among old till receipts, mouldy sweet wrappers, manky makeup and broken biros, to see my phone light up before it started to ring. Spooky, I thought, as I fished it out feeling a warm rush of triumph. I bet it is Tor thinking of me in the same instant I'm thinking of him. Wrong. I glanced at the caller ID. It was Scott Henderson.

My heart began to flutter, and I started to twirl my hair nervously.

'Hello,' I said.

"Hello to you too," replied Scott, in his familiar Australian drawl.

"What can I do for you?" I asked rather ungraciously, as my romantic wishing moon hardened into a lump of metaphorical cheese.

"I thought we had that conversation when I gave you a lift home from the Hunt Ball," he said.

"I was pissed as a fart," I replied.

"You don't look pissed now," he said. "Although you do look hot and bothered."

My hand froze in my hair and I sat, stock still. "Are you…?"

"Yes," said a voice behind me. "I've been watching you from a distance. Quite the little virago."

"When I'm in the right," I sniffed. I looked up at him quizzically as I chucked my phone back in my handbag. "How come you're here?"

"Konnie," he replied. "I gave her my number when I was at your place."

My eyes went heavenward. "Why am I not surprised?" I said.

"So, what was the contretemps that caused such a fuss?" he asked looking at me intently.

I waved my hand and explained it was a long and boring story.

"He's my ex," I said, as if that explained everything.

"Are you still pining for him?" he asked in a sympathetic voice.

"You have got to be kidding," I spluttered.

"And the other one, the night of the Hunt Ball?"

"The jury's out on that one," I replied, crossing my fingers behind my back.

Fortunately, I was saved from further interrogation when we were interrupted by Konnie and Jake who walked over to us, their arms lovingly entwined.

"Jake has apologised, and he's promised to be nice to you in future," said Konnie looking up at him adoringly.

"Jake, nice?" I said half-jokingly. "I'll believe it when it happens. It's hard to teach an old dog new tricks."

Jake glared at me and then turned to Scott. "Are you Rebecca's latest victim?"

"Maybe," he said. "Who knows? Being Australian I've bivouacked in the outback, so I'm used to prickly things with a sting in their tail. But I've got a tough hide, I've learnt to handle most things. It's just a question of technique." I flashed him a grateful smile.

Konnie turned to Jake and introduced Scott. "Rebecca's written a story about Scott's traumatic childhood as a migrant orphan in Australia, it's going in the paper next week, do you remember me telling you about it?"

Jake said he did and showed genuine interest. He talked in-depth to Scott about his experiences and asked if he would be prepared to visit the university to join in one of his tutorials.

"Your story would make a great PhD thesis," he observed. "In fact, my partner," he stumbled over his words, "rather my ex-partner and colleague, Sabrina, has just spent two years at an Australian university teaching cultural studies, I'm sure she'd be fascinated."

I instinctively looked up at the ceiling and, like Chicken Licken, expected the sky to fall on my head. I didn't have to wait very long.

"I'd be more than happy to do that," Scott said. "It needs debating back home as well as here, if you'd like to give me her address and number, I'll look her up when I get back."

Jake took a long swig of his beer and then wiped his hand across the back of his mouth before replying, "No need, she's back here in this country, been back a week or so. Leave it with me, I'll arrange a meeting."

There was an ominous silence before Konnie said quietly, "You never told me that Sabrina was back in the country."

"Didn't I?" said Jake shrugging. "I thought I did. Anyway, why should I, it's not as if it's relevant."

"Have you seen her?" asked Konnie.

"Of course, I've seen her," said Jake in a blustery voice, "she teaches at the university remember, I can hardly not see her, can I?"

"I mean, see her, as in see her," said Konnie, her voice rising.

"Oh, you mean, see her as in having sex with her?" said Jake defensively.

"No, of course not," said Konnie anxiously. "I mean, have you seen her alone, privately?"

Jake shrugged, "So what if I have? I didn't realise having dinner qualifies as a betrayal."

Konnie's eyes filled with tears. "Bastard!" she shrieked, before running from the room. Jake dutifully followed her out.

"Here we go again," I said. "Action replay, Act I Scene I. Konnie had better get used to living in the farce lane."

Just, then I noticed Mervin walk into the room with his latest love interest, Henrietta.

"Oh look," I said, turning to Scott. "Here comes Rent-a-Shag." I went on to elaborate how Mervin had recently morphed from a big fat fossil to a 21st century babe magnet. I caught Mervin's eye and he left Henrietta with Delia, to wander over and say hello. I slapped his arse and gave him a massive wolf whistle. "Well, well," I said with an admiring glance at his new waistline. "From fat and free to fat-free."

Mervin laughed and struck a model-like pose. "Missed your chance, I'm in great demand," he said as went on to simulate rhythmic sexual thrusts by writhing his hips and pumping his arms like pistons. "Anyway, I've brought Henrietta who I met at the Hunt Ball, it's early days so I've dressed to impress, can't put a foot wrong tonight."

"No gain without pain," I said poking his stomach. "Just think what you were like a few months ago." I took a swig of wine, "Then again, perhaps better not."

"You're right you know," said Mervin thoughtfully. "I mean look at Delia and Gareth's relationship and all they've been through. It didn't occur to me, you know, the turmoil, or that Delia was a married woman."

He looked earnestly at Scott. "I used to be oblivious to the fact that married woman have needs, during my Mr Blobby days that is. But since posting a picture of my new image on the internet," he coughed coyly. "I've received several requests for my company from such ladies, and my eyes and my flies have been opened, so to speak."

"Naughty," I teased. "And have you obliged?"

Mervin smiled smugly. "I may have given one or two ladies a little bit of comfort." He smiled knowingly at Scott, "Let's just say I've had to buy my condoms in bulk." Delia, who had wandered over followed by Henrietta, overhead Marvin's remarks and asked him to elaborate on his theory about married women's needs.

"Have you got a new job as a gigolo?" she giggled.

Mervin, glancing anxiously at Henrietta, went bright red and started spluttering some feeble tale about lending a sympathetic ear to married women who had confided in him about their loneliness and isolation. As he blathered on, I suddenly became aware of a pungent smell. I turned and whispered to Delia.

"Have you farted?"

She sniffed deeply. "No," she said wrinkling her nose. "But you're right there's a right old whiff in here."

"Is it you?" I asked holding my nose and turning to Scott.

"Certainly not," he said indignantly.

"I bet it's Moira," I said. "She's a vegetarian. If you ever go into the loo after her at work," I flapped my hand under my nose. "Toxic."

We all started to sniff the air.

"It smells like dog shit," Scott said.

We all looked down at the carpet and then started to examine the soles of our shoes.

"It's you," shrieked Delia, pointing at Mervin.

All eyes fastened onto the bottom of Mervin's trainers to see the tell-tale traces of dog poo ingrained in the soles. He started to hop about on one foot. All of a sudden Gareth rushed into the room holding a cloth and a bottle of disinfectant.

"It's all up the stairs," he said, his eyes wide with horror. "And on the Persian rug in the bedroom." He rushed off.

Mervin took off the offending trainer, revealing a huge hole in his sock and then looked wildly around the room. Suddenly, on impulse, he rushed over to the Aga, lifted the lid and nonchalantly popped his trainer inside and then walked back to us with a lopsided gait.

"All dealt with," he said wiping his hands together. He looked at Henrietta. "Buy another pair. It's only money. Eighty-five quid actually, but hey," he shrugged and then held his hands up in the air. "I'm loaded."

It didn't take long for the realisation to sink in that Mervin's idea wasn't the best one he'd ever had. If the smell had been pungent before, it ripened into a really rancid odour. Konnie and Jake emerged from the back room as if they'd been smoked out like a plague of rats.

"What in God's name is that God-awful stink?" asked Jake clutching his throat.

"It's roasted dog excrement," I said with a hint of relish.

"And a rather sweaty trainer I'm afraid," said a shamefaced Mervin. There was nothing for it, we all had to evacuate the house.

"It's an omen," Mervin whispered to me in an agonised voice as we stood shivering outside.

"What, for the end of the world?"

"No, no," he moaned. "My relationship with Henrietta, why would she want to get intimate with me after a humiliating experience like that?"

He was absolutely distraught, but I could offer little solace. After all, he had made a complete arse of himself.

As soon as we got the all-clear, we trooped back inside. Gareth had gamely fished Mervin's charred trainer out from the Aga, thrown all the windows open and then sprayed the rooms with air freshener. But the smell still lingered.

"Which pillock was responsible for that shit?" said Jake, his gaze sweeping the room like a mine sweeper. His eyes swept past Mervin and then swung back to fasten on his trainer-less foot. "I might have known it was that berk."

Konnie turned to Jake and said with feeling, "At least he's not responsible for sending people up shit creek without a paddle." Jake looked deeply uncomfortable and took a swig of beer.

Delia inhaled deeply. "I think this bad smell's going to hang around for ages, don't you?" she said to Konnie in an effort to change the subject.

"Not if I have anything to do with it," Konnie replied. "As far as I'm concerned, the solution is quite simple." She looked at Jake. "The door's over there."

He opened his mouth as if to say something, took one look at Konnie's face, shut it and then meandered out with his hands in his pockets with a well-shifty looking expression on his face.

"Have you been on the receiving end of a massive willy-wobble?" I asked sympathetically.

"You could say that," she replied with a crestfallen face. "I'm pregnant."

Chapter 25

I never, for one moment, anticipated the huge media frenzy that Scott's story would generate when it hit the streets. The calm, quiet, untroubled waters in Wethershire where we fish for stories was suddenly turned into a seething, foaming maelstrom as shoals of news-hungry journalists from the metropolis, swarmed into town like ruthless piranhas alerted by the smell of fresh, bloodied meat. Poor old Gladys, she never stood a chance.

The piece was the best I'd ever written. "It deserves a double-page spread," I argued with Keith as we made up the pages. He waved a photo of Percy handing out rosettes at a gymkhana under my nose. "Even if it means consigning your pin-up to the back page?"

I picked up Percy's picture and drooled over it for a few seconds before chucking it down on the desk. "He's gorgeous but disposable Keith. We live in a disposable age, disposable nappies, disposable razors, disposable men. They only have shelf life of ten years max and then the tedium sets in. The buzzword is recycling."

The best I'd hoped for from the story was selling it to a national for a nice injection of cash to put towards a new stair carpet. I didn't anticipate that it would spark an international incident and incite the country to turn into a nation of vigilantes, baying for the blood of the man who'd betrayed poor old Gladys. Requests for interviews started to pour in from regional radio and TV with the nationals hot on their heels.

"I'm sorry," I said for the hundredth time to Scott who had taken refuge in my house after he was besieged by journalists at the Doom and Gloom.

"They won't rest until they find out who my father is," said Scott, running his fingers through his hair as he paced the floor. "Gladys will rue the day she ever saw my face."

"The best you can hope for is a terrorist incident or a train crash, or maybe an oil slick," I said as I examined a swatch of carpet samples. "That will divert their attention for a while, after that your story will be old news, consigned to lining the bottom of the proverbial budgie cage."

Scott stared at me as I held a sample of coir matting next to the hall curtains.

"What do you think?" I asked.

He snatched the book of carpet samples from my hand and threw it on the floor.

"I think you are absolutely, unbelievable." He clicked his fingers in front of my eyes. "Wake up Rebecca, wake up, why don't you come and join us in the real world?" He grabbed my hand and placed it on his chest.

"People are real you know, flesh and blood, they have feelings and get hurt. Think about Gladys."

I went on the defensive. "Ever heard the saying, don't shoot the messenger'? I'd like to point out a few small, but significant facts. I wasn't the one who breezed in from the other side of the bloody world to The Herald and asked if I was interested in my life history was I?"

My voice rose. "And I wasn't the one who shagged Gladys all those years ago and sent her down the swanny, was I? I'm just the storyteller, doing my job, the medium not the message, get it? I'm nothing to do with you."

I suddenly realised that I'd still got my hand on his chest and was just about to snatch it away when Scott grabbed my wrist. He shoved my hand back.

"Feel that," he said. "Go on, feel it."

I could feel his heart racing beneath the palm of my hand.

"So what?" I said in a voice like a spoilt kid.

"So, you do have something to do with me, because you make me angry and you make me exasperated," he answered roughly.

He loosened his grip and his voice softened. "And you make me laugh and you make me feel as if I've known you forever." He looked into my eyes. "And you make me want to kiss you."

Before I could stop him, he put his arms around me and pulled me to him, kissing me full on the lips. My arms seemed to sneak up around his neck against my will, and before I knew it, I was kissing him back. It was the most beautiful, most devastating, most terrifying kiss I'd ever experienced. My eyes filled with tears and I pulled away, shaken to the core.

"Rebecca," he said softly, as I stood with my arms wrapped tightly around myself.

He moved to touch me.

"Don't," I said.

I bolted up the stairs and flung myself face down, Joey style on the bed. I heard him climb the stairs. He stood at the door of my bedroom.

"I'm not coming in," he said. "I'll leave you now. Will you be okay?"

I refused to answer. I heard him sigh as he turned and left. I listened as his footsteps descended the stairs and then I relaxed as I heard the front door closing. I lay there for what seemed like ages until I suddenly became aware that Joey was standing next to the bed.

"That Mr Henderson isn't a Spam Man is he Mum?"

I turned to look at him. "What makes you say that?" I asked curiously.

"I've just seen him on the telly. He's…" He closed his eyes tightly to help him concentrate.

"He's Scott Henderson, a multi-millionaire with business interests in Australia and the Far East." His eyes widened. "He's absolutely loaded."

Keith beckoned me into his office as soon as I walked into work the next day. "Well done, this is the best story we've had in years. Now the thing is, there's this sixty-four-thousand-dollar question that everyone wants to know the answer to. Who is Scott Henderson's father? Any ideas?"

I shifted uneasily in my seat. "No," I lied.

"Well, that's your next job and I've made it easier for you because Henderson rang me yesterday and requested your presence as he gets to go on all those national interviews. Says his mother needs support."

"But some will be in London," I said. "He's been asked to go on breakfast tele."

Keith got a fag out of its packet and pointed it at me and said facetiously, "You know I've always suspected you were smart, now you get the train tomorrow and stay in a hotel. I want the name of that man's father by the time we go to press. I've got my eye on you for promotion, so don't let me down."

Nice one. I've been gagging for promotion and now the chance has been dangled under my nose it means I have to shaft two people who have already had more than their fair share of shafting to last a lifetime. Scott would hate me, and it would destroy Gladys. Or maybe not. It would certainly destroy the reputation of Scott's father, of that there can be no doubt.

Scott took the media by storm as his rags to riches story went from regional TV to the national news. He became an instant housewives' hit as the subject of migrant children went to the top of the news agenda. He could charm the knickers off a nun, I thought, as each female interviewer simpered and flirted with him without fail throughout each interview. But Gladys didn't get such an easy ride.

I noticed she'd blossomed after being reunited with Scott. How come I'd never taken the time to treat her as someone other than Cess's wife, a village woman in an overall, who had led a completely uneventful life. How wrong could I be? Photos of her in my article as a young woman, show a strikingly beautiful heart shaped face and brown expressive eyes, fringed with impossibly long lashes. Hardy's Tess with her long wavy hair and natural, unspoilt grace.

But her small frame seemed to shrink with fear under the hot studio lights as she sat like a frightened rabbit caught in the headlights of an oncoming juggernaut. She became more and more agitated as the media pressure intensified. "It'll soon be over," I tried to reassure her as she emerged from yet another interview.

"I'm not sure it'll ever be over, my dear," she replied enigmatically. "I had no idea it would generate this amount of interest." She sighed and looked at me beseechingly.

"Love makes us do some foolish, silly things."

"Tell me about it," I said ruefully.

The public were baying for blood by the time most of the interviews were over. TV and radio switchboards were jammed with calls while the British and Australian politicians were slowly roasted under the TV grill over compensation, reparation and issues of culpability.

Scott was euphoric as we returned to the hotel for lunch. He punched his fist in the air. "That's for every one of those buggers who made my life hell," he said. "May they get what's coming to them."

Gladys' face went white. "Do you fancy a lie down before lunch?" I asked her. She looked at me gratefully and slipped away to her room, Scott looked mortified. "I've been a selfish, thoughtless bastard, haven't I?"

"You said it," I replied as I wandered off into the restaurant. He sat torturing himself with recriminations while I read the paper as we waited for Gladys to rest. He kept pacing the floor like a condemned criminal.

"You'll wear the carpet out," I observed.

"She's got nothing to worry about," Scott said earnestly, as he came to sit beside me, "there's no reason for anyone to find out who my father is, is there?"

I looked at him candidly.

"No!" he said in a shocked voice. "Please God, tell me Gladys doesn't know. You wouldn't, you couldn't?" He gasped.

"My editor wants to know by Thursday. I'm thinking about it."

He went nuclear. There ensued a row to eclipse all rows. We were arguing like cat and dog when the manager came over and asked us to leave the restaurant. We continued fighting in the lobby and then I took massive umbrage and marched off to my room after Scott offered to pay for my silence.

"How dare you insult me?" I hissed, as I went to slam the door in his face.

"How dare you sell my mother's good name down the river for thirty pieces of sliver?" he yelled as he shoved the door open and then marched into my room before kicking it shut.

"Who invited you in here, get out," I yelled.

"I'll do what I damn well please," he retorted.

"Then so will I," I said. "Don't you see, if I don't do the story, they will? I mean it isn't rocket science, is it? The Catholic organisation that arranged to have you sent to Australia was in County Kerry, wasn't it?"

Scott nodded.

"And your father's wife, who was a Catholic, came from County Kerry. Didn't she?" Scott stared at me impassively. I rummaged about in my handbag and flung a copy of the newspaper containing the article onto the bed.

"I couldn't work it out for ages, who you reminded me of," I said, pushing my hair back distractedly from my face.

"And then everything clicked into place when I saw this picture of Percy lying next to yours on the editor's desk."

I turned to the back page and pointed to the picture of Percy. Scott looked at me and looked down at the picture. "He's your half-brother, isn't he?" Scott looked stunned and said quietly in a broken voice.

"If you think anything of me at all you won't do this." He held out his hand. I knew in that instant that if I took it my promotion prospects and my independence would be dashed.

I turned to Scott. He's handsome and rich, I thought, and he wants me. Take that hand and you'll be made for life. For a moment, I visualised myself as a 'lady who lunches,' wandering, perfectly groomed into designer shops to spend a fortune on fripperies. Not me, I thought, as I slowly put my hand behind my back and looked him squarely in the face.

"You once said that we were alike, that you understood me. You were right."

175

His face lit up and he moved as if to take hold of me. I took a step back and held up my hands.

"So, don't stop me from doing my job. It's not between you and me, it's between you and your father. You haven't done anything wrong, you're not a small boy anymore, it's your father who's responsible. It's not for me to change the story."

Scott lowered his hands. "I trusted you."

I instinctively moved towards him and gripped him by the arms and said earnestly.

"You can trust me; I won't ever lie to you. I'm doing what I think is right." I looked him straight in the eyes. "I don't want to hurt you, please, please believe me."

He looked down at me, shook his head slowly and then pushed my arms away before walking to the door. He reached for the handle and then turning, pointed a finger at me before saying: "Prove it, or I'll sue."

"Shit," I thought. "You've burned your bridges now girl."

Chapter 26

How many times have I heard that stupid phrase, 'with the benefit of hindsight'? Too many. Please, can anyone tell me what the hell it means? Obviously, it's possible to benefit from hindsight if you don't go and make the same stupid mistakes again and again, but it's completely pointless saying, 'I would do such and such differently, with the benefit of hindsight. With the benefit of hindsight, I wouldn't have married that person and had thirteen children, or, with the benefit of hindsight, I wouldn't have run amok in the street with a machine gun and chillingly mown down dozens of innocent people in cold blood.'

How can you benefit from hindsight that wouldn't have happened if you hadn't been a complete prat in the first place to do what you would have benefitted from hindsight before you did it?

How can it improve your life to know that for years you made a complete balls-up of it, and, but for a different set of circumstances, twist of fate, arbitrary decision, you wouldn't be having to pick up the pieces now? Cold comfort, that's what I call it. It's cold comfort to know that if I'd had the benefit of hindsight, I wouldn't have married Giles. But I did and no amount of hindsight benefits me knowing that because of it, I'm now going to have to endure an excruciatingly embarrassing dinner with him, Mum, Joey and his new fiancé Fiona.

It's going to be teeth-grindingly, awesomely, jaw-breakingly, yawningly boring.

And I hate, more than anything, being bored. Which reminds me why I left Giles. I was fucking bored.

I was employing my strategy of staring vacantly out of the window hoping that the answer to all my problems would come knocking at the door, when my phone buzzed. "Sabrina, claws, Scott, urgent," read Konnie's text. What the hell does she mean? I called her up.

"She's after Scott, said Konnie in a breathless voice, Jake says he used Scott as juicy bait in an attempt to offload her and she seized on it instantly. She's got him in her sights and is going in guns blazing. It's serious because she's wearing a smudge of lip-gloss which she's always claimed is a symbol of female oppression. Why doesn't she just get her jugs out and be done with it?"

"Because she hasn't got any," I replied as I felt a pang of irrational jealousy. "Anyway, so what?"

"So, let him know you're still available, shag him quick before she worms her way in there for God's sake."

I reminded her that she had overlooked one slight detail. Tor.

"Tor's a sweetie, but he's just a distraction. You are not getting any younger, leave it any longer and you'll miss the boat. You mark my words."

I was outraged. "You sound just like my mum."

"You've got a wise old mum then," said Konnie. "Maybe you should listen to her more often."

Feeling distinctly uncomfortable, I decided to change the subject and asked how she was getting on in Ireland. She'd beetled off there to join Delia and Gareth in their hideaway to sort her head out about Jake and the baby. I'd decided it was payback time and asked her to do some digging about Gladys and Sir Walter. She's having a child with the love of my life, the least she can do is snoop around to find some hard evidence to prove the old goat is Scott's dad. Poetic justice or what?

"Well, to be honest, I'm having a lovely time," she said. "You wouldn't believe the pile that Seamus' family live in, it's vast, like Buckingham Palace and the countryside is breathtakingly beautiful and the people so friendly and the air so clean and…."

"I get the picture," I said.

"There's only one fly in the ointment though," said Konnie slowly.

I hazarded a guess. "Is it Jake? Is he being uncooperative?"

"Oh no," Konnie assured me. "The lines of communication are still open there. No, it's Seamus."

I speculated if it was anything to do with the altercation between him and Percy.

"I don't know," she said. "Although Percy is over here and they seem very friendly, if you know what I mean. Very affectionate."

I said that I hadn't the faintest idea what she meant.

"Well, openly affectionate."

I pointed out that they had been friends since childhood. "They are almost like brothers," I reasoned.

"I mean touchy feely, affectionate. Brothers, well they don't," she stopped.

"Don't what?" I asked.

"Snog," she said.

I felt as if I'd just jumped out of an aeroplane at 30,000 feet without a parachute or that my brain had shrivelled instantly, like a strand of hair on a hotplate.

"Really," I squeaked anxiously.

"They are in a relationship," she said, annunciating every syllable slowly as if I was half witted. "He's a problem because he doesn't like me snooping around about Gladys. He accused me of abusing his hospitality and said that if I carried on, I must go home and never darken his door again, or something equally dramatic."

"That's a real drag, there must be some ancient bloke or toothless old crone who can remember Gladys staying in the area all those years ago. After all, it must be like Wethershire , not much can happen here that misses the eagle eye of the locals."

I kicked the kitchen table in frustration. "Looks like the old bugger will get away with it after all," I said despairingly.

"Well, I tried my best before Seamus knobbled me," Konnie said. "I talked to a few old codgers in the pub and gave out copies of your article. But I daren't risk doing any more, although I would love to help Scott, I kind of identify with him, you know, because of my baby."

I told her that I understood completely and that was the reason I suppose I was so intent on getting justice done.

"If you say so, you poor deluded woman," said Konnie cryptically.

"Talking about deluded women," I said, ignoring her rude remark. "I'm off to the Doom and Gloom in a while for dinner with Giles and his prospective new bride."

"Have fun," said Konnie. "And just remember, no Giles, no Joey, it wasn't all bad."

She's right, I thought as Joey wandered downstairs, his gait and the way he held his head, so reminiscent of his father, a small chip off the old block.

"I'm going to have steak with French fries and coke," he said. "And a strawberry knickerbocker glory."

I ran my hand over his head affectionately and ruffled his dark brown hair.

"Okay," I said. "So long as you eat your veg."

What an ordeal, I thought, although it's got to be done, for Joey's sake. Show that we can all be adult and sensible and rational and reasonable. All the traits that made Giles such a suitable husband for me, a wayward, wanton young thing who, in the eyes of Mum and Dad, wanted to do outrageous things. Like go out with a boy with long hair.

It all seems so tame now and so long ago, although at the time it was heady stuff, listening to Orlando reading acres of Keats while I lay on the floor of his grotty flat in my pink half-cup bra and frayed jeans, looking up at the starry sky through the grimy skylight. Beautiful, fragile, sweet Orlando, who kissed me in the new mown hay and embroidered my hair with daisy chains, his hair soft-lifted by the winnowing winds, innocent, halcyon days, a virgin and a gypsy. Clever, sensitive, poetic, Orlando. A dreamer.

"But he's a school dropout and he smokes goodness-knows-what," and Mum held her breath and exhaled slowly. "He isn't a churchgoer. An infidel."

That was it. I was young for my nineteen years and afraid, afraid of all the wickedness, the unspoken deeds done by men. And so, I married respectable, responsible, reliable Giles and said goodbye to Orlando who watched secretly in Hartborne churchyard as I came out a bride.

"Giles and Rebecca had a lovely wedding," Mum informed Fiona, as we studied the menus. "It cost an arm and a leg, such a waste. I suppose you'll have a registry office 'do' seeing as Giles is divorced. Not that it was his fault," she said earnestly, leaning forward over her menu and nodding in my direction, her eyes going heavenward.

"I take the blame. She was spoilt, an only child, we tried for another, but I reached forty and then, well it's not nice and that was it. God's will. I think I'll have the steak," she said turning to the barman.

"It's off," he said bluntly. "The delivery van broke down."

Joey's face registered disappointment.

"Never mind," said Giles in a placatory tone. "There are lots of other nice things on the menu like pasta, or fish."

Joey looked mutinous. "I want meat, I don't like pasta, it's got bits in. Or fish. It's got bones."

He behaved in a perfectly beastly fashion until he was finally persuaded that a pork medallion, minus any sauce, was a fitting substitute for steak. When it arrived, he looked at it suspiciously, poked it, took a nibble and then decreed it wasn't to his taste.

"It's rank," he said. "Leather."

Giles was hot and flustered with embarrassment. "It's lovely, look," he said taking a bite. "Umm."

Joey made a face. "Yuk! It's covered in spit."

He elaborately sliced a two-inch margin off the meat and then plonked it on Giles' plate claiming it was, 'contaminated.'

This is a lot more entertaining than I thought it would be I decided, as Mum waded into the fray with hobnail boots on and gave Joey a lecture about the War and how they survived on powdered eggs and the family pig's chitterlings that she used to turn in a bucket every day with Thelma until they were ready to cook.

"Father would kill the pig and we'd scrub off all the bristles," she said with relish. She looked at Fiona who sat listening impassively. Mum elaborated in case she'd missed any vital piece of information. "The chitterlings were the pig innards," she explained. She turned to Joey who was obviously impressed. "Nothing was wasted, not even the brains. And we'd boil the head for soup. It was delicious, delicious, Fiona."

"I'm a vegan," she said, pushing a stuffed mushroom languidly around her plate.

Mum didn't reply but pulled a disapproving face.

"Well, this is lovely, isn't it?" said Giles brightly. Nobody replied.

"I think this place has gone off, since Joey's grandpa died," Mum said looking around. "They didn't play this awful pop music for a start. Can you tell them to turn it down?"

Giles, ignoring her remark, motioned to the barman to clear the plates and asked him to bring the pudding menus. I used this as an interval to go to the loo so I wouldn't miss any of the second half. I was just reapplying my lipstick in the mirror when who should walk in but Sabrina. You could have knocked me down with a feather. She looked startled and as pleased to see me as I was to see her.

"Oh," she said. "What are you doing here?"

I glanced at the toilets and then turned back to the mirror. I couldn't bring myself to speak to her.

"I'm here on a date," she said. "With Scott." She gave a tight smile. "We have so much in common, Australia, music, food." She put on a tragic face. "And we've both been betrayed in love."

I registered interest. "So, it's off with you and Jake then, over?"

She looked uncomfortable. "Well, it had come to its natural conclusion. And really, he's such a Philistine. I've had a lucky escape."

I turned to go.

"Anyway," she said as I opened the door. "He's rushed off to Ireland for some reason, urgent business apparently. He was always wedded to his work."

I stopped in my tracks. I wonder if Konnie knows, I thought. She didn't mention it earlier. I took out my mobile and sent her a text message and then wandered back to the dinner table making a detour to pass by Scott's table on the way.

"You look happy," I said. "I assume it's nothing I've done."

"Well, you haven't been able to expose my secret, so there's no reason to be angry now. Let me buy you a drink as a peace offering. I'll be going back Down Under shortly."

I declined and warned him not to get too complacent. "I'm working on it as we speak," I said.

"I'll believe it when I read it," he replied, raising his glass in salute.

"Save it for your girlfriend," I remarked as I saw Sabrina emerge from the toilets. His face darkened.

"Isn't that gentleman Gladys' secret love child? I saw him on breakfast telly," Mum said, craning her neck around to look at Scott. "Such a nice man." She waved to him and mouthed 'hello.' He smiled and raised his hand.

"Ask him over," she said. I remonstrated and told her that it was rude as he was obviously entertaining. "Give over Mum," I said, as she beckoned to him, waving her arms like a policeman directing traffic.

I could see Scott smirking as he got out of his seat to wander over, followed by Sabrina.

"Nice to meet you," simpered Mum.

"My pleasure," said Scott as he took her hand and kissed it. "My pleasure."

Mum insisted on introducing him to the rest of the table. I could see Scott looking at Giles with interest as they shook hands.

"Do feel free to join us," said Giles, earnestly, obviously keen to divert Fiona's attention from Joey's naughtiness and his ex-mother-in-law's nuttiness.

"Thank you," said Scott. "Don't mind if we do, we haven't eaten yet."

He pulled over a chair for Sabrina who sat down with a scowl.

"Are you celebrating?" asked Scott politely after he had introduced Sabrina.

"Oh yes," said Mum. "Giles has found happiness second time around with Fiona.

Much more suited to him than Rebecca I have to admit, though I am her mother."

Mum gave Fiona a motherly smile, "Fiona's getting to know us. I look after Joey a lot you see, they rely on me, I'm indispensable aren't I dear?" she said turning to me.

Before I had time to answer, she continued without pausing for breath. "Fiona's parents live in France and Giles' parents are long gone." She leaned over to Scott and hissed loudly behind her hand, "Rebecca was a child bride, Giles was a father figure. A mistake."

Giles, who had obviously overheard her indiscreet remark, tried to steer the conversation into neutral waters by politely asking Sabrina if she lived locally. Sabrina took the opportunity to launch into her life history. By the time she'd finished we'd learnt that she was divorced, had two gifted children at university who were little short of geniuses and that she'd got a PhD.

"And how did you meet Scott?" asked Mum. "Is it a love match?"

Sabrina explained that they'd been introduced by a man called Jake Manderson at the university where she worked.

"Isn't he the horrible man that you left Giles for?" added Mum with alacrity. "He's a dreadful man." She said to Sabrina. "A communist."

"I know," Sabrina replied. "He left Rebecca for me. And I left him…"

She left her sentence hanging in the air as she looked coyly at Scott.

"Well," said Mum looking a bit shell-shocked. "What a small world. I keep telling Rebecca that she'll get left on the shelf if she doesn't get a move on."

Scott turned to me and said in a rush, "I thought you were seeing someone called Tor?"

Mum squinted at me as though she were looking for something in the dark. "Rebecca?"

I dismissed Scott's remarks with a wave of my hand. "No one important, forget it Mum."

"He's not getting you mixed up with your friend Konnie, is he?" she asked looking confused.

"No," said Sabrina. "She's having a relationship with Jake. Whether it will last or not remains to be seen. I have my doubts."

Mum sat looking nonplussed with her mouth open, lost for words.

"Konnie's having Jake's baby," said Joey, as he scraped the last vestiges of strawberry ice-cream from the bottom of his knickerbocker glory. "I heard Mum talking about it to Delia on the phone."

Sabrina went as white as a sheet. "I don't believe it," she said through clenched teeth. "He wouldn't be such a fool."

I looked daggers at Joey, as I flapped my hands against my ears. "You must have made a mistake," I said. "Got the wrong end of the stick."

"You're telling fibs," said Joey. "You're a big fibber." He starred at me with narrowed eyes and pursed his lips, liberally rimmed with strawberry ice-cream. He looked at the people sitting silently transfixed around the table, waiting for his next remark which he milked for all it was worth. Going for the greatest impact he fixed his eyes on Sabrina and delivered his punchline.

"And Mum snogged Mr Henderson."

Sabrina's face flushed bright red. Fiona looked pleased, Mum looked bewildered.

Scott threw back his head and laughed. "And very nice it was too Joey."

Sabrina stood up sharply. "I need to make a phone call," she said, rummaging about in her handbag.

"Don't you dare repeat what Joey said about Konnie, if you're thinking of calling Jake."

She flashed me a look of pure venom. "Well, if it isn't true, it doesn't matter does it?"

"Just keep your sticky beak out of it," I said wearily. "It's none of your business now."

She turned and marched off to the toilets.

"I really can't keep up with all these shenanigans," sighed Mum. "That Jake Manderson sounds like a bad lot and she's a hoity toity piece."

She turned to Scott. "Make sure you don't make a mistake. Rebecca had a lucky escape. She almost married a wastrel. Didn't she Giles?"

Giles surprisingly disagreed. "I'm not so sure Vera. Orlando may have been rather wild, but no doubt he would have settled down in due course. Rebecca would have grown out of him, forgotten and moved on. As it is…" he stopped.

"Did he leave you too?" asked Scott.

I looked down at my hands. "You could say that," I said quietly. "He hung himself on my wedding day."

I vaguely heard Mum wittering on in the background, "No consideration for those left behind, she really never got over it."

I took out his letters when I got home and read the faded script.

"Forgive me, I loved you too much."

I lay in bed, trying to sleep as the minutes turned to hours. No, there can be no consolation in the benefit of hindsight, I thought, thinking of Orlando, immortalised forever in my mind, young and strong and true. Beauty is truth, truth beauty. A hermeneutic circle that no benefit of hindsight could break, or ever bring back.

Chapter 27

"Oh, what can ail thee, knight-at-arms, alone and palely loitering?" I asked Mervin with a smile as I answered the front door to find him standing outside wringing his hands.

"I'm expanding in direct proportion to the torment I'm experiencing. I licked all the chocolate off a packet of digestive biscuits and I'm gagging for a fry-up. I need your advice before I metamorphosise into my old repulsive self."

I asked him to elaborate as I invited him in for a cup of tea.

"Can't talk long," I said. "I'm off to Mucklesbury for inspection by my lover's daughter, Freya. She sounds delightful."

I listened as I busied about putting on the kettle while Mervin beat his breast, gnashed his teeth and bemoaned his lot with a plethora of dramatic gestures and deep expansive, shuddering sighs.

He wrung his hands and recounted how Henrietta had said she couldn't possibly take him home to meet 'Mummy and Daddy' when he's so obviously a Heinz 57 variety and didn't have a pedigree. "I told her my aunty Jean and uncle Ken live in a five bedroomed detached house in Solihull with an indoor pool, but she said that was so nouveau."

I passed him his mug of tea and asked him how he could fancy such a snobby bitch. He looked shocked. "I love her Rebecca, with a frenzied passion. It was love at first sight, but she's too good for me, too above me, too out of reach."

"But she's got no neck," I said.

His throat gobbled like a turkey. "You are talking about the woman I love."

"You've got it bad," I said sympathetically. "Have you tried to get her out of your system, you know, other women, fuck-to-forget jobby?"

Mervin perked up. "Yes, I have sought solace with a few of my net mates, Wendy, Lorna, Greta and Janet, or is it Janice? Or is it Janet and Janice? I forget, they all merge. But they welcome me with open, well open arms."

I bit my lip. Typical, rushing off on a marathon humpathon to deposit his seed into some warm and willing woman just because he can't cope, a mega minge-winge. He must meet them on some fetish site like spamman.orgy.co.uk, why else would they want to sleep with him? They can't all be that desperate to settle for a shag with a DUD.

I counted slowly to ten and then told him he was suffering with a bad dose of lust.

"Henrietta's blinding you. Get a grip, you need to stand firm, call her bluff, tell her that she's a social dinosaur and you've got other women queuing up. Treat 'em mean and keep 'em keen. Play it cool. Women like her don't rate wimps."

His ears visibly wobbled with angst. "Do you think she'll fall for it? Can I afford to risk it? My ardour is red hot. Searing."

Horrible thought, I shuddered, as I assured him that she'd come to heel. I recalled her at the ball; frumpy, plain, late thirties and single with the hint of a moustache.

"And don't forget, you mustn't succumb to oral temptation," I teased as I eased a chocolate finger in-and-out of my mouth. "You and your willy have only just made eye contact again after many years, it would be a shame if the blubber made a comeback and cast a shadow."

"You're looking at Mr Ice Cool Purvis," Mervin said as he squeezed me in a bear hug on the doorstep. "You're a star Rebecca, I owe you one."

"Invite me to the wedding," I yelled as he slid into his Ford Probe.

Two hours later I had first-hand experience of how Mervin must have been feeling as I felt my belly distending in proportion to an acute attack of anxiety triggering trapped wind, as I stood apprehensively on Tor's doorstep. It felt as if my stomach lining was corroding with nitric acid.

Why is it much easier to give advice that take advice, I thought as Tor opened the door and invited me in.

"She's not nearly as pretty as Mummy," said Freya when Tor introduced me to this diminutive little tot with pale blue eyes and sticky-out pigtails.

"Rebecca is a beautiful person inside," said Tor smiling at me.

"Wrong answer," I thought grimly as I smiled benignly at them both like the Virgin Mary.

"Your mummy is very pretty," I said to Freya. "Wasn't she a model?" She nodded in agreement.

"You could never be a model. You're too fat."

I laughed. "She's just like Joey," I said gaily to Tor whose face had gone ashen. I gave Freya a description of Joey. "He can be a bit naughty sometimes, but he can be funny and clever when he wants to be."

"I don't like boys. They smell."

"Ha, ha, ha, ha, ha," I laughed hysterically like a hyena.

Sensing that the two women in his life weren't going to instantly hit it off, Tor suggested we hit the road so that we could go for a walk at Freya's favourite country park.

"We used to go to Jail Gate Common all the time with Mummy," Freya explained as we drove along. "That's where you used to walk with Mummy before I was born. When you were in love, wasn't it, Daddy?"

This has to be the most sophisticated form of torture, I decided as Freya parried verbally with Tor to make sure I felt as unwelcome as possible as she repeatedly kicked the back of my seat until I could endure it no longer.

"Is that wise?" I asked her politely.

"I don't know what you mean," she lisped innocently. Tor craned his head around to look at her sitting demurely and as quiet as a mouse.

"Be a good girl for Daddy," he smiled encouragingly. "We're nearly there."

I thought, 'Brace yourself' as I heard faint sounds of sniffling and snuffling being emitted from the back seat. I glanced warningly at Tor who just smiled lovingly and squeezed my hand. Dumbo. Undeterred, Freya embarked on counter offensive Mark II with small, sniffy sobs which earned her a solicitous enquiry from Tor who asked her if she was going down with a cold.

Aware that extreme measures were needed, Freya opened her mouth as wide as the Channel Tunnel. 'Here she blows,' I whispered under my breath as she emitted such a high-pitched fit of wailing and boohooing that Tor was forced onto the hard shoulder as she collapsed into a paroxysm of body-racking, ear-splitting howls.

"Daddy's darling, sweet girl, what is the matter?" he asked urgently, swaying dramatically backwards and forwards as he cradled her to his chest while she continued with her Oscar winning performance.

"She's so horrid," Freya gasped jerkily through rasping sobs.

"O my pet lamb, Daddy's sweetie pie," said Tor as he rained kisses down on her face.

Pass me the sick bag I thought, as he eventually placated her with rash promises as he unpeeled her fingers one by one from around his neck so we could continue the journey.

The little minx caught my eye in the mirror as Tor got back into his seat and stuck out her tongue until it reached right down to the bottom of her chin. I gave her a conspiratorial wink, which made the tongue go in but her bottom lip stick out. Stress or what?

By the time we reached the country park my belly was rumbling and gurgling like an overheated old water cistern that was just about to blow. "I'll just nip to the loo before we start," I said, rushing away to let off steam. My poor old bum hovered gratefully over the toilet bowl to no avail. Not even a peep. I squeezed and pushed and prayed for a blast. 'Damn', I moaned, admitting defeat as I struggled to zip up my jeans over my distended belly. What would I give for a decent fart?

Every step seemed to pump up my rock-hard stomach as Freya continued on her Rebecca demolition derby and deification of Rita.

I've got to sit down, I thought, or else I'm in danger of whizzing off into the sky like a massive balloon when its air is exhaled all at once. Tor gave me a queer look when I asked if we could sit down to admire the view. We'd only walked about five hundred yards.

"Let's go and sit on that outcrop of rock," I said as playfully as my paralysed bowels would allow. But Freya had other ideas and literally dug her heels in and refused to budge.

"Rebecca's fat and lazy," she said, as Tor pulled her gently by the hand.

"Now now, sweetie munchkins, let's go and have a nice climb," he wheedled.

I almost farted audibly with shock when Freya took one step and then tripped and collapsed into a heap on the floor. Fortunately, it was a false alarm and my tummy just rumbled like distant thunder as Freya accused Tor of pulling her over on purpose. She embarked on a second seizure of copious weeping and wailing. "I'm going to tell Mummy of you, you're a child abuser."

Tor turned white as he frantically rubbed her little knees and kissed them.

"See," he said almost manically. "Not even a scratch."

But Freya wasn't having any of it. Sensing victory she dragged her leg behind her, claiming she'd gone lame as she made a pathetic attempt to hobble a few steps.

'Poor kid,' I thought, as Tor indulged her deception. She's going to grow up an insecure, demanding diva like Rita to use her feminine wiles to make mincemeat of wimpy men.

"I think her leg ought to get checked out at the hospital, maybe she's strained it. I can't afford to take the risk," Tor said in a broken voice as he scooped her up into his arms. I was gobsmacked, surely not.

As we turned back, Freya gave me a triumphant little smile over Tor's shoulder as I trudged behind while he murmured sweet nothings in her ear.

'Be honest,' I said to myself as I put my seatbelt on. 'Do I want to put up with this crap or not? 'No,' I decided. Given the choice, I'd rather have my teeth extracted without aesthetic.

"If you don't mind, I'd be grateful if you'd drop me off at your place first so I can shoot off," I said. I got such a look of complete incredulity that I could be so selfish in the teeth of a crisis that Tor was lost for words. "I've got things to do," I explained lamely.

"As you wish," he said formally.

I closed my eyes as we motored back to Mucklesbury in complete silence, except for the occasional little whimper from Freya as she remembered her potentially fatal injuries.

"Be brave, we won't be long now baby," said Tor as he pulled up outside his house.

"Are you sure you won't come and support me?" he said pointedly as he turned to face me.

"Maybe another time," I said weakly.

"O my God," he said with feeling as a look of horror crossed his face.

"Okay, okay, I'll come then, but to be honest I've got rotten guts ache," I replied thinking his expression was way OTT.

Tor swallowed slowly and then pointed his finger over my shoulder, I turned to see the Grim Rita emerging from behind the hedge. Cripes.

"Mummy," squealed Freya as she flung open her car door and ran like the wind to meet her.

"My darling baby," said Rita. "Are you alright, have you missed your lonely mummy?"

"She seems to have made a remarkable recovery," I remarked dryly to Tor, whose eyes popped out in disbelief. Some children do 'have 'em', I observed wryly as I got out of the car to follow him up the garden path. All hell broke loose when Freya informed Rita about her little mishap, especially when it turned out that it was remarkably all my fault.

"I knew you were trouble when I first saw you," Rita hissed. "Freya doesn't like you; you don't gel, you're making a fool of yourself."

Tor dithered around as if he was treading on broken glass, frantically trying to shoo Rita away by flapping his hands, "Please Rita, some other time," he begged and then begged some more, and when that didn't work, grovelled. She wouldn't budge. It was a meltdown of Hiroshima proportions.

"Having trouble, are we?" said a familiar voice. We all turned to see Ted standing on his doorstep with a teapot. "Fancy a cuppa Rebecca?" he asked.

"I'd love one," I called as I decided a bit of confrontation was in order.

"I'm going to see Ted for a cup of tea, you've got half an hour to cut the crap or we're through," I declared to Tor as I looked at my watch, leaving him to inveigle, plead, implore and beg Rita to bugger off. To no avail.

"He's a right milksop," said Ted. "Drippy as a wet weekend. Don't know what you see in 'im. I'd have been a much better bet."

And then he informed me with undisguised glee that even if I wanted him now, he was no longer on the singles market.

"I took Molly to Falaraki and it did wonders for her psoriasis. She was very grateful if you know what I mean, and friendship turned to lust and lust to love, like, and we've been inseparable ever since. Except for now, she's gone off to Aldi to get some mince."

I congratulated him as he gave me the low-down on their relationship which he said sizzled with intensity. "The sparks fly I can tell you, we 'ad to get rid of the nylon sheets or else we'd have been electrocuted."

"Fascinating Ted," I said as I looked at my watch. Tor's half an hour was up.

"This is it," I said. "I wonder if he's got shot of her?"

Ted escorted me to the door. "She's the one with the balls, she's got summat on 'im all right that he can't shake off. Don't know what, she's a right tin ribs."

I swallowed hard and nodded. All seemed quiet when I knocked on the front door. It opened a crack.

"Daddy says to wait here while he takes Mummy home for a chat," said a somewhat chastened Freya.

I followed her into the kitchen where she sat and stared at me with undisguised loathing. I tried to be nice.

"It's such a pity about your poorly leg," I said. "We were having such a lovely time." Silence. She stared at me intently.

"Would you like to see my room?" she asked. I was taken aback.

"Yes," I said, accepting her olive branch gratefully. "That would be nice."

She took me by the hand and led me up the stairs.

"That's my room," she said, pointing to the end of the landing. "It's next to the room that Daddy keeps locked. He wouldn't want you to go in there."

She turned to go back down the stairs.

"Tell me if you like my Barbie doll," she said.

I was intrigued. What's she playing at, I thought as I made my way along the landing, past Tor's room with his antique bed and then the locked room where he apparently wouldn't want me to stray. Except that it wasn't locked. The key was in the door. What a dilemma, as temptation seeped into my consciousness like mist over a moor.

I took a deep breath and marched past into Freya's room to inspect her Barbie doll, but all the while, before my eyes, hovered the key in the lock.

"He'll never find out," I reasoned, as I stood clutching Barbie to my chest. "But what if there's something in there that you'd rather not know," another little voice echoed in my head. I put the doll down and marched from the room, past the locked door, to the top of the stairs.

"You're being ridiculous," I chided myself as I put my foot on the first step. "What can be in there that can possibly hurt you? The beastly child is trying to wind you up."

I took a deep breath as I turned back towards the room to turn the key in the lock. I sauntered in, to be confronted by Rita. A kaleidoscope of her. Painting after painting, sketch after sketch, sculpture after sculpture. I walked up to an easel where a canvas stood with a magnificent oil painting, a bravura of colour, texture and intensity. Rita, naked, erotic, sensuous, beautiful, wild. And desired. I touched the canvas; the paint was thick and wet.

"Rebecca, Rebecca." I turned to see Tor standing on the threshold, his face full of fear. "I can explain," he said.

"You don't need to," I said sadly as I walked past him.

"Don't go," he pleaded. "I need you. Please. I love you."

He chased after me as I ran down the stairs, out of the house to my car.

"I don't love her," he said, as a sob caught in his throat. "I hate her, she's destroying me. You're my sanity, my generous, kind, beautiful Rebecca."

I turned to him. "Not so sane that I don't feel like punching your lights out. We're finished," I declared with more conviction than I felt as tears stung the back of my eyes. I wildly put the car into first gear, but hot with hurt and confusion the clutch slipped, and it stalled.

'That child's possessed,' I muttered through clenched teeth as I kangarooed off down the road past Freya who stood smiling enigmatically and waving gaily as I bounced past. I felt numb all the way home.

I need to talk to the girls, I thought as I picked up the phone when I walked in, breathing a sigh of relief when I realised I'd got a message from Konnie.

"Hi Becks, give us a call, I've got some good news and some weird news. Speak to you soon."

I needed something to steady my nerves, so I poured myself a strong cup of tea, sat down with a packet of Jaffa Cakes and gave her a ring.

"Hi Konnie," I said when she answered. "Did you get my message about Jake before he arrived. Did it help?"

Apparently, she'd received it just in the nick of time although she feigned surprise when he pitched up. "Anyway, before my news, how are you? You sound down in the dumps."

I told her of my encounter with the frightful Freya and the gruesome Grim Rita from the initial hostile reception to my undignified exit.

"How awful," said Konnie as she started to snigger.

"It didn't seem funny at the time," I spluttered as I began to see the funny side of things. I started to titter. Good old Konnie, just talking to her made me feel relaxed. Thump, thump, reverberated my bum with pleasurable ecstasy as my belly slowly stared to deflate.

"I think we've got a bad connection," said Konnie. "The reception here's really bad, can you hear that awful noise at your end?"

I placed my rear end on a cushion to muffle the rip roaring wind as I excused the noise by saying the central heating was on the blink.

"Anyway, tell me all your news, it sounds most intriguing," I asked to distract her. It was in fact, much more intriguing, it was an eye opener.

Konnie explained that she'd been stopped in the street by one of the old codgers she'd questioned about Gladys.

"His name's Darragh and he worked at the O'Connor's place. It was one of the only places for miles around where there was any work available, and he vividly remembers Gladys who went to work in Ireland from Wethershire as some sort of lady's maid to Venetia O' Connor. He remembers the scandal and is as outraged about it now as he was when it happened over fifty years ago."

She went on to explain that Sir Walter had stayed all summer at the O'Connor's place. It was an open secret among the staff that the two were lovers, he was besotted with Gladys who was a stunner, with men buzzing around her like bees round a honeypot, including Darragh. But Sir Walter was under pressure to marry Venetia to tie two powerful dynasties together. As soon as Gladys got pregnant, she was shipped off to a Catholic care home in Dublin for unmarried mothers. Darragh took her to the station in the O'Connor's Bentley as Gladys sat on the back seat, crying the whole way. She was sent back to work at Hartborne Hall under the watchful eye of Venetia O'Connor who married Sir Walter not long after.

"Venetia sounded like a cold fish," said Konnie, "not right for a hot-blooded squire like Sir Walter. No wonder he was tempted with Gladys."

"Bingo," I said. "We've got the bugger."

You could have knocked me down with a feather. No wonder Sir Walter was determined that the truth wouldn't come out.

"Are you alright?" asked Konnie with concern.

"Never better," I said.

"Anyway, talking about babies, I told Jake about ours when he came over to Ireland to surprise me."

"Will he help you?" I asked.

"He'll do more than that," Konnie said in triumph. "He wants to marry me."

She laughed gaily. "We're getting hitched next weekend in Newton Saucey registry office and of course you're invited. I'm so happy."

I congratulated her fulsomely and when the call ended, I asked myself, 'Be honest, how do you feel about that?' A thump reverberated in my pants. That about sums it up, I thought, as I stuffed a whole Jaffa Cake in my mouth and got up to put the kettle on for another cuppa.

Chapter 28

I woke up on the morning of Konnie's wedding feeling like a dodo teetering on the edge of a cliff. The last remaining singleton on planet Wethershire . Apart from Moira, but she doesn't qualify.

Still, I had Joey, I reminded myself, that was some consolation. "Are you ready for Konnie's wedding?" I asked him as he sat on the sofa excavating toe jam from between his toes.

"Nah, I'm not coming. It's boring. I'm going shopping with Dad to look for my Christmas present."

"Fine," I said. "Suit yourself. See if I care."

He shrugged and sniffed his fingers.

I stood tapping my foot impatiently on the floor while I allowed him a few minutes to see the monumental error of his ways before resuming my perfectly legitimate request.

"After all, I don't often ask you to do anything for me, but on this occasion, I would like you to be there with me. For support, as you are my son. Please. Mega beg."

"Nah."

A most unsatisfactory and unreasonable response I decided. There followed a flurry of soul searching exercises to see if I was in any way to blame for his unspeakable selfishness. Maybe I needed to put my foot down or else he would grow up to be a complete brat. Yes. But just as I opened my mouth to speak, the doorbell rang.

"Bye," Joey yelled as he got up and raced out of the door.

"Chill," I said to myself in the mirror as I took deep calming breaths, you can do it. Draw on those inner reserves of strength, independence and fortitude. My lip wobbled. Okay. I admitted defeat. You're just going to have to bullshit your way through it. Bring on the understudy, the real Rebecca Pearce is currently out of service, normal transmission will resume shortly.

Knowing that I was only operating with half a brain, I double checked everything at least ten times before I left the house and got into the car to drive to the registry office in Newton Saucey. Confetti, wedding present, card, I muttered under my breath as I switched on the engine. Then I remembered I'd forgotten a hankie. I'm entitled to blub a bit I told myself as I went and fetched a box of tissues, after all, one of my best friends, heavy with child, is going to marry someone who I thought, with such unshakeable conviction, was the love of my life. I can shed a few discreet tears, no one will deny me that, surely?

I scanned the row of wedding guests as I arrived and saw a spare seat next to Moira.

"Hello dear," she said. "What a happy occasion." I gave her a tight little smile as I looked around at a sea of happy couplets, Delia and Gareth, Mervin and Henrietta, Percy and Seamus, Sabrina and Scott. Scott caught my eye. I looked away. Let him think what he likes, I thought as I proudly lifted my chin and gave Keith and Dick a jolly wave.

But I couldn't help asking myself why I was all on my little ownio as Konnie arrived, a vison of loveliness in a designer frock, to claim my ex-lover. Who, by a horrible and perverted twist of fate, was standing feet away from the women who he betrayed me for? Who, by an even crueller, sadistic coincidence, to add insult to mortal injury, snaffled the most eligible man ever to appear on my romantic radar, right from under my nose. Because of your irritating habit of self-sabotage, I chided myself. And fear I conceded, unadulterated, bone crushing, stomach churning terror. I thought of Orlando and switched off.

"How cute," I said dry-eyed as I handed Moira my box of tissues.

"I always cry at weddings," she blubbered. "Such a happy, happy day."

I stuck to Moira like glue as we all assembled outside for the photographs. They seemed to last for an interminably long time. Konnie and Jake with her mum and dad, Konnie and Jake with his mum and dad, granny and grandpa, aunties, Uncle Tom Cobley and all.

At last, it was finished. Konnie smiled and waved her bouquet in the air. "Catch it if you can girls," she shouted, as she hurled it directly at me.

There was a scrum as it flew through the air. I instinctively ducked to miss it. Henrietta pushed in front of me with a passable impression of a rugby forward in a World Cup final with the scores draw-all, seconds from the whistle.

But Scott beat her to it and swiped it from her outstretched hand.

"I think this was meant for you," he said as he handed it to me with a bow. "Thank you," I said blushing a deep red. "But I don't think I'll be needing it." I handed it directly to Henrietta who grabbed it gratefully.

Delia who saw the exchange, came up between us and turned to Scott. "She does fancy you darling, but she's in denial, she just needs to be ravished. If you want her, you'll have to do the chasing, she's not the marrying kind." She smiled sweetly and turned to put her arm through Gareth's just as Sabrina pitched up to claim Scott.

"Very chivalrous of you," she said, clinging onto his arm like a limpet. "But I think Rebecca's already spoken for. She is embroiled with an artist, I believe." She looked at me down her nose. "He's not much in evidence today. Finding it hard to hang onto him, are we? As usual."

I winced. What a twenty-four carat gold cow. "Actually, I don't believe it's very dignified to hang onto men," I said, glancing at her vice like grip. "In fact, I am unexpectedly back on the market. On the prowl for a hunky man."

I smiled sweetly and slowly licked my lips as I glanced at my watch. "Isn't it time to drive over to the reception? Just as well, I've got an insatiable hunger." I flashed Scott a hot flirty look and reminded him that he'd promised to take me and Konnie to dinner—as a foursome. Sabrina looked daggers.

The Doom and Gloom was packed with revellers as the beer and wine started flowing freely. "So, this is where it all happens is it?" asked Keith as I stood with him and Dick at the bar. "The hub of the Wethershire gossip machine, churning out scandal as it happens. Tell me who's who."

I pointed out the notable key players in a rollcall of the Wethershire soaps. "That's Percy," I said as he walked into the snug with Seamus. "And that's Scott Henderson."

Keith recognised them both from their pictures in the papers. "And you say they are half-brothers, sired by this Sir Walter geezer?"

"Sssssh," I said putting my fingers to my lips. "You'll cause mayhem."

"It's a fantastic story," Keith replied, "I think it's time one of us gave Sir Walter a visit."

"Here comes another scandal," I whispered, as Delia wandered over with Gareth.

"Delia has traded in her impotent old husband for a younger more virile model. If Henry caught a whiff of the fact she was here, he would trample down anyone in his path to get his fingers round her throat."

"Civilised lot in Wethershire then," said Dick dryly as Delia joined us with the devoted Gareth in tow, followed by Mervin and Henrietta.

I asked Delia if she was wise to come out so blatantly. "Well, I'm following Percy's example," she said as she glanced over to the bar where he was laughing and flirting with Seamus. "He's told Sir Walter and it's gone 'live' on the Wethershire grapevine. Not that everyone didn't know already, with the odd exception," she laughed gaily as she caught sight of my crestfallen face.

"You mean Lover Boy?" Keith interrupted. "Well, I'll be. How could you get it so wrong Rebecca?"

Tell me about it, I thought as I looked over at Scott. How could I have been such a bloody fool?

Just then Konnie strolled over with Jake and introduced him to Keith and Dick. "Are you another of Rebecca's victims?" Jake asked Dick with his usual lack of originality.

"Do you always have to say that every time you see me with a man?" I asked, instantly on the defensive. "Dick happens to be my deputy editor and he thinks very highly of me. Don't you?" I said, turning to him earnestly. Pathetic. I could have kicked myself. Sad approval seeker.

Jake laughed. "Boss's pet?" I stood and seethed. Dick jokingly said I intimidated the hell out of him. "Keith keeps warning me she's snapping at my heels, it's only a matter of time." He drew his finger dramatically across his throat. Keith laughed.

"You and Rebecca were an item once, isn't that right?" asked Keith.

"Yeah," said Jake nodding. "In fact, another of my ex's is here, Sabrina." He turned to see her standing close by the bar with Scott. "All terribly civilised."

Scott, realising that he was under discussion wandered over. "I was just remarking how civilised it all is," said Jake. "You know, Rebecca and Sabrina, all hunky-dory at my wedding. Kinda smart."

Keith looked at Scott. "It's all rather convoluted and incestuous though, isn't it?"

Scott asked him what he meant. His voice held a touch of menace. I tugged at his sleeve.

"The fact that Jake's had his wicked way with Sabrina, Konnie and me. He's a tart basically."

"He didn't mean that," said Scott, looking down at me. He looked at Keith, who looked over at Percy. "Sibling rivalry, both with a touch of the Oedipus Complex me thinks."

I told Keith to shut it. He shrugged and turned his back on Scott to face the bar. Scott mulled over what Keith had said and then grabbed my arm. "We need to talk," he said, dragging me out of the bar in the most undignified manner.

He was breathing heavily when we reached the small reception area.

"What the fuck have you been up to?" he asked.

"Me?" I squeaked.

"Yes, you," replied Scott. "You know something and I'm going to find out what it is. But not here. Come up to my room."

Scott slammed the door behind him.

"I think we've been here before," I remarked. "So, there's no point in going over old ground."

Scott poured himself a whisky from a bottle near his bed. "Just spit it out. Cut the crap." He took a massive swig from his glass. I looked at the floor. "Well. go on, I'm a big boy, I can take it."

I went over to the window and looked out over the darkening sky and recounted Darragh's story. He turned to face me. "Does that editor of yours know?" I nodded. "If he publishes, I'll sue the fucking pants off him." He turned and marched out of the door.

'Shit,' I thought. 'Bad, bad karma.'

I could hear the shouting before I'd even reached the reception. I poked my head round the door of the bar room to see Scott holding Keith firmly by the neck of his shirt, shaking him like a rag doll.

A crowd had congregated to watch the action. "Let me pass, I'm a journalist," I said as I elbowed my way through the throng.

I came up behind Percy and Seamus who were watching with interest. "I always said he was an oaf," said Percy in a loud voice.

"Excuse me," I said poking him in the ribs. "Would you mind moving? I want to reach your half-brother who is busy defending his mother's name against muckrakers like me." I gave him a shove.

"What did she say, have they finally worked it out?" asked Seamus. "You heard," I yelled in the heat of the moment, as I pushed my way forward. "Sir Walter is Scott Henderson's father."

Silence monumentality fell over the bar and then it erupted in a frenzy of wagging tongues. Percy and Seamus followed me to the bar shouting 'slander.'

I was breathless by the time I reached Scott and Keith who were having a right dingdong. As I struggled to intervene, my eye was caught by a person waving at me from behind the bar. It was Mum.

"I got in the back way. It's an emergency. Henry's on his way." I froze. "I tried to get you on your mobile." She gabbled on, "Mrs Hoare heard from the farm worker and he phoned Thelma, who…"

I turned and frantically tried to fight my way back from the way I'd come but it was gridlocked by the general fracas as people started to take sides in the argument after Percy staggered back into the crowd after a sharp shove from Scott.

I waved frantically to Delia who was sitting away from the rabble sipping a glass of Bolly. She gaily waved back. I gesticulated wildly, starting with a penis shaped gesture from my forehead followed by a strangling impersonation. Delia laughed.

Just as I managed to scream, "Henry!" loud enough above the din, I heard a familiar brutish sound from behind.

"Where is that son-of-a bitch who is fucking my wife?" Gareth looked as if he'd wet his pants. The mob, already inflamed by the Scott and Percy altercation, were ripe for further action and gleefully turned on their once most venerated master with undisguised pleasure and refused to let him pass.

I could see poor Konnie standing at the back of the bar with her mouth the shape of an O as she vainly pleaded with everyone to calm down. Too late, whipped up by a combination of beer and bloodlust the reception turned into one unholy brawl.

Dick gave me a wink as he captured everything on his mobile phone's camera.

"Hold it there, please," he said, one hand outstretched, just as Henry was about to punch the lights out of Mervin who looked frozen with complete terror. "I'd leg it if I were you," I advised Dick when Henry turned a baleful red eye in his direction.

"That's if you ever want to have children."

But Dick kept dodging and weaving, snapping away all the time at the complete mayhem around him. Five minutes later Keith casually strolled over, brushing down his jacket to say he'd got the story in the bag for Friday's front page splash and it was time to leave.

"Nice one mate," he said to Jake, who for once was completely speechless, as he sauntered out of the door.

"Do you need a lift?" asked Dick.

"No thanks," I said. "I sort of feel a bit responsible. I can hardly do a runner now."

The atmosphere was almost carnivalesque as I returned to the bar. The fighting had stopped, and people were picking up the overturned tables and chairs. Percy, Scott and Seamus were nowhere to be seen.

"Delia got away," said Konnie as she rebuilt her wedding cake which had toppled over like a skyscraper in an earthquake. She bent down to pick up the ceramic decoration of a bride and groom that had stood on the top of the cake. It had spilt in two. "Hardly an auspicious start," she said as she began to cry.

"Hey baby," said Jake, tenderly. "Fuck the cake." He took her face in his hands and tenderly kissed away her tears and then held her tightly in his arms. He looked across at me affectionately and smiled. I smiled back.

They're going to be okay, I thought as I drifted off to sleep that night, dreaming that I was flying, flying high like a bird in the sky.

Chapter 29

Monday morning. The tumultuous events of the weekend seem like a distant memory, but it's more likely I've put them in my memory drop box and conveniently forgotten the password. I'm worried I've turned into a worrier. The worry lines on my forehead seem to be getting deeper by the day. It worries me. It won't be long before I can screw my hat on my head if I'm not careful.

But everything ebbs and flows like the tide, I tried to reason with myself, as I sat at my computer on auto pilot, keying in facts about the boring humdrum activities that preoccupy people's daily lives and the mundane petty crimes that make useful little newsy nibs.

Newton Saucey man Ron Stubbs was accused of telling porkies at the Broadmarket Magistrate's Court this week after he was accused of stealing two packets of bacon from the Co-op,' I typed. He was grilled by the prosecution who gave a sizzling summing up as he accused the defendant of being 'an habitual liar.'

I pinged it over to the subs desk.

Then, the phone rang.

"Hello, I want the obituaries. There has been a sudden death."

I engaged my most solicitous voice and explained that the lady who usually took the details was away from her desk, but if they would like to give them to me, I would pass them on.

"Well, my name is Ethel Hoare and I want to report an unexpected death."

My heart froze as the worry beads started to rattle. I was gripped with a horrible premonition that I wasn't going to like what I was about to hear. I felt, with a sure conviction, that the contents of my bowels were about to make a premature appearance.

"Well, it's Sir Walter Albion-Hartborne, he passed away suddenly, late last night."

"What was the cause of death?" I asked, my pen shaking in my hand as I prepared to write it down.

"It was a massive stroke, he died in an instant, it was a blessing he didn't suffer."

I made an urgent visit to the loo before I went and told Keith the momentous news.

"It's curtains on the Gladys' story. We'll never get to the truth now. Sir Walter's inconveniently keeled over and died, taking all the answers about Gladys with him to the family crypt in Hartborne churchyard."

"Inconsiderate old bugger," said Keith, scratching his head. "Doesn't he know I've got a newspaper to write? Having said that," he ruminated, "you can't libel the dead." He stood up and rubbed his hands in front of his chest. "This will be manna from heaven for the nationals. Gladys' secret lover was a knight of the bloody realm." He grinned, cupped his mouth with one hand and yelled across the floor to the subs desk, "Hold the front page!"

Then, turning and pointing to me, he uttered the words I dreaded the most. "We need a statement from the family, so you, Rebecca, you're going to have to go and do a death knock."

I motored over to Hartborne Hall full of trepidation, wondering what kind of reception I would receive. After all, according to chaos theory, I could be accused of being the prime suspect for causing Sir Walter to fall prematurely off his perch. Little did he know when he met me, that I would be the author of his death. That the wearing away of the tread on my stair carpet, acted like the seeds of time counting down to his demise. I'm sure that if he'd known that lurking in the next village, lay the woolly impetus to the exposure of his earlier misdeeds, he would have offered to buy me a new one. But he didn't and it's a reminder to all of us that we are hostage to the same vagaries of fortune. Maybe at this very moment, a small but insignificant incident somewhere on the planet has ignited a train of events that will lead to a major catastrophe. And there's nothing we can do to stop it.

The first thing I noticed when I pulled up on the drive was the pitiful sight of Sir Walter's empty wheelchair. The tassels on his tartan rug, discarded on the seat, were shivering in the wind.

I waited in the cadaverous stone porch as I rehearsed my cunning plan of action. If I asked Percy outright if he would confirm Darragh's story in Ireland regarding Glady and Sir Walter's love affair, I'd probably be shown the exit pretty quick sharp.

No, I'd ask for a loving tribute statement, and once that was in the bag, ask the question that every national TV breakfast host was gagging for; 'can you confirm that Sir Walter is Scott's dad and ergo, Scott is your half-brother.' At least I wouldn't go back to the office empty handed.

I took a deep breath and lifted the heavy door knocker and listened as the sound of it echoed around the porch. The wooden nail studded door opened slowly, creaking on its ancient hinges, as Mrs Hoare's weather-beaten face peered out from between a small crack. As soon as she saw me, she opened it wider and without a word shuffled off down the passage in her slippers towards the drawing room.

I followed, bracing myself as I approached the open door, worrying about the kind of reception I would receive.

The first person I saw was Scott. He was standing and looking out of the graceful French windows on the south facing wall of the drawing room. They framed a timeless view of the stone terrace leading to lush green lawns that swept down to a stone-built ha-ha, bounding a flower filled meadow where longhorn cows grazed.

"This terrace would make a great spot for a barbie," he remarked, turning to Percy who was sitting opposite Seamus. They were both warming themselves in high-backed chairs either side of an ornate marble fireplace where logs burned brightly in the grate to take the chill off early winter.

As Percy rose to join Scott at the window, he saw me, lurking, white faced, in the shadows.

"Look who we have here," he remarked, raising an eyebrow to Scott. "Rebecca dear, you look worried," he said, as he ushered me into the room, beckoning to a vacant chair near the fire. My nerves felt as taut as the cables holding up a suspension bridge. Any sudden shock and they could snap like knicker elastic. I felt the onset of palpitations as my adrenal glands went into overdrive.

"Coffee anyone?" asked a voice behind me.

I almost jumped as high as a froghopper as I turned to see Gladys, minus her apron.

"Yes please," I replied, feeling most discombobulated as I tottered over to the chair proffered by Percy, tentatively perching on the edge and keeping one eye on the door in case I needed to leg it quick. I glanced at the ornate ormolu clock on the mantelpiece, calculating I'd got twenty minutes max to get a tribute statement before pressing the nuclear button.

"So, what do we owe to the pleasure of your visit?" asked Scott, as his eyes bored into me as if he could read my mind. The pictures reserved for the front page splash of his altercation with Percy at Konnie's wedding, flashed across my mind.

The guy can read me like a book, I thought, as I schooled my face into a steely gaze.

I turned my attention to Percy, adopting a sympathetic tone of voice, dripping with feigned sincerity as I expressed my sorrow over Sir Walter's unexpected death.

Then, whipping out my notebook and pen I explained I'd pitched up for a tribute statement and braced myself to frizzle like a fish in a frying pan for my brazen impertinence.

Before Percy had time to reply, Gladys walked in carrying a tray with cups of coffee and a plate of her legendary melting moments. She placed it on a small wooden ornate table inlaid with mother of pearl, before sitting in a vacant chair next me.

"Sugar?" she asked as my mouth literally dropped open.

"No thanks," I stuttered as Percy rose from his chair and plucked my notebook and pen from my hand like a seagull swooping down to pinch a chip.

He turned to Scott. "What shall I write for Rebecca, do you think she deserves anything after her dogged persistence to expose our family secrets, digging away like a ferret down a rabbit hole?" He feigned mock outrage, placing his hand on his chest saying theatrically. "What a silly sausage I've been. I thought she loved me!"

Seamus threw back his head and laughed while Scott, looking with amusement at my angst-ridden face, made a riposte akin to poking a hornet's nest. "I would advise anyone who sups with Rebecca to do so with a very long spoon. I've been a victim myself. It can be very seductive but lethal, creates havoc with your blood pressure."

I was stung. "It's not funny," I blurted out ill-advisedly, seeing as I was officially at work. I gave Scott an adversarial glare as I braced myself on the arms of my chair.

"You're all rich. I've got a mortgage, a kid and the wage of a regional journalist, as in a pittance."

Immediately aware of the error of my ways, I feverishly tried to backtrack, but Gladys intervened before I had time to gather my thoughts.

"Good for you dear, tell them how it is. How the other half lives," she turned to give me a reassuring smile and squeezed my hand. Unrepentant, Scott leant forward in his chair. "Hothead," he said provocatively, as he flashed me a look that would score one hundred degrees Fahrenheit on the flirty thermometer. I flushed deep red like a schoolgirl but was saved from replying as Percy handed my notebook to him with a flourish.

As Scott scanned the page, a smile spread slowly across his face. "Looks good to me," he said, as he moved from his chair to hand the notebook to me. I read through Percy's elegantly written script.

Sir Walter, Peregrine, Charles Albion-Hartborne died suddenly aged 89 at his residence, Hartborne Hall in the village of Hartborne, Wethershire .

Sir Walter was married to Venetia O'Connor, late of County Kerry, Ireland. He had a distinguished Army career where he was a recipient of the Military Cross for his gallantry in the Battle of El Alamein. He was master of the Newton Saucey Hunt for over thirty years where he had a reputation as a renowned and fearless huntsman. He loyally served the county of Wethershire as Lord Lieutenant and a local magistrate for many years. He leaves behind two sons, Percy Charles Albion-Hartborne and Scott Alexander Henderson.

As I lifted my eyes from the page, they filled with tears. "She does have a soul," exclaimed Percy excitedly. He clasped his hands together, scanning my face apprehensively like a small trembling dog, anxiously looking to its owner for approval before it can wag its tail.

"I did love you," I said impulsively, as Percy's face broke into a wide smile, before the clock chimed the hour and my professional instincts took over.

"A picture, a picture of you both together," I said excitedly as I wiped my eyes and fished my mobile out of my handbag. Scott duly obliged, rising languidly from his chair to stand next to Percy in front of the fireside.

"What about Gladys?" I asked cheekily. "Don't push your luck," said Scott smiling as I clicked away. I was so excited as it dawned on me, I'd bagged a major scoop. 'I can't wait to tell Keith and the guys', I thought triumphantly as I uttered the most profusive gratitude and quickly gathered my things together. I'd got what I wanted. It was time to scarper.

"I'll see myself out," I said breezily, as I backed out of the drawing room, waving a jolly goodbye. I turned to race down the passage, forgetting, as I felt the heady elixir of getting a good story, that I might never see Scott again.

I drove back to the office with a sense of euphoria. All my hard work and worry had paid off spectacularly. I made a vow that I would never allow myself to be gripped by unnecessary worry again. As I drove back through the fuzzy felt patchwork of green meadows and brown fields harvested of crops, my mind drifted to the seismic shock I'd just witnessed to Wethershire 's social hierarchy that has gone all topsy-turvy since Scott rolled into town. One minute Gladys was wandering around Hartborne Hall with a mop and bucket. A minion. Now she's the mother of a love child, a multimillionaire, born after a fling with the master of the house. I can't wait to see her at the top of Percy's table asking Sir Lady Howgrave if she'd mind passing the salt. And Henry Fielding, landed gentry and local magistrate, spent the night in the local nick as a guest of His Majesty's pleasure after his fracas at Konnie's wedding. He won't be bothering Delia again in a hurry.

A smile flickered around my lips as I reflected on Mum's forebodings that sees all the recent shenanigans as a sign of the end times that were practically foretold in the book of Revelation. If she's right, I mused, Gladys is the Whore of Babylon, Sir Walter is the antichrist and the four horses of the apocalypse will be paying a visit to Wethershire any day now. Just wait until she hears about Sir Granville Bland.

I sauntered into the office when I got back, to see the picture of Scott and Percy at Konnie's wedding replaced by the images I'd sent over on my phone with the story to match. "Nice one, Rebecca," said Keith, as he beckoned me into his office and shut the door behind him. "I'll miss you when you're gone," he said, as he rummaged around on his desk for his fags.

I instantly felt gripped with worry. "Am I sacked?" I managed to whisper in a strangled voice, as my fingers fluttered at my throat. "Eh?" said Keith, looking confused. "Don't be daft, what made you think that? No, it's when you swan off to some glossy daily one day soon and leave us old provincial hacks behind. You're promoted. Senior Reporter. We'll talk salary later." With that, he gave me a wink. "Time for a fag," he said, as he opened the door, waved me through and followed me out.

I was dog tired by the end of the day with all the emotional highs and lows. My eyes felt stiff with starch. I craved sleep. But as I crawled into bed, my mind started whirling as it frantically tried to make me face the music in the last chance saloon, regarding my feelings for a certain person. Round and round the room it whirled, dancing with the memory of Gladys minus her apron, pirouetting at Scott and Percy's newfound friendship, and doing a right old boogie-woogie over my promotion. Frustrated, it finally forced the issue, putting on massive clod hoppers and frogmarching me with a paso doble to recall my pas de deux with Scott Henderson, earlier in the day, at the door of Hartborne Hall.

"Having trouble?" I remembered the sound of a familiar voice behind me as I struggled in vain to open the heavy oak door after I hurriedly left the drawing room. I turned to see Scott who'd followed me down the passage. "Thanks, I can manage," I said, flushed with confusion.

"There's a knack," he explained, as he stood close behind me, placing one hand lightly on my shoulder. I stiffened. "Why don't you let me show you?" he cajoled softly, as his other hand brushed past my waist as he moved even closer as he put his hand on the doorknob and effortlessly opened the door. Lust licked along my veins like wildfire as I felt his body heat. His arm encircled me as we partnered in a casual embrace. He moved, gently pushing my hair back from my face. Nuzzling my neck, he whispered in my ear, "Will I see you at the funeral?" I nodded dumbly and ran.

I rolled over in bed and clutched the pillows. 'Be brave, I said to myself, face the music. Admit it. You fancy the pants off Scott Henderson.' The lust that had licked through my veins as I stood close to him, reignited with a vengeance. My bits were suddenly plugged into the mains. Wow. If I'd felt a spark with Tor, this was a high voltage surge with enough terawatts to short circuit a power station. I couldn't help but indulge. Slowly, deliciously, mind-blowingly, back-archingly, toe tingly, stomach meltingly, fiercely and satisfyingly epic. For an instant, I almost lost consciousness with ecstasy. I lay back exhausted, sated with pleasure. That was a petite mort experience, the sensation of post-orgasm, the little death, I mused. I squirmed uncomfortably, realising I'd got off on looking forward to seeing Scott at Sir Walter's funeral. But in the midst of life, we are in death, I reasoned prosaically. And then, pondering on this profound discovery, I lay wide awake all night worrying. Worrying that I'd missed the boat with Scott. Maybe Mum was right after all.

Epilogue

The day of the funeral was unseasonably warm for a winter's day. The air was oppressive and humid, with occasional gusts of wind that lazily picked up fallen leaves, swirling them around into little flurries of fury that hinted at menace.

I was in an agony of indecision about what to wear. My bedroom looked like a jumble sale by the time I left the house. Clothes and shoes were strewn everywhere with complete abandon. It was tough striking a balance between wearing something demure and understated to show respect for the dead and looking sultry and sexy to set the pulses racing for the living. As in Scott's. Sod it I decided, as I poured my myself into an LBD. It's do or die and I'm not ready to peg it in the relationship stakes just yet.

I pitched up at Hartborne church to see TV journalists, foraging like crows, trampling over the graveyard looking for little snippets to feed their news hungry viewers. There were still plenty of juicy pieces of flesh to pick from the bones of the Gladys and Sir Walter saga before it was dead and buried.

Feeling a tad responsible for a day of grief turning into a media circus, I zipped into the church and scanned the pews to see if Delia and Konnie had arrived. I searched among a sea of bald heads lined up like eggs in boxes, sprinkled with a variety of ladies' hats that nodded brightly like alpine plants in a rockery. It didn't take long to spot them as two hatless blonde heads stood out in relief amongst the sea of dirge.

The organist blasted out Elgar's Nimrod to herald the arrival of the cortège. It was as if a touch paper had been lit when the congregation saw Percy and Scott as head pall bearers. They jolted upright like electrocuted mummified remains as the news fizzled and crackled down the pews like exposed electrical wires. The pall bearers navigated the coffin, past the Zimmer frames and walking sticks that cluttered the aisle, to place it at the altar where Sir Walter's illustrious forebears gave witness, with stone effigies and family monuments dating back to the year dot.

Delia gave me a hard nudge in the ribs and licked her lips lasciviously behind her order of service as Scott walked solemnly towards the family pew. As I looked across at him, he turned and our eyes met briefly.

"A serious house on serious earth it is, in whose blent air all our compulsions meet, are recognised, and robed as destinies," intoned the vicar's opening words. I shivered.

"I can smell rain," I said as we left the church and headed to the Doom and Gloom to take advantage of a free bar and nibbles, laid on to celebrate Sir Walter's long and riotous life.

It seemed quite a jolly affair for such a sad occasion as people swapped amusing anecdotes about Sir Walter, many of them retold from down the years, woven into the patchwork tapestry of Hartborne's history.

"Bottom's up girls," said Delia as she downed a pink gin, winking as she cast an appreciative eye over Thomas the stable hand who was nursing a pint at the bar.

Konnie looked at me intently as she stirred her orange juice with a straw. "On the topic of hot guys, have you shagged Scott yet?"

I hastily looked around to see if Mum or aunty Thelma were in earshot, before explaining that I hadn't had the opportunity and if I did, I'd probably bottle it.

"We can't have that," she said stroking her enormous baby bump. "I've worked it all out. If you manage to bag Scott, then we could have five weddings and a funeral."

I looked at her in confusion. "Delia and Gareth, Mervin and Henrietta, Percy and Seamus and you and Scott. I'm already hitched to Jake. A blockbuster epic to Wethershire 's longest running soap opera."

My mouth dropped open. "Has Henrietta agreed to marry Mervin?"

"According to Gareth," said Delia. "He popped the question and she said yes. Mervin's all a quiver with desire and can't wait to get her down the aisle."

It seems it's my destiny to be on my own I concluded as the afternoon wore on with no sign of Scott. I escaped from the reception to the back of the square tower at Hartborne church. I needed to clear my head. It seemed everyone was pairing up, even ex lardy bucket Mervin.

"But I like being on my own," I said out loud to Sheela na Gig, a pagan stone fertility goddess that's stood behind the tower since the Victorians dug her up in the graveyard. No doubt she outraged their sensibilities, a powerful naked woman with a serpent carved between her breasts.

"Can anyone join in this conversation?" a voice said behind me.

Scott's voice made me jump, catching me unawares. "Do you have to keep creeping up on me?" I asked breathlessly as he woke me out of my reverie. "And who told I'd be here?"

"Your mum thought this is where I'd find you," he said apologetically as his eyes earnestly searched my face to see if I was okay with the intrusion.

"I've been coming here and sharing my secrets with Sheela since I was a little girl," I explained, smiling to put him at his ease. "She's pagan, an earth goddess who births us and takes us back into her at death. She intrigues me," I said, as I traced her breasts and the coiled serpent. "Legend has it that she's here to warn against lust and evil." I flashed him a megawatt bulb flirty look.

I felt him move imperceptibly closer. "I can assure you I am innocent of the latter sin, but I have to confess to being guilty of the former."

I felt an overwhelming impulse to strip naked, drag him to the floor and mate. There must be some mileage in the pagan fertility goddess myth I thought, biting my lip as my fanny flaps burst into flames. I'm sure I could get pregnant just standing next to him. I gasped inwardly as I felt the magnetic power of attraction and went all of a quiver, just like Mervin.

"Are you cold?" asked Scott solicitously as he opened wide his black Crombie coat.

I hesitated. For a moment. I recalled the last time I accepted the offer of sanctuary in a man's overcoat. But this time it was different. I felt safe. Well almost. Scott held me close.

"I will never let you go," he whispered passionately, kissing my hair. "My fierce, brave, independent Rebecca. You followed the right path that led us here. I would never ask you to sacrifice anything for me. Can you ever forgive me?"

I stared intently at his coat as I fiddled with a button. "I'll consider it," I replied half-jokingly. "But I'm like a butterfly, you mustn't hold me too tight." I pulled away. He put his hands up and stepped back.

"It's been a helluva journey for me too, coming here. But I've learnt a few things. Like letting go of the past." I turned as he pointed over my shoulder, to see Gladys leaving flowers at the entrance to Sir Walter's family crypt.

"Let it go," he said gently, as I glanced at Sheela with a warm memory of Orlando as he crowned her stone hair with a wreath of flowers. I stood there feeling torn as the sound of thunder suddenly rumbled in the distance.

Scott looked up at the darkening sky, pulled up the collar of his coat and turned to go. "But what about Australia and Sabrina and Percy. I need to update the girls," I blurted out before I could stop myself.

He halted in his tracks and turned around and said roughly, "There was never and could never be anything between me and Sabrina." His tone softened. "If you want to hear more about my reconciliation with Percy and my plans to move into the east wing at Hartborne Hall, then why don't you come to my room at the Doom and Gloom." He held out his hand.

"Will you be giving me another bollocking?" I asked suggestively.

"Well, I wouldn't put it quite like that," said Scott, his face breaking out into a wide smile. I slowly reached out and put my hand in his and we ran as fast as we could, back to the Doom and Gloom, just as the heavens opened and the rain began to fall.